WIRED IN

A PARADISE CRIME NOVEL

TOBY NEAL

WIRED IN

A PARADISE CRIME NOVEL

TOBY NEAL

"Computers are useless. They can only give you answers."

~ Pablo Picasso

Chapter 1

The child had curled her body around an old stuffed rabbit as if protecting it. She lay on a bare mattress in a walk-in closet whose gloom was held back by a night-light, her thumb in her mouth. Blond hair gleamed silver in the grainy video feed.

Special Agent Sophie Ang swiveled the tiny video cam snaked through a hole bored in the drywall of the ceiling. She checked all four corners of the small space, and there was nothing to see but empty shelves. She brought the camera back to rest on the tiny figure in the daisy-sprigged nightgown she'd been wearing when they took her.

"Primary feed established," Sophie whispered into the comm unit.

She took one more look at the child, visible in a window on the monitor, before crawling along the floor of the apartment above, pushing the floor schematic ahead of her.

Sophie drilled her second hole right near where the living room light fixture should be. She leaned all her body weight onto the silent, battery-operated pneumatic drill. The dust and wood of the subfloor and ceiling material of the unit below blew past her on a jet of warm air, making her nose tickle with an incipient sneeze. She turned her head hard, pressing her nose against her shoulder and holding her breath until the urge passed.

Sophie felt a sudden give as the drill punched through and instantly let up on the pressure, holding the drill in place so it could suck the last bits of ceiling material out of the hole. She fed in the camera on its stiff, flexible cable, looking to see what was happening in the room below on the monitor.

Directly beneath the eye of the camera two men lounged on couches set at right angles facing a flat screen TV. Sophie rotated the cable slowly, watching in the monitor. The camera scanned the room, taking in guns set carelessly on the coffee table beside empty pizza boxes and a pyramid of beer cans.

"Secondary cam installed and operational. Two unsubs in exterior room, armed," Sophie whispered.

"Roger that. Return to base when camera secure."

Sophie opened the black tool backpack she'd carried in for the operation. Inside were a battery-operated cutting saw, pliers, and the camera equipment's plastic case. She stowed the drill in the backpack and glanced at the two open windows of the video feed, now streaming wirelessly to the surveillance van parked outside the apartment building.

The little girl rolled over, looking at the ceiling, the rabbit clutched in her arms.

"Mama," she whispered. "Mama." Her eyes were black holes in the low-resolution image. Tears shone on her cheeks. Sophie felt something painful tug at her as she read the girl's lips. She endured a flash of unwanted memory.

Something was happening in the other video feed.

Both men had picked up their phones and were reading what looked like a text message. Sophie saw them look up at each other, and through the floor beneath her, voices rumbled to accompany her lip reading.

"The FBI is onto us. You ratted us out!"

One of the men leapt to his feet.

"No, you did!" the other one yelled. "You even got the payoff!"

Sophie whirled and grabbed the saw out of the tool backpack. She ran back to the hole directly above the child even as her earbud crackled with orders for the rescue team. *"Move, move, move!"*

Sophie flipped on the saw, set at top speed, yanked off the vacuum piece that suctioned out the dust. She brought the chainsaw-like tool down, whining like a dentist's drill. The saw bit into the wood, tearing though it like an electric bread knife through dinner rolls. She hauled the saw up out of the hole, threw it out at another angle, and drew it toward the end of the last cut.

The girl only had moments.

Sophie made the third cut of a triangle as the room below echoed with yelling, then the deafening *bam-bam-bam* of the kidnappers firing on each other.

Sophie leapt to her feet, threw aside the saw, and, hoping like hell the child had the sense to get out from under the hole appearing in her ceiling, she leapt with both feet and all her weight onto the rough triangle she'd made.

The fall was short and hard and she landed facing the closet door as she'd planned, knees bent to absorb the landing, the mattress taking some of the shock.

She hadn't landed on the child. That was all she cared about as a tumult of wood, drywall and dust followed her down. She drew her weapon, and the closet door opened.

Sophie fired at the dark silhouette in the doorway. She fired until the shape fell backward out of sight, and then she spun to find the girl.

Anna Marie Addams had folded herself into the corner of the

closet and her rabbit was tight against her chest. She lifted her head, eyes huge. Sophie squatted down, touched Anna's hair and whispered softly, "Don't look. You're safe now. But don't look. And put your fingers in your ears."

Anna obeyed, putting her head down over the rabbit and her hands over her ears. Sophie turned and faced the door, blocking the girl with her body.

"Package is secure," she said into the comm.

Her earbud crackled. "Roger that. Breaching the apartment."

Sophie felt Anna shudder with terror, pressed against the back of her legs, as the door cannon boomed in the exterior of the apartment.

This time the doorway filled with nothing but a man's arm, firing into the closet. Sophie fired back, but her breath was stolen by a blow to the chest that knocked her back against the child and the wall.

Sophie felt Anna squirming beneath her. She couldn't speak, couldn't breathe, and an endless long moment passed as black spots filled her vision and her hands scrabbled for the Velcro closures of the vest. Then hands lifted her off of the child, dragged her over the bodies in the doorway, and ripped open her Kevlar vest.

Sophie's diaphragm finally started working and she dragged in a breath. Her squad commander, Agent Gundersohn, leaned down into her face. "You're okay, Agent Ang. The vest caught the round."

"*Demon spawn of a pox-ridden sailor,*" she cursed in Thai, her voice a thin wheeze.

"What?" Gundersohn cupped his ear.

In the closet, Anna was screaming.

Sophie hauled herself to her feet. Her ears rang from the gunshots in the enclosed space. Her ankle buckled when she stood and it hurt like hell to breathe—but Anna was screaming. She stumbled back into the closet, pushed her way through the two team members trying to calm the girl, and dropped to her knees in front of the child.

Anna's head was down and her hands were still over her ears. A high-pitched cry ululated from her tiny body. Sophie put her hand on the child's head and leaned close, into the screaming.

"Hush, you're safe now. They're gone."

A second later the shrieking stopped. The rigid little body uncurled. The small white arms reached out. Sophie stood up with the child in her arms.

"Don't look," Sophie whispered.

Anna pressed her wet face into Sophie's neck and shut her eyes, clinging like a baby monkey with her arms and legs. Sophie carried the child past the two sprawled bodies in the doorway, past the pizza containers and fallen beer cans and the man with his throat ripped open by bullets, leaving arterial spray across the couch. Past the black-clad Hostage Rescue Team members in their FBI-emblazoned Kevlar. Down the hall and a flight of stairs, through the push-handled exit, across the foyer of the building, out the glass front door, onto the sidewalk, and into the sunshine.

* * *

The Information Technology Lab was cool and quiet, the light dim, the carpet sound canceling. The hiss of air conditioning and the low hum of computers at work were welcome relief after the chaos of the afternoon. Sophie opened the tool backpack and took out each item, wiping it down, replacing it carefully. She wrapped the cords, stowing each device in its compartment, clean and tidy.

Hours earlier, Sophie had ridden in an ambulance with Anna to be checked out at the hospital and have her own injuries treated. The child would not let go of her. The trip had been emotionally harrowing, as was the scene when the girl's parents burst into the cubicle in the emergency room.

The girl's mother swept Anna off Sophie's lap and into her arms. Tears flowed as the father joined their hug, but when Sophie tried to get up and quietly leave, Anna reached out and grabbed her arm. "No. Don't go."

"I have to. Your mama and daddy are here now." Sophie gently peeled the little fingers off.

"Here. You need Bun-Bun to take care of you." Anna thrust the stuffed rabbit, damp with snot and tears, into Sophie's arms.

The woman raised brimming eyes to Sophie. "Thank you for saving our daughter's life."

Sophie had walked out with the rabbit tucked under her arm, battered but feeling good. Done cleaning and stowing her equipment and debriefing completed, Sophie got into the pearl-colored Lexus SUV her father had given her upon graduation from the FBI and went home, protocol after an injurious shooting incident.

The penthouse apartment she lived in belonged to her ambassador father, who was threatening his long-planned Hawaii retirement any day now. She entered her elegant building's elevators from the parking lot, and as the doors shut, she realized she was tired. She was both physically and emotionally sore, worse even than after one of her mixed martial arts fights.

Maybe it wasn't such a bad thing that Special Agent in Charge Waxman had sent her home. She'd hooked the kidnappers' phones up to a write blocker extraction device that copied their contents for easy review on another computer, and the results would be available for her to work on tonight at her home computer lab, a clone of her FBI workspace.

She heard the patter of Ginger's toenails inside the red lacquered door as she unlocked it. The lab bounded into the hall the minute the door was opened. In spite of two rounds of obedience school, Ginger continued to be impulsive and embarrassingly affectionate. As much trouble as the dog was, the Lab's joyful enthusiasm was a balm to her soul.

Sophie grabbed Ginger's leash off a hook by the door as the big dog lashed her legs with a happy tail. Sophie had a pet service walk the dog every day around noon, but Ginger still acted like they'd been parted for years anytime Sophie returned.

They walked down the cooling sidewalk in the rich blue of evening in Honolulu. The moist, plumeria-scented air touched Sophie like a gentle hand, and vivid orange clouds massed in the darkening sky of sunset between the high-rises. She felt the swing of her stride loosening tight, hurt muscles. Exercise had always been the way out of pain for her.

Fellow pedestrians smiled at Ginger or petted the dog as they passed. Being a dog owner had changed Sophie's life. She felt like a real part of her neighborhood. She'd hardly noticed the colorful section of Honolulu she'd lived in before she'd adopted Ginger from the Humane Society. Now she knew every fire hydrant and strip of grass for blocks around her building, and all the people who liked dogs: old Mr. Arakawa at the corner store who wanted to pet Ginger daily, Missy Kaina who ran the coffee shop and saved bones for Ginger, and the twin Vietnamese toddlers who belonged to the woman who ran the nail salon and pasted their identical faces against the glass door in rapture as Ginger passed by.

Back at her apartment, Sophie fed the dog and freshened the water bowl before stripping off her clothes and dropping them straight into the washer along with the filthy stuffed rabbit. She padded naked across the burnished teak floors of the immaculate space, enjoying the view through massive seamless windows. The moon gleamed a silver path over the burnished black sea, gilding the iconic silhouette of Diamond Head in the distance.

After her shower, wrapped in a dragon-embroidered silk robe that her aunt had sent her from Thailand, she sat down at her home office station, a networked duplicate of her FBI work bay, ringed in three monitors.

Sophie's computer friends were waiting. The one she'd named Amara was currently sifting through the copied hard drive of a laptop that had been brought in for evidence, Janjai was running a write-blocker from another computer, and Ying, with the most powerful processor, was secretly running an off-the-books copy of her Data Analysis Victim Information Database, DAVID.

DAVID was supposed to be locked up in the Bureau vault under technical review, awaiting approval to be used. She'd built the program herself here in her home lab, used it on a few cases and, when she'd had to disclose it, the Bureau confiscated the program.

But not before she made her own copy.

DAVID was just too good to be mothballed forever due to concerns about consent and confidentiality that were unlikely to be resolved. Built off the FBI's Violent Criminal Apprehension Program, DAVID went one better than ViCAP. The program was able to burrow through mountains of online data and local law enforcement firewalls to look for commonalities and keywords, detecting crime patterns nationwide. Using a confidence algorithm, DAVID developed probability ratios, an invaluable tool assisting Sophie in narrowing down variables on a case.

Sophie turned on the three computers that matched her rigs at work in exact configuration with an electronic key fob she'd developed. As the rigs hummed into life, she reflected on the barren months she'd spent trying to comply with SAC Waxman's dictum that she not work on FBI business anywhere but in the office due to security concerns.

That dry period had led to her getting Ginger, a decision she couldn't regret even as the dog padded in, belched, and swiped Sophie's leg with a raspy tongue before flopping at her feet under the desk. She'd also discovered her love of hike-running the gorgeous trails of Oahu, and she couldn't regret that either. But in the end she'd caved in to her compulsion to be online working cases at any hour of the day or night.

The security issue was a real one, so Sophie had turned her skills to developing an encryption for her rigs with so many layers to it that she was almost ready to submit it to one of the hacker festivals as a challenge—but like her mixed martial arts fighting, as long as she was with the FBI she couldn't draw attention to herself with public displays.

She pulled up the kidnappers' phones' content list and ran a simple comparison program that isolated the phone numbers the phones had in common on their contacts list. Following that, she input the text messages' content and crosschecked senders.

The fatal text message the kidnappers had received had originated at the same number. Someone had set them up against each other. She now had a number for that unknown caller. She put on her headphones, logged into her own virtual private network to mask her location and IP address, input the number, and dialed.

The phone rang and rang. No voicemail. She ran a location algorithm but it came back *User Unknown.* "Probably a burner," she muttered.

It was time to put DAVID to work. She switched to Ying and

checked in with DAVID's monitoring subprogram, looking for trends. Months ago, she'd input a variety of law enforcement and news agencies and set them to be monitored with keywords. These were running constantly in the background via DAVID. When a statistical probability trend was tripped, the information landed in an 'attention cache' for her review, DAVID's terminology for collection of query data.

She checked the cache now, scanning through a series of probability ratios on crimes that DAVID had matched to perpetrators with known *modi operandi* from the ViCAP database. She routed these to appropriate agents in their respective states. Her FBI colleagues across the U.S. had come to count on this data sifting from Sophie, which she had explained as a simple subroutine that operated off keywords.

DAVID was never mentioned, and if some suspected Sophie was still using the rogue program, no one checked too closely. Her intel was too valuable to be dismissed.

A red alert icon pulsed next to a probability ratio in the cache box set to Honolulu, keyword "simultaneous."

She frowned, and clicked on the alert. Her kidnapping bust was listed already. The bare bones of her case as her SAC had entered it popped up, but DAVID was able to compare and analyze only information that had been inputted, and hers was too fresh for much to be available. However, a second case was listed in the cache. DAVID had discovered another trend: rival gang leaders in Hawaii were murdering each other at a statistically unlikely rate.

"What does that mean?" Sophie leaned forward as she pulled up the threads of the news items that had tripped the alert. She scanned the articles.

Two rival gang leaders, one from the Tong Triad and one from the Boyz, had shot each other alone in an alley in

Waikiki. No witnesses, and no other gang members involved. Similar occurrences had happened on the Big Island, in Kona and Hilo. A total of six gang members had canceled each other out.

Sophie sat back, giving her eyes a rest by focusing them on the view of the city's sparkling lights seen through the nearby window.

The gangs would be scrambling to reorganize themselves. This provided an opportunity for both law enforcement and rivals to pick off the groups that weren't able to replace their leaders.

Her phone rang. FRANCIS SMITHSON appeared in the ID window.

"Hello, Dad."

"Sophie." Her father had a resonant, Morgan Freeman-like voice. The sound of him saying her name summoned him immediately in her mind's eye: his strong-featured brown face, a little creased with age but still handsome, silver wings developing over his ears in black hair cropped as short as hers.

"Nice to hear your voice. What's new in your world, Dad?" He'd always wanted her to call him the American name for father even when her mother had objected early on. Remembering the constant frosty atmosphere of her parents' silent warfare growing up, she was glad they'd finally divorced when she was at boarding school in her teens.

"I'm coming for a visit next month. Hope you can fit me into the apartment."

Sophie smiled. "That would be wonderful! And of course, your bedroom always awaits. This is your place, not mine."

"Well." He harrumphed. It was an old argument. She still sent him a monthly rent check, which he then stuck in a pile, un-cashed, and returned to her on his visits. "I've put my retirement papers in. So we are going to be roommates, one way or another."

"I look forward to it, but I'll believe it when I see it." He'd been threatening to retire for years, but kept getting sucked in by the latest drama of his ambassador job. Currently he was stationed in what he called "that hotbed of iniquity," Washington, D.C.

"How's the hound?" Her father had been surprised when Sophie brought Ginger home from the Humane Society, but had fallen in love with the Lab when he'd met her on his last visit.

Sophie looked down. Ginger looked up, eyes liquid with adoration, tongue hanging. "She's fine. It'll be great for you to take her out during the day when you're here. She'll love that."

"So. I have news about your mother."

"Oh?" Sophie frowned, her eyes on Ying's screen. She had DAVID open and working now, burrowing into the actual case files on the gang murders—hence the confidentiality concerns of the Bureau and other law enforcement agencies. Her screen filled with gory crime scene photos from the Honolulu murder.

The Triad leader had fallen in the gutter, his bloody head propped up by the curb at a strange angle. The Boyz leader, in a characteristic black shirt with a red bandanna, had fallen face down. A blood pool spread beneath him.

"She's not feeling well."

"Not feeling well" was code for Sophie's mother's depression, sometimes so bad she wouldn't get out of bed for days at a time.

"She's often not feeling well. And I didn't know you two were talking." Pim Wat Smithson was an elfin beauty. To see Sophie's tall, muscular black father beside her petite, exquisite Thai mother was to see two completely different examples of humanity, not just in looks, but in temperament. Sophie knew she was their combined DNA in every way: similar in build and intelligence to her father, but with her mother's facial features, golden skin, and tendency to depression.

"She's worse than usual. They have her in a place." 'They' was Dad-speak for Pim Wat's powerful Thai family.

"What kind of place?"

"They're calling it a spa, but I think it's the other kind of place."

"A psychiatric facility, you mean." Silence met this. Sophie shut her eyes, rubbing a bruise on her chin she didn't remember getting. "That's a good thing, Dad. Maybe they'll get her on some medications that work."

"She tried to kill herself this time. Said no one loved her."

"Ridiculous." Sophie opened her eyes. The gruesome crime scene photos were still there from the Honolulu gang killings, distracting her. She minimized them. "She's a drama queen." That American phrase described her mother well.

"Your Aunt Malee called me. She asked me to let you know."

Sophie was silent, sorting through complex feelings about her mother. She'd tried to make Pim Wat smile for most of her childhood, turning herself inside out to be perfect. Sometime in early adolescence, she'd begun to realize making her happy was impossible. Something was broken in her mother, and nothing Sophie did could fix it.

Sophie shook herself back into the here-and-now, looking down at the tattoos in calligraphic Thai on the insides of her arms to re-orient herself. One arm reminded her, hope and respect. The other, power and truth. On the exterior of one thigh, freedom. On the other, courage. Circling her navel in tiny writing, where no one saw them but herself, were love, joy and bliss.

"You should be worrying about yourself, Dad. Your high blood pressure. Following through with actually retiring."

He sighed. "I know. Co-dependent, and we've been divorced ten years. She does that to me."

"She does that to everyone. It's how she survives."

"That's harsh, my dear."

"I'm sorry. I can't do any better than that."

"You're angry at your mother because of the marriage to Assan Ang. I never thought it was a good idea, as you know, but no one knew what he was like."

"It happened. It's not going away."

"Well. I have a source that keeps me informed on him, and he's married again. We tried to warn the young girl's family."

"No!" Sophie stood up in agitation and felt her stomach knot as a surge of rage and horror hit her bloodstream.

"Yes, I'm sorry to say. His new bride is seventeen. Her family wouldn't listen. Your mother tried to kill herself after she heard. She took a whole bottle of sleeping pills."

"Oh, God." Sophie tried to calm herself, one hand gently rubbing her bruised sternum. Ginger, sensing her agitation, whined.

Assan had another bride.

It was untenable, unbelievable, and had already happened.

"Pim Wat blames herself for pushing you into that marriage."

"Well, she did push me into it. But I'm out of it now." Sophie felt herself going alternately hot and cold with flashes of memory. "Someone should help that girl."

"We've done all we can. He's taken her to Hong Kong."

Sophie remembered that palatial downtown apartment all too well.

"It's not right." The realization broke over Sophie that it wasn't enough to have escaped Assan herself. He was still free, and he was still doing whatever he wanted to whomever he wanted. She wondered how she'd blocked that out of her mind for so long. "What can I do?"

"I don't know, dear. But I wanted you to be aware."

Sophie blew out a breath. "Upsetting as this is, I'm glad you let me know."

"Your mother—she can't help how she is. She has a sickness of the soul."

That was a new way to look at it. "Yes, it is that. Thanks for calling, Dad."

Sophie hung up, her mind going back to the apartment in Hong Kong. Acres of marble floor, black lacquered furniture with white leather, stylized Asian art, and a shiny stainless steel kitchen, everything top-of-the-line. All of it concealed the darkness that lived inside. She knew too well the ways Assan could torture and conceal.

"Enough," Sophie said aloud. "Enough. He's taken up enough space in my head." She looked down, rubbed her tattoos. They reminded her of her truth. Here. Now.

That poor girl was not her problem. Her family had even been warned. What more could anyone do?

Sophie refocused on the case files. She ran a few more programs, trying to track the sender of the tip-off email that had come to the FBI. She still couldn't trace it. She wondered if the tipster was also the inciter of the kidnappers' turning on each other, though there was no way to be sure at this point. At a dead end with the kidnapping case, she went back to DAVID's gang murders.

She studied the crime scene photos and the evidence processed at the scenes.

Everything pointed to the rival gang leaders meeting at an appointed place and some sort of trigger setting them off against each other. What had happened? Some sort of double cross? And why had they met in the first place?

It reminded her of what had just happened with her kidnapping case.

She scanned the photos and spotted a phone on the ground, fallen out of one of the men's pockets. Maybe there was something on that phone—a photo? A text message? She could verify that the phone had been logged into evidence, but other than a list of phone numbers from the chip that had been uploaded as part of the case file, the phone's contents remained on the actual device in an evidence locker at the Honolulu Police Department.

"Foul stench of a three-day corpse," she muttered in Thai. She had no justification to go poking around the HPD.

Her eyes were growing heavy. She slid into a silky sleep tee and as she did so, her fingers brushed the tattoos around her navel. She wondered if anyone would ever see them, would ever touch her besides Assan. That phone call had released memories that had no business surfacing. She shook her head to clear him away, but the ache in her soul remained.

If only her mixed martial arts coach Alika Wolcott would ask her out. She'd had a crush on him for years now. She brushed her teeth and revisited the painful memory of a few nights ago.

She'd just finished a bout in the ring with a heavyset Tongan girl nicknamed Jezebel, which had ended quickly and badly for the Tongan. Alika had stepped through the ropes, wearing his fight gear: split-fingered gloves, an open padded helmet, Lycra shorts, and nothing more. "Got energy for a couple of rounds with your coach?"

"Sure." Sophie's pulse went into overdrive as she circled him, trying not to fixate on how gorgeous he was. Warm brown eyes, intent on hers. His smile, with a dimple in the wall of his cheek, the way his dark hair waved off his brow, the grace of his movements as he swung a little from side to side, trying to tempt her into some foolish opening move. His skin was like caffe latte with butter in it, gleaming over world-class muscles.

There was a distracting shine of sweat on Alika's shoulders as she charged, only to be brought up short by the breathless thud of him tossing her onto the mat. It infuriated her, even more so when he yelled, "Getting sloppy, Soph!"

She tried to punch him in spite of having the wind knocked out of her, and she'd have had him too if his rubber guard hadn't protected his mouth. Then they were grappling in earnest, the twin fuels of anger and sexual frustration making Sophie even stronger than she knew she was.

She took down a man of six foot two, two hundred twenty pounds, and she made him eat the mat. But it felt like an empty victory when he thumped, and she let him up from the facedown reverse arm restraint that settled things. He sat up, dark eyes flared. Took his helmet off, shook his hair back, and glared at her.

"We're done here," he said.

She knew he meant he was done coaching her. Just like that, she'd graduated.

Done.

He'd never acted on the chemistry between them over the years or even acknowledged it, and she was too messed up to act on it either. Now she'd worked so hard under Alika that she'd defeated him for the final time. He wasn't her coach any longer.

"Done. Okay." She'd walked out of the ring like it didn't matter.

Sophie slipped into the wide, empty bed. No, Alika had never asked her out and now she wasn't sure he even wanted to be a friend. She pressed a button on the wall and the blackout drapes she needed to sleep swished closed. Ginger, seeing these activities, jumped up on the bed.

"No, Ginger. Down." Sophie pointed. Ginger hunkered and flattened herself out like a big, tawny-yellow fur rug. "Down!" Sophie exclaimed, smacking the smooth jade-green coverlet. Ginger looked guilty and slithered off, the picture of reluctance. "You'll wreck the material," Sophie told the dog, dimming the lights. "You can lie right here next to me."

This was a conversation they had every night. Ginger pressed her cool nose into Sophie's hand as if agreeing—but Sophie knew she'd wake up to the dog lying across her feet in the morning.

Chapter 2

The Ghost rose from behind the Asian-styled black lacquer desk of his seldom-used official office. He walked around to the front, hand extended. "Thanks so much for coming to check out our company, Mr. Hansen."

Hansen was a small gray man ill prepared for the humidity of Hawaii in a gabardine suit and shiny black dress shoes. Pearls of sweat adorned his bald pate and the hand he extended the Ghost was damp. "Thank God you have air conditioning in here."

"Every comfort for our clients, and for our computers, of course." The Ghost gestured to a seating arrangement around a low table featuring a vase of ikebana bird-of-paradise. "Why don't you tell me how we can serve you."

"I'm here on behalf of a client. My client prefers to remain anonymous, and has security concerns."

"Of course he does. You've come to the right place."

The interview proceeded well, and ended with the Ghost's assistant bringing in contracts for Hansen to sign by proxy for his powerful, rich, anonymous employer.

Under the Ghost's elegant black silk shirt, his heart thudded with excitement. He kept his body still and breath controlled with the core of inner discipline he'd cultivated through years of martial arts and meditation training.

This big fish that had just swum into his net had connections in Europe and Asia, and if he were happy with the Ghost's services, more would come. Ushering Hansen out after another unpleasant handshake, the Ghost returned to his desk and sat down to develop an expansion plan.

* * *

Ginger was draped across Sophie's feet when she woke, much later than usual without her alarm. Sophie clicked on her rigs and did her morning bathroom business, feeling bruises from yesterday's rescue op throb at her from various areas. She took a couple of ibuprofen and changed into exercise clothes.

She sat down at her work area, putting on her headphones. "Call work," she said aloud, pressing a button at her ear, and the phone feature rang. She pulled up Visual and moments later, she was looking at Waxman in the conference room. Her boss's silver hair showed comb tracks, but tiredness showed in the pouches under his gray-blue eyes.

"Good morning, sir. Just checking in. Do you need me to come in today?"

"No. Internal is still processing your shooting. You have an afternoon psych debrief scheduled with Dr. LaSota."

Dread tightened Sophie's belly. LaSota, one of the FBI's psychologists, was not known for her bedside manner.

"Yes, sir. Just wanted to let you know I extracted the data off the phones. The text messages the kidnappers received were sent from the same source."

"Did you get a number?"

"A burner. And no luck tracking that tipoff email either. Did Gundersohn and Yamada come up with anything new?"

"Yes. They found the lessor of the apartment and are tracking that to a holding company. They may route data later today to your workstation at the office to track the company further if they get stuck. We're still trying to find out who's running this supposed kidnapping ring, but until then, rest your injuries. How's the chest, by the way?"

"Sore." She rubbed the bruise she'd spotted in the mirror this morning, lurid against her tawny skin. "But I'm fit for duty whenever you clear me. Send me material to work on at home."

"I thought we discussed that."

"We did." Sophie kept her face impassive. She knew what her expression looked like. Assan had taught her that face, and she continued to find it useful. Eyes slightly down, submissive. Brows arched, alert as if waiting for directions. Mouth firm but slightly smiling, as if in a good mood. Oh yes, she had this mask practiced and she could keep it up for as long as she needed to. "I told you then about VPNs. My work station is secure."

"Agent Ang, we have policies for reasons and they are bigger than you. When you're cleared for duty and back at your desk in the office, that's when you'll get more data to process."

"Yes, sir." Sophie bit down on her frustration. She had no intention of following restrictions and policies developed by old white men who never got out from behind their desks and were unfamiliar with the new frontiers of tech. This was part of the reason the FBI was losing virtual battles online. "Call me when you're ready for me to come in."

"I will." Waxman sat back, smoothed a steel blue tie that exactly matched his eyes. Sophie wondered if his wife had picked it out for him. It seemed like the kind of thing a wife would do, the kind of thing she'd have done if Assan had been worthy of it. "I feel bad that the review process of DAVID is taking so long."

"Yes, it is." Sophie kept her face immobile, unreadable. "I'm sorry about the delay as well. What's the problem?"

As if it didn't much matter, when it was everything.

She had to get through the meeting with Dr. LaSota and stay cleared for duty. She was hiding a lot lately, and planning to keep on hiding it.

"It's the consent issue that's slowing things down the most. What we need to do is to set up blanket consents for DAVID to access other agency and law enforcement databases at will and as needed, and that's really meeting some resistance. There are many who think DAVID could be a threat in the wrong hands."

Sophie's muscles tightened with frustration. "I've developed some really good encryption software. I have every intention of guarding DAVID with the best protection the Bureau can come up with."

Waxman sighed, rubbed his chin. A slight rasp to the sound, amplified by the video feed, told Sophie he hadn't shaved, unusual for such a tidy man. They must have been up late and back in the office early. "Of course. But that's not the only issue. The bigwigs I've heard from are concerned it gives our agency too much power, having a program like DAVID that searches their databases for information for our cases, and not vice versa. So I don't know what to do next to advocate for use of the program."

"DAVID works. It will catch criminals that would never be detected otherwise," Sophie felt her cheeks heating. "Isn't the greater good worth fighting for? It's been almost a year. DAVID could have helped us find a dozen criminals already, by now." And it had, she hoped, through the forwarding of *modus operandi* trends she'd sent to FBI offices all over the country.

"I have the lawyers working on it. I've gone up the chain of command as far as the Director. I don't know what else do to." Waxman spread his hands on the desk. He had long-fingered hands, elegant and smooth as a concert pianist's. There was no wedding ring on his finger. "I'll keep working on it, but I want you to prepare yourself for the worst."

Sophie shot to her feet, pushing back her chair. "DAVID is mine. It's not work product developed on the job. I made it in my spare time, at home. I own it, and I can get a patent on it."

Waxman's eyes narrowed. "And do what with it? It's built off of ViCAP, and that's the Bureau's proprietary database."

"There's a lot you don't know about DAVID. What it can and can't do. And no, it's not dependent on anything. DAVID just needs a host computer and it can analyze whatever database I send it to, working off hypotheses or keyword searches."

"Well. Perhaps you should do a presentation. Educate the higher-ups on how DAVID works and how it can serve the greater good."

Sophie sat slowly back down. "I can work on a presentation with some possible case scenarios."

"Good. I'll set it up. The Director and the branch chiefs are coming out for a summit in Honolulu in a few weeks. We can plan a roll-out then."

Sophie's hands prickled with sweat. A public presentation to the Director of the FBI and his branch chiefs terrified her. "I'll get something ready."

"Good. And keep it in mothballs until then." Waxman did a slow wink, a settling of one eyelid that told her he was perfectly aware she was still using the program. "I wouldn't want you to get into trouble."

"Of course. Anything else, sir?"

"Don't forget your appointment with Dr. LaSota."

"Yes, sir." She cut the feed.

Now, between the situation with her mother, being stalled on the case, and the news about DAVID, she really needed the distraction of going to the gym. But before she did, she called the patent lawyer her father had recommended to get the ownership of DAVID started.

* * *

Sophie was warming up at the speed bag after her jump rope routine when Alika came out of his office, striding toward her. He was wearing his usual gym clothes when he wasn't fighting—a loose pair of nylon workout shorts and a black tank with the Fight Club logo emblazoned on it. Sophie never got tired of just watching him walk around the gym.

She kept up her speed bag workout, soothed by the rapid thumping of the swinging leather against her fists.

Her former coach came to stand beside her. "Sophie, can I have a minute?"

"I have another five minutes on the bag." She didn't look at him.

"Okay, five minutes, then." Alika went on around the room, speaking a word of encouragement and correction to the various people working out and sparring in the ring. Sophie was due in the ring for a sparring match in forty-five minutes, up against a Brazilian girl with a black belt in jiu-jitsu. Sophie could tell the girl had an attitude by the aggressive stares the Brazilian kept giving her from her stationary bike in the corner.

As if it didn't matter and she had all the time in the world, Sophie finished her five minutes on the bag and walked back to Alika's office, stepping inside it to shut the door. She was surprised when he got up from behind his desk and pushed the switch on the wall that frosted over the viewing window into the gym, ensuring privacy.

"Have a seat." He gestured to one of the molded plastic chairs in front of his desk.

She sat, pulling the Velcro tabs that secured her split-fingered gloves open and easing them off.

"I wanted to have a chance to congratulate you properly on graduating from coaching." Alika's voice was carefully neutral as he sat down behind his desk. "I think we ended things on a—well, a tense note. I was angry that you beat me in the ring, and I don't think the way I ended our coaching relationship acknowledged what a remarkable athlete you are and what a milestone you've achieved."

"Thank you." Sophie didn't know how to respond to this formal speech. Alika pulled open a drawer and removed a parchment certificate, heavy with gold leaf. He handed it across the desk to her.

Sophie Malee Smithson Ang has achieved the highest level of Mixed Martial Arts training available through Fight Club, the paper read. It was dated and signed *Alika Wolcott: Coach, Owner, and Operator.*

Sophie blinked. The black letters of her name swam in front of her eyes.

"Thank you," she whispered again. "I will treasure this."

"You should. I've never given one out before." Alika smiled, and she liked the way a dimple creased his cheek, tiny fans of good humor highlighting golden-brown eyes under black brows. "I thought that, now that you've graduated, we might spend some time doing other things."

Sophie's heart lurched and sped up. "What kind of things?" Her eyes went back to the certificate in her hands. The paper trembled.

"I don't know. A run-hike on one of the trails. Something." He shrugged, elaborately casual. "I think I'll miss our bouts."

"I'd like that." Her voice was thready. "We can still spar, right? I need a partner who can really give me a workout."

A long pause followed this and he didn't answer. Finally, she raised her eyes to his. They locked on hers in a heated gaze she'd only ever imagined he'd give her, a look that dried her mouth and loosened her knees. She was glad she was sitting down.

"I can give you a workout you'll never forget. Any time." His voice was a rough whisper.

Sophie shot to her feet, terrified by the intimacy he hinted at and her response to it. "Thanks for this," she stuttered, waving the certificate, and fled.

* * *

Dr. LaSota was a woman made up of angles. Her asymmetrical bob lined up with her jutting cheekbones, and a sharp collarbone provided a counterpoint. Her well-marked eyebrows raised as she pointed a pen at Sophie. "Why don't you start by telling me about the kidnapping bust."

Seated on an industrial-beige couch in the temporary office the peripatetic psychologist used when she was in Honolulu, Sophie wore her expressionless mask. She'd showered and changed at the gym, and carefully and professionally dressed for the interview in her FBI non-uniform.

Sophie crossed her legs and swung one foot a little as she described the tipoff email to the FBI, the surveillance of the address, her role of going into the apartment above the kidnap location and installing surveillance feeds.

"So there was no intention to raid the place. Cause loss of life."

"No. We just wanted to get a visual on what was happening inside. We had already verified that the girl was missing, though her parents hadn't reported it due to the kidnappers' threats. We'd identified the kidnappers entering and exiting the apartment unit."

"So how did you know to drill into the ceiling of the walk-in closet?"

"It seemed a logical place to stash a small child. Only one exit, and any noise would be muffled." Sophie's leg swung a little faster. She slowed it consciously.

"So you speculated and made your holes for the surveillance camera based on logic."

"Yes."

"Interesting." A long beat went by. Dr. LaSota eyed her, and Sophie held her gaze, demeanor compliant. She could feel Dr. LaSota waiting for her to disclose more, and finally the psychologist said, "Tell me more about what you felt when you saw the child in the closet."

Sophie shrugged. "She appeared to be adequately cared for. She wasn't injured." She knew Dr. LaSota couldn't see how fast her pulse was racing if she kept her breathing even.

"Tell me about the decision to saw through the ceiling and try to rescue the child."

"I was monitoring the surveillance of the kidnappers. I saw them get the texts that set them against each other, and speculated the child only had a few moments before the kidnappers tried to take her out."

"I reviewed the recordings and also the reports from the field. You could have crushed the child by landing on her."

"I was aware of that, yes." Sophie's foot swung faster and she couldn't seem to slow it. "It seemed worth the risk."

"You're a tech agent. Other than your training at Quantico,

you have not had an active role in operations in the field. I'm interested in what made you take such a risk—both to yourself and to Anna."

Sophie knew the woman's use of the girl's name was deliberate, and she felt the name like a deeply struck chord. Her mind filled with the sight of the child's tear-streaked face, calling for her mother.

"It seemed worth the risk," Sophie repeated woodenly.

"It didn't have anything to do with the fact that you were kidnapped and held in a closet at the age of seven?" Dr. LaSota said gently.

Chapter 3

Dr. LaSota's words sliced through Sophie's self-protection, a razor slicing a veil. Sophie had never disclosed her own kidnapping during any of her psych interviews or on her Bureau application, but it was a matter of record in Thailand. Dr. LaSota must have located that record. Sophie had hoped it had been obscured by her parents' influence.

"I don't know if it had anything to do with that ancient history." Sophie's lips had gone immobile, and she could barely force the words through them, but her foot wouldn't stop swinging. "It doesn't much matter, does it? It worked. I saved the child."

"It all matters. How our agents react in the field is critical, and nothing is off limits in this interview. Nothing." Dr. LaSota flipped open a folder on her lap. Sophie had the sense she was only doing that for effect. "It appears that you also have a history of domestic violence."

"I fail to see how that's relevant. Were any of my actions in the field inappropriate?"

"Not necessarily." Dr. LaSota kept her eyes on the folder, but Sophie felt the sharpness of the woman's full attention trained on her. "Have you ever had any therapy for your past experiences?"

"I have not needed to."

"What constitutes 'needing to'?" The psychologist closed the folder and gazed at Sophie with pebble-hard eyes.

"I don't know. Symptoms. Difficulties with relationships and getting along with others. Panic attacks. Impairment in normal activities." Sophie willed her foot to stop and it finally did. "I handle uncomfortable feelings through exercise."

"And what an exerciser you are." LaSota opened the folder again. "According to your coworkers, you take exercise breaks throughout the day an average of four times."

"Who told you that? Bateman?" Sophie felt heat suffuse her. "I could be standing around or getting coffee. I choose to stay fit for my job, instead. The FBI would be lucky to have the rest of its employees stay as fit as I do."

"Feeling defensive?"

"I don't like being spied on."

"You aren't. All agents are under assessment to a degree. We monitor our agents' mental, physical, and emotional health. And I wonder if this exercising strategy is not just a little excessive." She mock-consulted her file. "Apparently you are something of a mixed martial arts contender in the Hawaii fight scene."

"SAC Waxman is aware of my hobby and we've discussed it. I don't fight in any public exhibition matches."

"And it never occurred to you that taking up a form of aggressive hand-to-hand combat after your divorce was a form of displacement?"

"Who cares what it is. It's my private life, and the way I've chosen to act in my private life enhances my job performance, not impairs it." Sophie locked eyes with the psychologist and this time, didn't back down. "Show me evidence of any wrongdoing or impairment, and I'll address it."

"Sophie." Dr. LaSota closed the folder and leaned forward,

the picture of sincerity, but Sophie felt nothing but clinical judgment. "it's my job to assess the mental and emotional fitness of our agents. If it was only physical fitness that was a yardstick, you know you'd beat half the agents here. But I worry that these un-dealt-with issues are a ticking time bomb, and someday, some time, they are going to cause you to slip up. To be frozen when you should move or, more likely, jump when you should take the stairs. It's just lucky that child moved out of the way when you came through the ceiling. Can you imagine how you would have felt if you'd crushed her? As it was, you pulled this off. I want you to know I've got a flag on your file."

"Noted." Sweat prickled under Sophie's arms. "What would reassure you that I'm handling my past perfectly well?"

"If you went to counseling, and showed some more normal relationship patterns. Dated a little. Were a little more interactive and connected with your peers."

"I have relationships—at my gym, and in the Bureau. I have a dog. A Labrador."

LaSota consulted the folder again and made a note. Sophie was beginning to hate whatever it contained, and the way LaSota used it as a prop.

"And have you dated since your divorce?"

"No. But I have—possibilities. Not that it's any of your business." Sophie kept her facial mask in place, glad something was finally moving forward, maybe a little bit, in her situation with Alika.

"That's interesting timing." LaSota made a note in the file. "Let me know if anything develops. I also see that you're friends with Agent Marcella Scott and former agent Lei Texeira. Both of them have had issues with men. Interesting choice of friends."

"Enough." Sophie's voice was firm and low. "They've handled their 'issues' as you call them, and so have I. We're doing our jobs above and beyond the norm. Until you can show some wrongdoing, I have no intention of allowing this invasion of my privacy to go any further." She stood. "I will let SAC Waxman know I complied with my post-shoot debrief. Good day."

She yanked open the office door but closed it very softly as she left, and had the satisfaction of seeing Dr. LaSota's eyes and mouth wide in astonishment.

Sophie called her friend Marcella Scott on the way home. "Just survived Dr. LaSota," she told her fellow agent.

She and Marcella had become friends over four years of working together in the same office, and now often met at the gym to spar or go on run-hikes together. They hadn't spent much time together since Marcella and Detective Marcus Kamuela got engaged, though, and Sophie missed her friend.

"Oh God. That woman. She has eyes like a witch pricker," Marcella said.

"A what?" Sophie frowned at the unfamiliar Americanism. She'd only been in the United States full time since she joined the FBI five years ago, and she still ran across colloquialisms she wasn't familiar with.

"Oh, never mind—a dark period in Western history, not your side of the world. How are you feeling? I heard your vest took a bullet."

"Bruised, but fine. You going to make it to the gym at all this week?"

"It's not looking like it, sorry. Got some hot cases, and when I'm not working on that, Mama is driving me nuts with wedding stuff. You're just lucky I haven't roped you in on any of it."

"I will help," Sophie said. "Just tell me what I need to do."

"Not yet. We still have time for flower choices and all that. Lately we've been visiting venues to try to pick a location for the ceremony. So what's new with your love life?"

"As usual, nothing. But I graduated from coaching with Alika and...it seems like he might ask me out."

"It's about time! I've been losing patience with both of you." Marcella's indignant tone made Sophie smile even as she turned into and navigated the parking garage at her apartment building. "Keep me posted, ok?"

"Will do."

Sophie said goodbye. Anxiety about her ex-husband, stirred up by the interview with LaSota, resurfaced as she settled in at her apartment after giving Ginger a brief outing. She needed to do something about Assan.

She keyed on the computers and while they booted up, she fixed a cup of tea and let herself remember him. He'd always been immaculately groomed, with a blocky face and deep-set eyes, so dark they were almost black. His sensual mouth held a cruelty not immediately evident.

Sophie had told herself he was handsome and rich, and it was the best she could hope for in an arranged marriage that she was cooperating with to please her mother. He'd given her a diamond bracelet and been gentle with her virginity on their wedding night, and she'd been hopeful and happy until after the honeymoon—when he took her to his apartment in Hong Kong.

Sophie shook her head to banish the memories and took a restorative sip of tea. Her fingers flew over the keyboard as she set up a secondary monitoring cache on Assan.

He was an importer-exporter with dual citizenship in Thailand and China, and he'd used that to bring all sorts of goods back and forth. Sophie had always wondered if his business was clean of contraband, but she'd never wanted to attract his attention by looking into it. Now, she needed to stop him from destroying another young woman's life, and the best way to do that was to use DAVID to find some dirt on him.

DAVID began sieving a number of items for review into the cache. Sophie shunted them to her FBI rig for tomorrow when she was back at work. She took a quick look at the "simultaneous" search, and frowned to see that there was yet another anomaly loaded in.

Several stockbrokers participating in an insider trading scheme had turned each other in—at the same time.

"Strange," she muttered. This new case had nothing in common with the other crimes, beginning to look fortuitous for law enforcement as kidnappers shot each other, gang leaders offed each other, and now stockbrokers turned each other in. It smacked of some kind of manipulation, and probably through technology. But what was the common thread?

She needed to find a way to get a look at the phones from the gang leaders. And maybe a call to the SEC to find out more about the way the stockbrokers had set each other up was in order, but it would have to wait until tomorrow. That agency kept decent business hours.

Sophie set up a query in DAVID about the probability that the cases were related, and while that worked, she put on her headphones. Ginger rested her head, appealing, on Sophie's leg. She'd been taken out briefly, but hadn't had a real walk.

The headphones beeped with an incoming call and she didn't check the caller window before answering. "Special Agent Ang."

"Sophie. It's Alika." That familiar deep voice, with its trace of warm humor.

"Yes." Sophie's voice came out flat and wooden, which is how she sounded when she was surprised. Surprised, and a little bit terrified.

He cleared his throat, laughed a little. "Okay, then. Happy to hear from me, I can tell. Well, remember how I asked you if you wanted to do something? Go for a run? I thought we could do a few miles before the gym tomorrow evening. If you're coming, that is."

Sophie stared at her monitor unseeing. "I planned to go to the gym." She still sounded stiff, even though this wasn't a real date. Just a run before their usual workout, something he might have suggested when he was coaching her. Nothing to be freaked out about, as Marcella would call it. "That sounds fine."

"Okay!" He injected his voice with cheer. "I'll see you tomorrow then." He hung up.

"*Flea-bitten meat-stealing mongrel covered in the spit of a thousand angry butchers*," Sophie hissed in Thai. "Dammit."

It occurred to her for the first time that Alika might not be the only one sending mixed signals.

Work finally done, Sophie brought the clean, freshly washed stuffed rabbit to bed with her. "No, Ginger," she said, as the dog looked at the soft, fuzzy animal longingly. "This is special."

Holding the rabbit as she got into bed, she had a flash of memory of her own kidnapping. The closet she'd been kept in was smaller than the one that held Anna, and no nightlight had been provided to ward off the dark. She'd cried at first, and called for her father. Even at seven, she'd known that her mother couldn't help her. Sophie still remembered the door opening, the figure silhouetted there.

"Shut up," the man said. "Or I'll shut you up myself." He'd cracked his knuckles as he said it. But he must have felt a little sorry for her, because he'd thrown a fabric doll into the closet. Sophie had wrapped her arms around the soft shape and been able to get to sleep.

She fell asleep with the rabbit in her arms, and dreamed of hunting viruses. All night she chased shifting patterns of electricity down the long gray corridors of a vast mazelike motherboard, frustrated that they were always out of reach.

* * *

The Ghost made a hand signal, and the Doberman came to him. Anubis's coat had a sheen to it like oil on the surface of black water, and he sat so perfectly still, ears pricked, that he reminded the Ghost of the Egyptian god he'd named the dog for. "Anubis, down."

The dog dropped flat, Sphinx-like. Intelligent brown eyes fixed on him, waiting.

"Patrol."

Anubis bounded up and trotted out of the tech lab the Ghost lived in most of the hours of most of his days. When Anubis was in patrol mode, he couldn't be petted or spoken to. He had a job to do, one he took seriously.

The Ghost turned back to his computers. He had several monitors ranged in front of him and multiple feeds running. He smiled, thinking of how well his latest project was going. The business more than paid for his lifestyle.

Anubis returned and sat beside him, sleek legs folded like springs. He flipped the dog a treat. "Good boy."

He knew the route Anubis would have taken: around and through the sprawling apartment with areas for all of the Ghost's interests: the double reinforced security door and entry foyer, state-of-the-art home gym, movie theater with recliners and surround sound speakers, a comfortable seating area around a coffee table for those rare times he had visitors, a gourmet kitchen, the tech lab, and of course, his bedroom.

A timer went off in the corner of one of his screens, set to remind him he had a rehearsal with the Hawaii Symphony. He got up, stretched powerful arms above his head, rotated his neck and wrists, and fetched his violin case from where it hung on a peg on the wall. He could never bear to be parted from it for long.

Anubis looked mournful, dropping to the floor and resting his head on his paws as the Ghost changed briskly in the walk-in closet in his gigantic bedroom.

"I'll be back in a few hours, boy." Securing the last button of his neat dress shirt, tucking it into tailored pants, he checked his appearance in the mirror. People told him he looked like that action hero from recent movies, but he thought he was better looking. He was taller, with an excellent body, and none of the debauchery around the eyes.

He strapped on his ankle rig weapon and picked up the violin case and his keys. Anubis followed him to the door, and the Ghost held his hand out.

"Gimme five." Anubis raised a paw and touched his hand. He rubbed the dog's chest briefly, then, snapped his fingers. "Patrol."

Anubis bounded away. He'd be in guard mode until the Ghost returned. The Ghost undid his various security measures with a button on his phone and stepped reluctantly out of his fortress into the night.

Chapter 4

Sophie sat down at her computer bay at the FBI offices the next morning and activated her clone rigs. While they whirred into life, she sipped a strong cup of Thai tea from her Thermos mug. The tea was sweet with honey and black as she could make it. The faint scent of jasmine rising from it never failed to remind her of her childhood home in Thailand.

They'd had a large family house, built in the traditional wooden style on raised pier posts with sharply peaked rooflines to handle frequent rain. Inside, the house was all gleaming surfaces of native woods. Inlays, carving and parquet work in shell, coral, and stone-decorated windowsills, and the floors were covered in luxurious matting and carpets.

The main house was divided into a series of mini-dwellings where different constellations of her mother's family lived. She and her parents had lived in one set of rooms on the side of the terrace facing the Ping River. Her grandparents lived in another subset of rooms, and there was a servants' suite as well.

The house was on a raised knoll, safe from annual flooding even with the monsoons, and Sophie had loved to sit on a bench in the window and watch flat-bottomed boats poling, sailing, or motoring by on the smooth, fecund, jade-green water.

The family spent time together in the central terrace in the middle of the house. The raised courtyard-like platform was built around the trunk of a huge magnolia tree that provided shade. Chairs, benches, and toys made the terrace a great place to play with her aunt Malee's children, who shared a nearby suite of rooms.

That early time in her life couldn't be more different from her current urban, high tech, isolated life. But her computers were all the company she wanted or needed, she told herself firmly, looking at the pile of hard drives on her work station awaiting her attention.

Ken Yamada, crisp in FBI gray, strode through the pneumatic doors of the lab and over to her bay. "Welcome back, Sophie. We have a meeting with Waxman to kick off the day."

"What about?" Sophie glanced at Yamada, alert.

"Reviewing where we are on the kidnap case. We're still treating the case as though this situation is part of a bigger network as the tip-off email indicated, but so far Gundersohn and I aren't finding anything to support that."

"Okay. I'll be there shortly." Sophie wanted to check her query caches before the meeting.

"Make it quick." He turned and left with his graceful stride.

Sophie turned back to her computers and opened up DAVID.

She pulled up her bank of keywords. She'd set DAVID to keep up its roaming monitoring of the words *simultaneous, murder, killing, confession, accusation, shooting, and disclosure*. She didn't remember why she'd thrown *simultaneous* in there. It stood out from the rest of the keywords like the anomaly it was. And yet, including it had shaken out patterns no one would have put together otherwise.

DAVID had also answered her query about the probability of the three cases having a commonality: 64%.

Not as high as she'd expected, but still a likelihood. Now if she could only figure out what that commonality was. She wished she had more time to come up with something useful for the meeting, but in checking her trace programs, she hadn't anything to bring to the table except that her kidnapping case was "probably" 64% related to some other interesting cases that DAVID had brought up.

Only she wasn't supposed to be using DAVID.

Sophie sipped the tea, shutting her eyes. Something had tipped the gangsters off that they were being double-crossed, and they had acted on that information. Someone had done the same with the corrupt stockbrokers. They'd been manipulated into outing each other somehow, as had Anna's kidnappers.

But how?

She wasn't going to know until she found out how they'd been communicated with, and how they were all connected to each other. She didn't have enough in the cache to mount a real investigation to take to Waxman yet, but this situation would certainly qualify as an FBI case if she could find those answers, crossing state lines and even crime genres as it did.

She set DAVID to searching for commonalities between the disparate cases. All this took time, because DAVID could work only with the parameters it had been given, which meant that she had to pause, consider, and look for databases to search and variables to enter.

Sophie plugged the write blockers into the new pile of hard drives from other cases. She would have to work on all this and check on what DAVID had collected on Assan Ang after the meeting.

A few minutes later, Sophie slid into her chair next to Waxman in the conference room. The meeting was underway, but the SAC acknowledged her with a nod. Ken Yamada and Gundersohn sat across from her.

"We're doing a recap of the kidnapping case so far."

"Yes, sir."

"How is your injury?"

"Just a bruise, sir, and I've had plenty of those."

"Excellent. Ken, would you put up notes for us on the whiteboard."

Ken stood and straightened his lapels, uncapping a pen. "Initially we focused on evidence collection at the scene and tracking the lessee of the apartment where the kidnapping was staged. Through interviewing the building manager, we determined that the apartment had been rented on a month-to-month basis with cash. The whole building is owned by a corporation, Takeda Industries. A real estate company manages the units."

"We are still operating under the assumption that the tipster who emailed this kidnapping in is telling the truth, that there's a network of professional kidnappers," Gundersohn said. "Which is going to guide our decisions to probe deeper than just the suspects that died at the scene."

"Speaking of, it would have been nice for you all to leave at least one of them alive so we could interview him." Waxman smiled, a humorless twitch of the mouth.

"Couldn't be helped," Gundersohn rumbled. Sophie was glad he'd chimed in on that. Next to Waxman, Gundersohn was the most senior agent of the Honolulu team and Waxman had never questioned his judgment that Sophie was aware of.

"Well, the other great thing would be to have a lead on this mysterious tipster, or even what set the kidnappers off in the first place. Agent Ang, got anything for us?"

"I'm afraid not, sir." Sophie fiddled with the controls on the monitor that marked her seat at the table. Crime scene photos of the dead kidnappers filled the screen, sprawled in the graceless poses of the unexpectedly dead. "I've explained to the team before about source information concealment in online tracking. Whoever sent us the tipster email knew what he was doing. I also extracted any relevant information I could find off the kidnappers' phones and identified that they received simultaneous text messages, telling each of them that they'd been betrayed, and that others had been paid off. I did retrieve the source number of that text message off the phones, but it led back to a burner."

"What I wonder is: who sent those kidnappers text messages at the same time? And who's our anonymous tipster?" Ken said.

"Do you think it could be the same person?" Waxman asked.

"But how would the tipster, who knew about this operation somehow, maybe through a connection to the family or some other way—how would that person have the kidnappers' numbers?" Sophie said. She was thinking of the coincidental cases—a connection she hadn't narrowed down yet, and couldn't disclose anyway. "Maybe someone monitoring the situation is the tipster," she said, thinking aloud.

"But even if he were, one presumes he notified us out of an altruistic motive to save the child. Why would he then endanger that child by sending those text messages to the kidnappers? If you hadn't been exactly where you were and thought of a quick way to rescue her, Anna Addams would be toast right now," Ken said.

"I know. It doesn't make sense." Sophie inclined her head.

"The ransom drop wasn't completed, so we have no further leads than the bodies and the evidence in the apartment," Waxman said, rolling a pen between his fingers.

"If I may, I'd like permission to go see the victim's family whenever someone from the team is going out to interview them." Anna's face had been on Sophie's mind more than she wanted to admit. She wanted to see how the little girl was doing, and return the rabbit to her.

"I'm going out to the victim's house today." Ken was making notes in a column of Tracking Leads. So far there wasn't much in the column. "I'll let you know when I go. Gundersohn is meeting with the medical examiner to go over the bodies of the kidnappers and see if they tell us anything, but we don't expect much since we know how they died."

"What about the trace in the apartment? Anything there?" Waxman had a line between his brows.

"Nothing that doesn't go back to the three kidnappers," Gundersohn said. "But we've found their prints in the system, so after the ME's and home visit, Ken and I plan to visit their addresses."

"Let me know if you need any help with that," Sophie said.

"The prints of the deceased are loaded into the case file already," Gundersohn told her. "They had false identification with them but the prints came back to solid IDs in the system. Career criminals, all three, with sheets ranging from breaking and entering to armed robbery. None of them busted for kidnapping before, but that doesn't mean they haven't done it before."

"So to conclude, there's no indication that this particular kidnapping is part of a larger network." Ken capped the dry erase marker with an air of finality.

"Let's check in tomorrow and see where we are then." Waxman retracted the screens with the press of a button. "Dismissed."

Chapter 5

Sophie put on her headphones and, to the opening strains of Beethoven, organized herself by making a checklist in one of her apps.

Done with that, and waiting on notification from Ken to go visit Anna and her family, she took a minute to check the cache for what DAVID had collected on Assan Ang.

Sophie read the news articles in Chinese, just to keep from getting rusty in her third language. There was a lot of information about his high profile life in Hong Kong, including a wedding announcement. His new bride looked tiny and way too young, and Sophie stifled a stab of compassion as she looked at the grainy black and white image of the two standing stiffly.

She discovered that Ang had regular shipments of "agricultural products" shipped to Europe and the U.S., even Hawaii, from Thailand. It might be worth a call to the DEA to see if anyone had checked the contents of those shipments, but she needed something hard if she was going to make a move against him.

She went back to the query in DAVID looking for a common denominator among the three "simultaneous" cases, and frowned as she saw a name pop up: Security Solutions.

She opened a file and began shunting information into it about the company. It appeared to be a multi-pronged agency that offered anything a client wanted from round-the-clock guards to Internet security for their data systems. Scrolling through the Meet our Staff column, she paused her mouse over a familiar face.

Lee Chan. She knew that face, that name. The smiling young tech had gone to programming classes with her in Hong Kong. She remembered his eager, awkward manner. It was nice to see he'd found a good job as Vice President of Tech Operations.

What was the connection between this company and her kidnapping case? She narrowed the search query parameters in DAVID. Once she was able to introduce that bit of information to the team, she could broaden the investigation to include that company without disclosing her use of DAVID. It was worth a call to her former classmate to try fishing for a little more.

She hit the phone feature on her headphones and asked to be put through to Chan.

"This is Lee Chan." His voice still sounded young and eager.

"Lee! Hello. This is Sophie. Sophie Ang, from Hong Kong."

A pause. "Sophie! How nice to hear from you. Are you in the United States?"

"Yes, right here in Honolulu. I found you on the staff listing for Security Solutions. I thought I'd reach out and say hi."

"Well, I'm so glad you did. Um—is there something I can help you with?" Chan must have run through his mental repertoire of why she could be calling and come up with how little they had in common.

"Yes, as a matter of fact." She fiddled with her mouse. Sophie wasn't glib, so she was afraid she sounded a little heavy-handed as she said, "I'm thinking about looking for a new job.

I've heard good things about Security Solutions. What kind of company are they to work for?"

"They're great." There was no mistaking the enthusiasm in Lee's voice. "Management is innovative, the monitoring software we're developing is state of the art, and we get stock options. Don't have any openings right now, but I'll keep you in mind if we are hiring any new techs. Got a number for me?"

"Great." Sophie gave him her personal cell number, wondering when she was going to have to disclose that she was with the Bureau. "Any downsides?"

"I've been with them four years. They're expanding into Asia, and the top management is gone a lot, so I end up working with a VP I don't care for much, but I've got my own department so it's not too bad. What are you doing these days?"

"Oh, thanks so much. I just wanted to see if it was worth putting in an application," Sophie said. "Keep me in mind!" She hung up with a cheerful goodbye.

* * *

Sophie stood beside Ken on the wide, bluestone lava steps of the island style mansion where the Addams family lived in the upscale subdivision of Kohala. She hadn't had time to go home to get the rabbit.

Anna's mother, Belle Addams, opened the door. Sophie had reviewed the file on the family prior to the visit because she hadn't remembered the parents' names in the welter of emotion upon meeting them at the hospital. They held up their cred wallets. Belle's wide blue eyes went straight to Sophie's face.

"Agent Ang! I'm so glad you're here. Anna is constantly asking for you."

"She is?" Sophie smiled. "I've been wondering how she's doing."

"Please, come in." Belle made a gracious gesture. They went into a sunken living area with glass sliders that overlooked a lush backyard with a pool. "She's actually at an appointment with her counselor right now. Dr. Souza. She's an expert in childhood trauma work. We're seeing Anna come out of her shell more each day." They sat on soft leather couches with Belle facing them. "Her father took her to the appointment," Belle said. "We're taking turns because she's going every day."

"That's good." Disappointment weighted Sophie's stomach that she wasn't going to see the little girl, but that made a personal visit to bring the rabbit back doubly important.

Ken cleared his throat. "We have some follow-up questions because, even though the kidnappers are deceased, we need to find out how they targeted your family. Do you mind if I tape this interview?"

"Of course not. Ask me anything. I'm just so glad you did what you did." Belle smiled at Sophie. "Anna thinks you are her guardian angel."

"Just doing my job." Sophie lowered her eyes in embarrassment. "I'm lucky I was in a position to act quickly."

"Well, speaking of that. We wouldn't have known your daughter had been kidnapped if a tipster hadn't emailed the FBI. Why didn't you report the kidnapping?"

"A tipster told you?" Belle's eyes grew wide. She addressed Ken this time. "I bet that 'tipster' was Charlie, my husband. We weren't supposed to communicate at all with law enforcement. When we first gave our statements to you and your partner, we told you this. They used one of those voice distorters to call us, and sent a snippet of Anna's hair and her nightgown, threatening more pieces if we didn't wire the ransom payment into a numbered bank account." She blinked rapidly at the memory. "Anyway, I never would have allowed Charlie to take that kind of chance, but he must have decided to tip you off anyway. I'll kill him when he gets home."

That explained the dangerous tension between the kidnappers' setup against each other and the tipster's motive in reporting the child's disappearance. She could tell by the glance Ken flashed her that he was thinking the same thing.

"We haven't been able to identify anything about the tipster." Sophie held up a cautionary hand. "It's best not to jump to any conclusions. I know Agents Yamada and Gundersohn must have asked you this, but is there anyone you suspect of being involved? Anyone we can re-interview? Most kidnappings have some connection to the family."

"No. Anna and our youngest, Kellie, have a nanny, but we trust her totally. We have some domestic staff. You're welcome to talk to them."

"Yes, I'd like their information, if possible," Ken said. "Kidnappings rely on a lot of knowledge of the family's movement patterns, so it's important to find out who or how that information might have gotten to the kidnappers."

"Who is your security company?" Sophie asked, prompted by the domed security camera she spotted through the window, an unobtrusive half-sphere the same color as the house.

"Security Solutions. They provide security for our house and business."

Sophie suppressed a start of surprise at hearing the name she'd just been researching. "Can I get the contact information for them?"

"Sure, I'll get that and all the staff's info too. Need anything to drink while I'm up?" Belle was doing her best to make this into a social visit.

"No thanks," Sophie and Ken murmured in concert, and she left. Ken narrowed his eyes at Sophie.

"Think there's something up with this security company?"

"This is a good lead. I found something in my online searches connecting that company with a number of irregularities," Sophie said vaguely. "Perhaps they have a breach of some kind. I'd like to run with this while you and Gundersohn follow up with the interviews of the staff."

"Sounds good."

They both sat up attentively as Belle returned with a handwritten list of names and numbers for Ken and a glossy, plastic jacket with promotional materials inside for Sophie.

"Security Solutions does all our services," Belle said. "Home alarm, Internet, and a fully integrated nanny-cam artificial intelligence program that sends alerts too."

The hair on Sophie's neck prickled with excitement. "That sounds innovative."

"Yes, it's really cutting edge. They film your normal patterns for a week, and then the program runs all the time in the background and sends you alerts on your phone about anything unusual that happens. It's so sensitive we had to keep adjusting it because it was too good, almost. It was always sending Charlie alerts when the girls did anything outside, since we have it set to notify us in case the girls get into the pool without supervision."

"I've never heard of anything like that," Sophie murmured. "Sounds unique. Is it exclusive to Security Solutions?"

"It is. We call our unit Helen. It's always analyzing." Belle had a warm note in her voice.

Ken frowned. "You don't find that kind of computer surveillance intrusive?"

"Oh no. It's like having your own eyes and ears everywhere in the house. This is a smart house in more ways than one."

They wrapped up the interview, and Sophie shook Belle's hand. "I have to return Anna's rabbit sometime when she's home."

"She asks about Bun-Bun but has told me you need him to keep you company," Belle smiled. "Don't worry about it. Whenever you have time."

Out at the car, Ken darted a glance at her. "Bun-Bun the rabbit for company?"

Sophie rubbed her shorn hair, ducking her head. "Yes. The stuffed animal was very dirty when Anna gave it to me. But it's washed now." She wanted to bring it back to the little girl, but there was no denying the rabbit somehow helped her sleep better at night. Sleeping was hard for Sophie, and her long ago kidnapping wasn't the only reason. "I'll have to come visit another time to give it back to her."

* * *

Back at her workstation, there were three new computers stacked in the reception area, and she still had final reports to do on the four she'd been working on before. Sophie plowed ahead steadily, taking fifteen-minute exercise breaks every hour to keep her brain and circulation sharp, drinking water and tea, and finally she'd made enough progress on the backlog to make a few phone calls.

She had a contact at Honolulu Police Department she could alert to this situation with the gang leaders. She hit a button on her headphone and said aloud, "Call Detective Marcus Kamuela."

The phone feature rang as she scanned the latest in DAVID.

"Detective Kamuela." Marcus Kamuela had a deep voice with an edge to it like bitter chocolate.

"Marcus, it's Sophie. I'm calling on official business."

"Excellent. What can I do for the FBI today?" Sophie could tell her friend's fiancé was injecting his voice with enthusiasm he didn't feel. She and Kamuela respected each other, but Sophie suspected that they were each a little jealous of the time the other took from Marcella. Now that they were planning their wedding, Sophie's time with her friend had become limited to working mutual FBI cases together and shopping for the wedding.

She told Marcus about the unknown relationship between the three murders. "Our computer analysis is telling us that the cases have to be related somehow. Those three situations just happening coincidentally, is unlikely. I thought I'd contact you about it."

"A real gift horse is what that is," Marcus said.

"Gift horse?"

"Yeah. You know. Don't look a gift horse in the mouth."

Sophie researched the phrase, her fingers flying as she said, "Gift horse or not, it's statistically unlikely for that to have happened without some kind of precipitating trigger."

"When given a horse, it would be bad manners to inspect the horse's mouth to see if it has bad teeth. This can be applied as an analogy to any gift: Don't inspect it to make sure it matches some standard you have, just be grateful," she read from the English Usage Dictionary.

"I'm well aware of the Triad and Boyz leaders offing each other here in Waikiki, but I'm not working that particular homicide. I'll check with our team about an "external trigger" as you call it, and contact Hilo and Kona too. But like I said, gift horse."

"I understand," Sophie said. And she did, perfectly now. "But sometimes even gift horses can bite you on the ass."

He laughed. At the deep, mellow sound of it, Sophie almost

smiled. Yes, Marcus Kamuela was "quite something," as her Geneva boarding school classmates would have said.

"I'll let you know if I find anything connecting the dots," Marcus said. "And thanks for the tip."

"No problem. See you soon."

"Yeah. The wedding stuff seems to be coming at us like an avalanche."

"I imagine." Sophie opened her calendar window in the corner of Jinjai's screen to check the date, still a few months away. "See you then, if not sooner."

She hung up with a sense of having done her duty. She'd passed this intel on, and likely nothing would happen from it. Marcus was a good detective, but he wasn't even on the case and it was a local PD matter. They hadn't asked for FBI support, a prerequisite unless a case automatically qualified for FBI attention. Because these murders were a 'gift horse,' investigators weren't likely to have dug too deep to find out exactly how or why the gang leaders were killing each other unless, further negative consequences were felt by the communities involved.

Sophie decided right then she needed to get a look at the gang leaders' phones in HPD evidence, no matter the challenges. She put a visit to HPD on the task list for the next day. She had another call to make before she met Alika for that run before the gym.

She hit a button on her headphones and called the Security and Exchange Commission, asking for the FBI liaison.

"Agent Kendall," a brisk female voice answered.

"This is Special Agent Sophie Ang of the Honolulu FBI. We've become aware of an interesting situation with one of your cases, and we're looking for some information about it," Sophie said. She named the defendants, the date and more. "This case intersects with one of ours, and I'd like to speak to the agent handling it."

A short silence. Then, "how did you get this information?"

"I prefer to discuss that with the agent I'll be working with."

"That would be me."

"Well, then, I don't think that's the most important thing about my inquiry. Why don't you fill me in a little more on the case, and I'll let you know what might be relevant from my end."

A short pause as the agent considered their stalemate, and then Agent Kendall snorted a laugh. "All right. As you mentioned, we had a call on the same day, close to the same time. Several traders who have been colluding with each other to manipulate the market each called in the other and reported. We've brought the defendants in and interviewed them separately. We're planning to prosecute them and are gathering evidence, evidence they've been submitting willingly."

Sophie rolled the stylus of the tablet she used for jotting notes between her fingers, her eyes wandering to the tall window in the corner with its ocean view. "Any idea what prompted these disclosures?"

"Yes. They each said they received a text that the others were turning them in."

This was consistent with what Sophie was finding from the other cases. "Do you know what, if anything, a company called Security Solutions might have to do with this case?"

"I believe one of the defendants, Tom Calhoun, uses Security Solutions for his home and his trading firm's security."

"Thank you, I really appreciate this." Sophie made a note of this confirmation on the pad.

"Wait a minute! So your case has to do with Security Solutions?"

"Yes. We're investigating them as having a possible security breach that's relevant to one of our cases."

"So what are you finding?" Agent Kendall's voice was sharp.

"Nothing specific yet." Sophie frowned, wondering if she'd just given away too much information.

"Well, I'll keep an eye out for activity from them over here for you if you do the same for us," Kendall said.

"Will do," Sophie agreed.

She still had a half an hour to kill before meeting Alika. She could poke around the mainframe at Security Solutions to see how tight it was boxed up. She opened up one of her hacker programs and dove in.

Half an hour later, Sophie sat back, impressed. The company website and its subsidiaries were shut up tight. She'd have to try again tomorrow. Security Solutions was going to prove difficult.

Sophie smiled. She'd come to like difficult.

Chapter 6

Sophie and Alika ran along the cement embankment separating the Ala Wai Canal from a strip of park and evening traffic in Honolulu's bustling downtown. Sophie wore light nylon shorts and the tight sports bra she wore for MMA, and Alika was in the loose nylon shorts and black tank that had become his Fight Club uniform.

Sophie sneaked a look at Alika as he ran easily beside her. His face was calm, and she liked the way the lowering sun gleamed along the muscles of his arms. He caught her eye.

"You're quiet this evening."

"I was about to say the same about you."

"Was wondering what you're doing later."

"Got a few practice rounds planned after this run with that Brazilian girl. She's been asking for another bout."

Alika snorted. "She ought to have learned her lesson the first time."

"Well, some people are stubborn. Like you." Sophie slanted him a glance.

"What do you mean?"

"Took you forever to ask me out. If this is even a date."

Somehow moving helped Sophie keep from getting all stiff with him. She was surprised when he laughed.

"I thought you… Oh hell. I thought you only liked me as your coach. So I dragged it out for way longer than you probably needed to work with me."

Sophie stopped in her tracks. The sunset of evening gilded the smooth surface of the canal, reflecting off of the shapes of coconut palms and skyscrapers, the sound of traffic a counterpoint.

"What did you say?" she exclaimed.

"Yeah. You were always so standoffish with me unless we were practicing that I thought you didn't like me that way. But then sometimes…" His voice trailed off as their eyes met. "Sometimes I felt something, and it seemed like you did too."

"I did feel something." Sophie took a tiny step toward him.

He reached out. Slowly he slid a hand up to her shoulder, back down again. She liked the feeling of his hand on her skin. She could feel how much he wanted her vibrating between them, see it in his eyes as he gazed at her mouth. She took another step closer. Their bodies, hot from the run, were almost touching now. She tilted up her face to look at him.

"I did feel something—and I might like to feel something more." She spun and ran away, laughing over her shoulder. He jetted after her, and they pounded full speed down the walkway, arrowing around other pedestrians and bikers. Sophie leaped over a park bench and did a flip off a low parapet. Alika whooped behind her.

Finally, the burst of energy worn off near a patch of park, Sophie bent over, hands on her knees as she caught her breath. Alika flopped on the grass at her feet, panting.

"I don't think I've got your cardio," Alika said.

"You don't."

He grabbed her leg and yanked it out from under her so that she landed on the grass beside him. "I have other skills."

"I'm looking forward to learning what they are."

Alika laughed. Sophie couldn't believe she was flirting with him like this, but it was fun.

"Serious, now. I have to tell you about something I know you might not like, but before we start anything, you need to know. It's another reason I took so long to ask you out. I was hoping to get things settled, but it's only been escalating." Alika's face was close to hers as they lay on the grass. She noticed gold flecks in his light brown eyes. She wanted to smooth the worried line of his brows.

"You're married." She tried to make it sound like a joke.

"God, no. You know my real estate development business is my main gig, right?"

"I know you build houses. That's all you've ever said about it."

"Well, there's an investigation into my business. It started some years ago, when I was going out with Lei on Kaua`i." Gravity brought his dark brows down like shutters over his eyes. "I'm over your friend Lei. It was a long time ago, but what got started then, back on Kaua`i, never really went away. Some detectives on the island have had it in for me for years now, always poking around looking for wrongdoing in my business. That's why I came to Oahu. But it seems trouble followed me here." He sat up, pushed a hand through wavy black hair. Sophie kept her neutral mask on, trying to really listen without reacting as she sat up beside him. "You should know this up front so you didn't think I was manipulating you or something."

"I wouldn't think that," Sophie said softly. "I've known you too long."

"You can check me out if you want. Run a background. I'll answer any questions you have."

Sophie frowned. "What are they looking at you for?"

"Smuggling drugs from Asia. Hidden in shipments of hardwoods I order from Bali and South America for my houses." Alika flipped over and began doing agitated pushups. "When I got here and set up my business, I refused to pay the "tax" the Boyz in Honolulu levy on the construction trade. Next thing I knew, some heroin trace was found by drug dogs that came around one of my warehouses. The cops were tipped off by an anonymous call telling them to check my shipments. And believe me, they have been."

"Okay. How can I help? I have friends in the local PD."

"It feels wrong to ask you for help. So far nothing has stuck, but I'm worried that if I don't pay the bribes, those drug dogs are going to find something more."

"To whom are you supposed to pay? What's the connection? Maybe I can do something from my end." Sophie bent over, grasping her toes in the sleek Nike running shoes, conflicted but knowing she trusted Alika. "If we had someone to go after, I'm sure my detective friend would act on it. He's straight. I guarantee it."

"I've been afraid to make the situation worse, because these gangsters have law enforcement ties, and I didn't know whom to trust. Anyway I'm telling you way more than I meant to. I just wanted you to know so you didn't think I was hiding anything. Because I'm not."

Sophie gazed up at him as they both stood. "I appreciate your telling me." Her eyes held his for a long moment. "I never did a background on you. I wouldn't. I don't think it's fair. But it's just stupid to have connections to law enforcement and not use them." She moved, and her shoulder brushed his. She felt the chemistry between them, magnetic and potent. It was not enough, and too much at the same time. "Can we get some dinner after my bout with the Brazilian?"

"You asking me out?" He grinned, and it lit his face.

"I guess I am." She smiled back. He leaned forward and set his warm mouth on hers. His lips felt firm and supple, and he seemed to be waiting to see how she'd respond. Sophie was surprised but stayed with it for a moment. Suddenly it was too much, too soon. She broke away and turned. "Let's get going."

* * *

Sophie inserted her key into the lock of the red lacquered door of her apartment after dinner, Alika right behind her. The meal had been simple and casual at a nearby Mexican restaurant, their heads wet from showers and the discussion mostly about her second trouncing of the Brazilian girl with the attitude.

"Brace for impact," Sophie said, and sure enough, Ginger hurtled into the foyer, colliding with Alika in excitement.

"Sit!" Sophie exclaimed, making a hand gesture that was supposed to signal sitting. Ginger just thrust her nose into Alika's crotch, inhaling loudly and thrashing their legs with her thick tail. Alika dropped to his knees and rubbed her chest, and the dog stuck her nose into his armpit, snorting in delight. He laughed.

"Two rounds of obedience school," Sophie said disgustedly.

"She's perfect," he exclaimed as Ginger flung herself onto the floor, exposing her belly in surrender. He rubbed the dog's tummy. The lab's leg kicked and her eyes rolled back in her head. Sophie had a sudden mental picture of throwing herself on the floor and letting him do whatever he wanted to her as enthusiastically as her dog. The thought made her smile.

She took the leash down off its hook on the wall. "Ginger needs a quick walk, like I said."

Alika stood. "Sure."

They got on the elevator and went down, Ginger cavorting
but settling down once the doors closed. Alika hooked an arm
around Sophie and drew her back against him as he leaned on the
steel wall. Sophie let him, her head resting against his shoulder,
the length of her body touching his, the leash loose in her hand.
She relaxed. She'd touched him often in the ring over the years,
but now she was getting to know his body in a new way. She
liked everything about it, and shut her eyes.

Ginger turned her head to look at Sophie with a question in
her expressive brown eyes as the door dinged, opened, and
another passenger got on. Sophie stiffened and tried to pull
away, but Alika tightened his arm across her. She settled back,
enjoying how they fit, realizing she didn't mind that a stranger
was seeing them together.

Alika was taller than she, broader across every muscled inch.
For once in her life she felt just right beside a man because they
were equals. She was desired, but also respected—everything
she'd never had with Assan Ang.

The other passenger rode down with them in silence. Sophie
flicked a glance to the side, registering a dark-haired man around
six feet tall, dressed in black, carrying a small duffel. Sophie and
Alika got out on the ground floor, but the other passenger stayed
in the car.

Night had fallen. Sophie and Alika walked down the still
warm sidewalk in the fragrant Honolulu dark, Ginger nosing and
smelling and squatting on all her usual spots. Alika took
Sophie's hand and swung it lightly. She liked the feeling, and
twined her fingers with his. He lifted her hand, and in the amber
light of a streetlamp, Ginger nosing around the base, he
inspected her long fingers.

"Such magic you do with these hands. Unlocking all the
secrets of the online world."

"And you." She turned his palm over and traced thickened skin at the base of his fingers, a hard ridge on the edge of his thumb. "I can see the tools in your hands from these calluses. You don't just use these hands for fighting. You build things."

He tugged her against him, her hand still in his.

"Kiss me," he whispered, as if he knew she had to be the one to do it. She leaned into him, wrapping her arms around the column of his neck and shoulders, drawing his head down to hers.

All was sensation, and light spangled darkness, and the feeling of falling and being carried at the same time, of giving and yet being given to. Finally she pushed away and laughed because Ginger, concerned by this unusual behavior, had wound the leash around and around their legs and now nosed at Sophie, whining.

"I have a chaperone."

They extricated themselves and when they were back at her apartment building, she opened her mouth to ask him to come up. He set his fingers on her lips.

"Not tonight," he whispered. "We're going to take this slow." And then he jogged away, as if he had to physically remove himself. She watched him go, smiling.

Chapter 7

*B*ack at work the next morning, Sophie re-engaged her hack on the Security Solutions mainframe. After an hour, she was frustrated at no progress. The team meeting this morning had been cancelled by Waxman, so she called Ken Yamada.

"I need to make a visit to the Security Solutions company headquarters downtown," she said. "Got the time to go with me? I'm finding some irregularities I want to check out."

"Sure. Speaking of home visit, Gundersohn and I are interviewing the staff at the Addams' house. Nothing interesting so far and stories check out, so maybe your security company was the breach after all."

They agreed on a meet time and Sophie hung up. She stood up, stretched, cracked her fingers, and noticed in the long glass window that it was another postcard-perfect Honolulu day. She'd been so preoccupied on her way into work thinking about the kidnapping case that she'd scarcely noticed.

Sophie sat down and loaded her best decryption software, a prototype she'd traded from a fellow tech agent. It was an off-the-books copy of a program her friend had written, and like DAVID, not a recognized FBI tool.

She'd never known it to fail.

The program went to work, drilling away at Security Solutions' defenses, and while that processed, she activated Ying and looked into the DAVID cache. It was time to sort through the data from the three "coincidental" cases and find out exactly how Security Solutions was involved.

Sophie pulled up the three files and set DAVID to work cross checking the data input on the cases. More information was available now, entered by the different law enforcement agencies in the intervening days. DAVID's little skull spun, and while the program was working on that, Sophie opened the cache on Assan Ang.

A good deal more information had collected, including links to Assan's shipping enterprises and retailers who received from him. Sophie pulled up the bills of lading. Wood for prefabricated "green" construction was listed, along with "textiles" and "assorted household decor." Most of his goods were warehoused in the Port of Los Angeles, where Assan had his own storage facilities.

Sophie was willing to bet, with the farmers he was contracting from, that at least some of the "assorted household decor" would be filled with opium poppy products.

But did she have enough to call in a DEA raid? And how bad would it be for her to use her connections in the FBI to do so, and have the raid come up dry? It would ruin her credibility, not to mention what might happen if anyone noticed that her last name was also Ang. She'd kept her husband's surname because she'd paid in blood for that name and wanted to remember the debt owed her.

But knowing Assan, if her ex-husband ever realized she was going after him, the world wouldn't be a small enough place for her to hide.

She was going to need some boots on the ground physical evidence before she made a move against Assan. In fact, even if she shut down Assan's import/export business in the U.S., how was that going to stop his abuse of a new child bride? Right now she didn't have anything to move on or an effective plan.

She needed a break to think.

Sophie set her security codes on her rigs with the key fob and left the IT lab, changing into exercise clothes in the locker room. In the elevator to the top floor of the building, she tried to calm her anxiety by shutting her eyes and controlling her breath.

The doors opened into a locked, bulletproof sally port. Sophie swiped her keycard, the pneumatic door opened, and she was on the roof of the building. She walked to the waist-high parapet surrounding the great open space, bare except for the big red X of the helipad. Near that, an open metal-roofed shelter held rows of bolted-down steel benches and tables for those awaiting transport or eating lunch.

She couldn't sit down anywhere right now.

Sophie broke into a jog around the track painted around the edge of the building. She wasn't the first to decide exercising outside was a good option. She'd use the company showers and locker room before returning to work.

The incredible vista of Honolulu, spread below in a 3-D patchwork quilt of color, movement and shape backed by the lush green Ko'olau Range, lifted her spirits in spite of her tension. As she lapped the hundred-yard circumference of the building, she took in the ocean view on the other side.

Towers of cumulous clouds, brilliant in the sun, blew across the cobalt sea like so many majestic galleons. Closer to shore, the water merged into shades of cerulean and turquoise. A sailboat as white and tiny as a child's toy tracked the edge of the horizon.

Gradually Sophie calmed as she ran, mulling over her dilemma.

She couldn't disclose the "simultaneous" cases and their connection to Security Solutions without disclosing DAVID's involvement, when she'd been specifically directed not to use the program just yesterday.

So what made the most sense was to keep working the straight end of the case as it pertained to Anna's kidnapping and see what she could see about the company with the full resources of the FBI brought to bear on it through the investigation. As things unfolded, she could use what they found to uncover the how's and why's of the "coincidence" cases.

Whatever happened, she couldn't talk about DAVID, or run the risk of losing her program forever—which reminded her that she needed to follow up on the patent application she'd started.

Sophie did one more lap, sorting through the threads of information and coming to the same conclusion once more. She stopped in front of the ocean view and bent to stretch, exhaling over her knees in long slow breath, and inhaling as she stretched high, filling her lungs with great breaths of moist, salty air warm from the beaches of Waikiki.

DAVID and the gift horse cases would have to stay her secret for a while longer, but that didn't mean she couldn't find some way to use a digital can opener to get inside Security Solutions and find out what the connection really was. She couldn't wait to go to the company's Honolulu office with Ken and see what she could dig up.

Sophie jogged on, her mind going back to Dr. LaSota's observations about her exercise habits.

"*Screw her*," Sophie muttered in Thai. She followed that with a string of other invectives. "Deformed daughter of a pox-ridden whore! Eater of Buddha's offerings! Demon-hag-witch who kisses the devil's backside!"

She was brought up short by Waxman's voice.

"You're pretty angry with someone," he observed.

"Sir! You startled me!" Sophie exclaimed. Waxman was wearing exercise clothes. He moved up to flank her.

"I'm wondering who it is that's kissed the devil's backside?"

"It sounds better in Thai, but it's Dr. LaSota." Sophie stopped, put her hands on her hips. "You might as well know, since my psych report probably went across your desk."

Waxman threw his head back and laughed. It was so full and rich a sound that Sophie found herself smiling. Waxman was younger than she'd assumed, with his silver hair. He'd always reminded her of the journalist Anderson Cooper.

"Nuff with the 'sir.' Call me Ben." Waxman dabbed his eyes with the edge of his shirt. "LaSota can indeed, be the deformed daughter of a pox-ridden whore at times. I've thought so myself. But she has her uses. Now what are you doing out here?"

"I needed to ventilate my brain. I've got a lead. I think." She might as well tell him about Security Solutions; he was going to have to know about the visit she and Ken had planned. She filled him in on the Security Solutions connection to the kidnapping case. "We're doing a scouting mission today."

She left off the 'sir' but felt it vibrating in the air between them. He was something more than a boss, it was true. He'd given help, encouragement, and support over the years. He was attractive. Sometimes she wondered what lay under his suit. But Waxman was her superior, and she was concealing a lot from him.

"Okay then. Remember, no more 'sir' in private. And let me know right away what you find." Waxman squeezed her shoulder lightly and she lifted a hand as he jogged on and she went into the sally port.

Her boss's hand on her shoulder reminded her how seldom she was touched. Except for Alika, last night. She smiled, remembering, as she stepped onto the elevator.

After a quick shower and change, Sophie sat down at her desk and donned her headphones. Her rogue program had broken the Security Solutions firewall.

"Excellent," she muttered, leaning forward, fingers flying as she surfed through various areas of their mainframe. Data began streaming across her screen, but without programs to define it, it was meaningless gibberish and wouldn't tell her anything. It was time for phase two of her breach, physical penetration. She hit the intercom button. "Ken? You ready for our field trip to Security Solutions?"

Chapter 8

Ken and Sophie rode up on the elevator of the elegant downtown high-rise where Security Solutions' Honolulu headquarters was located. She followed Ken into the offices and they held up their cred wallets at the gracious front desk.

"We'd like a tour of your computer lab," Yamada told the receptionist, a mixed-Hawaiian woman in a fitted sheath dress with a spray of jasmine tucked in a sleek bun.

"May I ask what this is regarding?" The woman's glossy smile twitched like a tic.

"That's a matter for your management," Ken said.

"Let me get hold of our vice president of tech operations, Lee Chan. Perhaps he can help you." She depressed a button on the phone and turned away with the receiver of the phone, muttering into it. "He'll be right out. You may take a seat."

Sophie frowned. Lee wasn't going to like seeing her in this capacity after her fishing expedition of yesterday. The reception area was designed to project wealth and authority, with its curved reception area, keypad door into the inner recesses, and deep-piled, silky beige carpet. Blond Danish furniture and an amorphous metal sculpture added to the modern mood.

"To what do we owe the honor of an FBI visit?" Lee Chan opened a door that led into the back, smiling, but that smile faltered as he recognized her. "Sophie?"

"Hello, Lee." She stepped forward, shook his hand. "It's great to see you again." Lee was wearing all black, and a collarless, button-less shirt that reminded her of photos she'd seen of Amish farmers.

"I take it you aren't really looking for a job," Lee said with a touch of acid in his voice.

"No." She turned and gestured to her partner. "This is Special Agent Ken Yamada."

Ken gave a disarming grin. "Perhaps we could speak privately?"

"Certainly. I'm eager to hear what brings you here." He turned and swiped a keycard through the combination door, leading them down a luxurious hallway covered in that beige carpet that didn't wear well but testified to the company's willingness to spend money on cleaning and upkeep. "What made you call me yesterday, Sophie?"

"I wanted a little informal background on the company. I didn't know, when I called you, that we'd end up having to visit in a formal capacity. I apologize for the subterfuge."

Sophie could feel Ken's vigilant attention on her as Lee came to a halt in the middle of the hall, turning to face her. His nose was shiny with stress. "You didn't need to lie to me. I'd have said the same thing to you in an official capacity as I said to you yesterday," the young man said.

"Again, I apologize. Your company is providing security for a family whose child was kidnapped. We rescued her, but are trying to find out how the kidnappers were able to take her undetected. Perhaps there was some breach they were able to take advantage of?"

Sophie thought Lee's color got a little waxy as he turned away. "I can't discuss individual clients' services without written consent from them, or a warrant." He resumed walking down a sound-deadening hallway rarified by classical Muzak piped in from overhead.

"We don't have that in hand, though we can easily get it. Can you just—show us around? Orient us on what you provide?" Ken interjected.

"Okay." Lee sounded sullen as he ran his keycard at another door and used a thumbprint lock.

"You were so enthusiastic about the company yesterday," Sophie said, trying to regain her former classmate's trust. "Tell us about it."

He opened the door for them. Inside, organically curved bays undulated around the room with tech people seated in them, headsets on. The lighting was low and the temperature cool. Sophie felt immediately at home.

"I imagine you did a little homework on us," Lee said. "In fact, I know you did."

"Just the basics," Sophie said, trying her most charming smile on the young tech. "You made the Fortune 500 this year. You're expanding your operations overseas and brought down some significant profits even in a rough year for the economy."

Lee gestured to the bays where the operatives were diligently working. "We have a lot of surveillance and alarm systems. We also provide personnel as needed throughout locations in the United States. And you're right. We're expanding, going global." His voice had warmed. He was getting over their initial setback, Sophie hoped. "We have a really unique surveillance monitoring system. It analyzes patterns in the home or business and can be set to send alerts wherever desired of anything out of the ordinary."

"We heard about that from the family who experienced the kidnapping," Ken said. "Kind of an artificially intelligent nanny-cam."

"Well, that's one way to put it," Lee said.

"All that must take a lot of memory. Where's your server farm?" Sophie asked.

"This way." Lee led them to another locked door, opened it.

Significant cold bathed them in a douse of refrigeration as they stepped inside. A tall steel rack filled with black, humming computers blinked with tiny red lights. Yards of blue cable wound like arteries around a heart.

Sophie peppered the IT tech with specifics about load and capacity and the current data storage of their system as Ken poked around. It turned out a lot of the company's actual data was stored off-site and this was just their backup, local server.

Which opened up interesting possibilities. If this was just Security Solutions' "front door," who knew how far, wide and deep their back door went?

"I'd like a software tour around one of your workstations." Before Lee could protest and while he still had to relock the server room, Sophie spun and walked to the nearest computer bay. She sat down, quickly plugging in a flash drive. The computer woke up immediately as she moved the mouse. A spyware program downloaded from the drive as she attached a tiny bug to the bottom of the keyboard to broadcast to her address.

She had the flash drive back in her pocket by the time Lee Chan had rejoined her.

"An interesting configuration," she commented. With Lee hovering at her shoulder, Sophie browsed through various security installations: scrambler satellite phones, encryption software for their clients, surveillance equipment for homes

activated by motion or heat and then run through an algorithm
for anomalous patterns by software so no human eye had to
watch the video. Essentially, the computer watched the video
and then alerted the company to oddities.

"Impressive," Sophie said. "Almost as good as AI"

"Our main programmer has a background in artificial
intelligence," Lee said proudly. "He's out of the country right
now, but he'd show you some stuff you've never seen before.
Course, then we'd have to kill you." He chuckled nervously.

"Never threaten a federal agent, even as a joke," Ken Yamada
said sternly.

"Of course not! Satisfied, Sophie? I mean, Agent Ang?" Lee
asked.

"Yes, I am. Though I'd like a meeting with your programmer.
To find out more about this artificial intelligence surveillance
program."

"I'll have him call you."

"We need to see the records and system our victim's family
had." Ken hooked his thumbs lightly in his belt, subtly pointing
to his weapon and badge.

"I'm afraid not, without a warrant. Or without their written
permission, as I said." Lee flashed his nervous smile. "If you
need further information, please call to set up an appointment to
speak with Frank Honing, our VP in charge of client operations."
The tech expert couldn't show them out fast enough. Sophie
didn't try to pretend they'd be friends again, and felt a twinge of
regret as she shook Lee's hand goodbye.

In the elevator back down, Sophie watched the numbers
change meditatively. Such a surveillance-monitoring program
would definitely be a strong selling point for clients. In effect,
the nanny-cam program could replace watchmen who tried to
pay attention to the same exhaustingly boring monitors hour

upon hour and let things slip by. Human error might be eliminated, and how much more efficient that would be.

Human error, waiting to happen. Her own emotions and needs, in a nutshell.

Ken Yamada didn't ask her until they were getting into the black Bureau Acura SUV. "You get in?"

"Of course."

He laughed as he turned on the vehicle. "Wonder what that meeting with their programmer will be like."

"Boring, I'm sure." Sophie reclined her seat a little, rolled her head from side to side. "Engineers and programmers are not usually great conversationalists."

"Present company excepted."

"Well, I grew up in a different culture and came to tech later than most. I had to learn social skills before I learned computers."

"Speaking of, you didn't tell me you knew Chan and had talked to him already."

"I should have. I apologize." She blew out a breath as they turned onto busy Kalakaua Avenue, the palm trees dotting the sidewalk gyrating in a breeze off the ocean. "We went to school together in Hong Kong. I was poking around the company website yesterday, and saw his picture. I called and fished for info without identifying myself as an agent. I didn't expect to have a reason to go to the company the very next day."

Ken smiled at her. "It's unusual, your background."

"I know." Sophie didn't elaborate.

"So how did that come about? It's time we knew the basics about each other, now that we're working together closely."

Sophie shrugged. "As you know, I'm half Thai. But I'm also half American. Which part led to all my tinkering and fixing as a child and my attraction to everything technology related, I don't

know. It certainly wasn't understood well by my mother's
family, but my father encouraged me. When I left for boarding
school at age ten, he sent me to an academy in Europe that
focused on math, science and technology so I got a strong
foundation in tech skills. I ended up getting married early, which
was a mistake, but during those five years in Hong Kong, I went
to classes in programming, which is where I met Lee. By the
time I joined the FBI I had a solid skill set in hard computer
science as well as software. You?"

"Much less colorful background. Grew up here in Hawaii. I
went to Punahou, one of our private schools here in Honolulu,
did undergrad at UCLA and majored in criminology. Never
wanted to do anything but be an FBI agent and come back to
Hawaii to work."

A short silence. Was disclosure time over? "So, what's your
take on Security Solutions so far?" she asked, to move things
along.

"I think they're hiding something," Ken said. "It's just a vibe
I picked up, though Chan gave us the red carpet treatment,
considering we showed up unannounced. I'm going to go back
with the consent from the family to check on their system. Do
you want to come for that?"

"No. You're okay at tech; but you can call me if you need
me."

Ken slanted her an ironic glance. "I'm considered pretty good
for a mere field agent."

Sophie ducked her head. "I meant no disrespect." She seemed
to be putting her foot in it.

Ken went on. "We can't assume it's anything unusual that
they want to protect their client list. Of course they're protecting
their clients, they're a security company. But that cyber-nanny
analysis program could have terrorist implications."

"I agree. If you could hack into someone's surveillance feed and then put the AI to work analyzing the patterns, it could be used to plot an assassination or a heist. A kidnapping. Anything." Sophie frowned, gazing out the window at the beauty of another downtown Honolulu day streaming by unnoticed.

"Anything designed to prevent a situation can also be turned against to create an opportunity," Ken said thoughtfully.

* * *

The Ghost sat down at his home workstation in the martial arts *gi* he liked to wear around the apartment. He'd completed violin practice, his evening run, and a shower.

An icon was flashing on his personal alert network. Annoyed, he opened the data stream to check it.

Someone had succeeded in breaking into the Security Solutions mainframe. As the alert program showed the list of programs that had been deployed to hack in, he frowned. Probably a government agency. He recognized signature coding on the decryption software.

He activated a backup program that imitated everything but the company's vital information and deployed that layer through multiple anonymous VPNs. Next time the hacker tried to get in, he'd be able to see everything of the company's interior workings—and nothing important.

The Ghost pushed away from his desk. Darkness was spreading over the city, but he wasn't ready to settle down to anything. Was it worth it to see exactly who'd broken through the company's defenses? He *was* concerned about the hacker's identity. This afternoon he'd also received a text from Lee Chan notifying him of an FBI probe. The hacker was probably a tech agent.

He went to his workout room and ran through a quick twenty minutes of strength exercises—stomach crunches on an inversion table, pull-ups, knuckle pushups.

His brain sufficiently aerated and emotion dispelled, he flexed his hands and sat down at his home rigs. Anubis followed him, intelligent brown eyes monitoring as he imported a video stream from Lee.

"Relax," he told the dog. Anubis settled immediately, resting his head on his paws, and the Ghost turned away and opened the security recordings Lee had forwarded of the FBI's visit to Security Solutions. He settled back with a protein shake to watch the FBI team.

There were two of them, a man and a woman. The man was Japanese and handsome in an austere way, his gray suit immaculate. The woman was riveting, even in the grainy video. He leaned in to get a closer look, blowing up his view.

Short dark cropped hair complimented a profile with high cheekbones, large dark eyes, a straight nose, and full lips. Her eyebrows looked like black calligraphy strokes. She wore neither jewelry nor makeup, just a simple button-down shirt, loose black trousers and athletic shoes, with the shiny FBI badge clipped to a small pocket.

The two of them followed Lee down the hall. The man looked competent, intelligent enough, but it was the woman he watched. She moved like water, and he noticed the darting of her eyes as she took in everything in the computer workroom. He could read lips, a handy skill, and she asked to see the server room. The Ghost cursed the budget choice that meant the surveillance feed lacked audio as he saw only the backs of their heads approaching the locked room.

Once in the server closet she checked the equipment briefly but then ducked back out, leaving the other agent distracting Lee.

The Ghost switched frantically to another feed to follow her. She moved quickly and sat down at the nearest workstation, her hands a blur of movement over the keyboard. Zooming in on the workstation, he replayed the video and caught the lightning movement as she plugged a flash drive into the computer.

"Shit," he muttered.

Her fingers flew over the keys and he saw her pull the drive out and hide it in her pocket. Her finger did something under the keyboard. *Probably hiding a transmitter.*

"Shit," he said again, but he was grinning now. He liked a challenge and so seldom got one. She was beautiful and dangerous, and he liked that.

Lee returned, fluttering and upset, with the male agent. The woman misdirected him and got him jumping through various hoops. Finally she appeared satisfied. She stood up, shook Lee's hand, and walked back out, leading the way.

She walked like an athlete, comfortable in her body. He wished he could see what kind of figure she had under those concealing clothes. Her triumph was obvious to him. She'd done what she came for, and Lee had no idea.

"Who are you?" He leaned forward, blowing up various views, trying to see more of her.

His security wasn't worth the electricity it took to run it. She'd set up a relay station, and now that she'd breached his network, all she had to do was clone the computer she'd infected to have a framework for processing the data she was stealing.

He picked up the phone and called Lee. The tech squawked and protested in dismay as the Ghost told him what he'd discovered. The Ghost switched to real time surveillance and watched the tech director go to the computer where she'd sat.

"Found the transmitter, sir. I'm sorry she got this far." Lee made as if to smash the tiny button on the floor.

"No!" the Ghost exclaimed. "Send it by messenger to my building. I want it. We can manipulate what they know."

"Shall I purge this unit's hard drive?"

"Yes, you can. But I want that transmitter."

"Yes sir, right away. She also asked to speak to the programmer in charge of our systems."

"Well, that's going to be impossible, isn't it?" The Ghost said.

"Right, I know. So how do I respond to her?"

"Tell her the truth. The man is gone out of the country and can't be reached. Now get me that transmitter." The Ghost paused. "And what's her name?"

"Special Agent Sophie Ang. I knew her before she was an agent. We went to school together in Hong Kong."

"And?"

"She's good. Very good."

"I can see that already." He hung up and surged to his feet, energized. He was going to find out everything about her. She wanted a meeting with the programmer? Now that would be interesting. But impossible, obviously.

He pulled a brand new computer out of its packaging and set it up in a corner of the lab. On one of his other rigs he set up another virtual private network and cloned the Security Solutions typical work hard drive she'd accessed. From one of his rigs he loaded a hard drive of data harvested some months ago. He could keep her off their trail with outdated data that would match what she'd been seeing before.

He went back to his main rig and began building an information file on Special Agent Sophie Ang. It made fascinating reading. The only interruption came when a bell dinged, notifying him that the messenger had delivered the package with the transmitter.

After fetching it, the Ghost retrieved the tiny, powerful transmitter and attached it to the keyboard of the new rig he'd set up. On his own computer, he followed the stream of data she was now receiving, and added a little something extra.

Chapter 9

*S*ophie was just settling into her Bureau workstation, reviewing the connections to Takeda Industries, the company that owned the apartment building where the kidnapping had taken place, when her phone rang. "Come to a meeting in the conference room in thirty minutes," Waxman's voice.

"Sure, Ben," Sophie replied, and he gave a short bark of surprised laughter, and hung up.

Losing the 'sir' was going to take some getting used to for both of them.

She only had half an hour, so she made the most of it, cycling through DAVID's search caches. Nothing new on Assan. She hadn't come up with any way to deal with him yet, either. But there was something in the "simultaneous" cache—a new case.

Three participants in an international child pornography ring had called to turn in other members to the FBI last night. The agents on duty had worked with HPD to respond right away, confiscating computers and arresting all three suspects with the evidence on hand.

Her pulse picked up when she saw that the case had come straight into their office. Perhaps this was what Waxman calling a meeting for. She'd assumed it was an update on the kidnapping case, which so far they still hadn't made a lot of progress on.

She ran a quick cross-check on the new case: one of the pornographers had a business that used Security Solutions computer security.

Now she had a formal way to connect all her cases. She didn't have to disclose DAVID's use at all. She could just say that her investigation into Security Solutions through the Addams family had led to her searching for a common denominator among some disparate cases, and now she had one.

Jubilant, she saved her files to a flash drive and jogged to the meeting. Ken Yamada and Sven Gundersohn were already seated along with Waxman, who had the screens up already.

"We have a new case." Waxman looked tidy and well-groomed, his silver-blond hair gleaming, but Sophie noticed a fleck of blood where he'd nicked himself shaving, right on the tip of his square chin.

Sophie waited while he went over all the information she'd already skimmed through via DAVID. She couldn't disclose that she already knew about this case and had run an algorithm on it. She was supposed to be getting the information for the first time at this meeting. She was going to have to wait, and work it in later.

Annoyance and frustration made her jiggle her leg under the table as she stared at her monitor.

"Thoughts on the tech aspects of the case? Will you take the lead on the pedophiles' computers?" Waxman's voice intruded on her agitation.

"Of course, sir. Nice that the perpetrators all turned each other in. How handy," Sophie said drily.

"I guess it was." Waxman rubbed his chin and the tiny scab disappeared. "I didn't think of it that way."

"Can we discuss the kidnapping case for a moment, sir? There might be a connection to this new case. I need to fill you in on some developments having to do with a company called Security Solutions." She made brief eye contact with Ken, enough to get a subtle nod. She explained the nanny-cam AI system and that Security Solutions might have been the way information was collected on the Addams family leading to the kidnapping.

Waxman frowned. "Gundersohn, Yamada. Anything from the staff interviews?"

Gundersohn shook his big, grizzled head. "No. Nobody's talking, and none of them have debt problems or other discernable motives. Their alibis are holding up."

"And we've identified the tipster," Ken said. "Charlie Addams, the father. He has some computer skills, and he admitted to me today that he sent the tip-off email. He didn't want his wife to know, but she figured it out when we asked her about it."

"That explains the disconnect between the motive of the tipster and the action of whoever incited the kidnappers against each other," Sophie said. "We still don't know who that person is, but as I've been probing into Security Solutions, several other cases have come to light with odd, coincidental commonalities, all of them tracing back to some connection to the company."

Waxman narrowed his eyes and Sophie could tell he was considering DAVID's involvement in the case.

"I'd like for us to backtrack to these other cases and try to find out from each client of Security Solutions involved with the case exactly how they were being set up to turn themselves in," Sophie said.

"I wouldn't be surprised if lawbreakers are Security Solutions' marketing niche," Yamada said. "Criminals R Us, Inc."

"So what was your impression of the company?" Waxman asked Ken. Sophie's fellow agent recapped their visit. He made no mention of Sophie's illegal hack on the security firm, to her relief.

"My sense is that there's a lot going on over there, and we're going to have to fight hard to access any of their information," Ken concluded.

"Let's focus on the kidnaping case and use that to get a look at the nanny-cam AI software," Waxman said. "That's a more promising way into this firm than their client list at this point. If we can find a connection between enough criminal cases and Security Solutions, plus some threatening spyware artificial intelligence program, search and other warrants are going to be easy."

"Agent Yamada and I will begin by interviewing the pedophiles, see what prompted them to turn each other in," Gundersohn rumbled. "Agent Ang can gather evidence off their computers."

"Yes, sir. And I've been wanting to go down to HPD and get a look at the gang leaders' phones in the Waikiki murder," Sophie said.

"Let's check in at the end of the day and see where we are." Waxman retracted their monitors. He cocked a brow at Sophie, and she knew it was on the tip of his tongue to ask her about using DAVID. She avoided eye contact and sighed a breath of relief at making it out into the hallway without him calling her back.

* * *

Sophie was pulling into the parking garage of the downtown Honolulu Police Department building when her phone rang. She grabbed the nearest parking spot and answered when she heard the ringtone she'd put on for Alika. It was a bit of the music from Rocky, because he'd always put her in mind, somehow, of that famous boxer, too stubborn to go down.

"Hello," she said, smiling.

"Did I kiss you last night? I had to call and check to see if I was dreaming."

"Yes, you did. With my dog chaperone tying us together with her leash."

"So I wasn't dreaming."

"You could have come up last night." Sophie bit her lip. She felt shy, but eager to shake off the last of Assan's shadow across her body.

He sucked in a breath. "You're supposed to play hard to get. We're going slow."

"You're the one who wants to go slow. And I am hard to get."

He laughed. "You are, indeed. Well, I called to see if you wanted to meet again tonight. Your choice of activity."

"Come to my apartment. We'll take Ginger out for her evening walk, go to a sushi place I know."

"Sounds like a plan. Switching gears here." His voice had gone serious. "One of my warehouses was sabotaged down at the docks last night. They burned a whole shipment of wood outside, spray-painted fixtures, wrote some really ugly graffiti. I already did the usual police report, but I wondered if you could give me your friend in HPD's phone number? I want to discuss what I know, try and get this stopped."

"Yes, call my friend Marcus. You met him at Fight Club with Marcella, remember? They're engaged. He's a detective with HPD." She gave him Marcus's personal cell number.

"Great. I'll let you know how it goes. When I see you later."

"Can't wait," Sophie said, and realized it was the truth.

She got out of the black Bureau Acura and slammed the door, beeping the vehicle locked and feeling a definite lift in her spirits at the prospect of seeing Alika.

She took the elevator down to the Evidence Room on the lower floor of the main HPD building and went through the rigmarole of identifying herself. She requested to see the evidence collected at the scene of the gang leader shootings and spoke with the sergeant on duty, explaining that she needed to examine the phones in connection with one of her cases. As the sergeant scrolled through the case listings for the right one, she mentally reviewed the earlier meeting.

Waxman had to know she was using DAVID on these cases. It was just a matter of time until he confronted her about it.

"*Dung beetles rolling great balls of shit uphill forever,*" she muttered.

"Excuse me?" The officer looked up sharply.

"Apologies. Just practicing my Thai. Got to keep it fresh."

"You Feds." He shook his head. "Wonder what brings you to a simple gang murder."

Sophie wasn't about to tell him. "Just checking a lead."

She was finally admitted into the depths of the evidence room and the sergeant pulled down the case box. "You can use one of the tables in front."

"Thank you. Okay if I photograph or make a copy of some of the things I need?"

"Yes, as long as you log it. We need to keep track of everywhere any of this information has been."

She snapped on gloves and carried the box to one of the steel processing tables with their harsh overhead lights. Inside the box was the bloodstained clothing the gangsters had been wearing, mercifully sealed in plastic—but the mere sight of the brownish stains made her nose wrinkle in powerful memory at the smell of old blood. The murder weapons had been logged and recycled in a gun return program after ballistics was checked. Sophie sorted through the various items and picked up the bag with the phones.

Glancing around to make sure she was alone, she pried open the first phone and took out the SIM card, slipping it into a slot on her reader. She copied both the SIM cards, re-inserted them into the phones, and checked back out of the station.

Back at her work bay, she downloaded the contents of the gangsters' phones to her computer and scrolled through the numbers and texts from the day the Waikiki gang leaders had killed each other. Sure enough, texts appeared from each other's numbers asking for a meet to discuss "new market developments."

Then, right at the time they were to meet, texts appeared from the number she'd already identified: *"You're being set up! He's going to take you out!"*

A similar one had appeared on the other gangster's phone.

Sophie sat back, considering. This was just like the way the kidnappers had been set up against each other. She booted up DAVID and ran a probability question regarding a saboteur within the Security Solutions company.

60% probable came back only after a few minutes. Perhaps DAVID was considering other scenarios, but unfortunately the program could answer only questions she put to it. Sophie called Waxman and the rest of the team and left messages about the contents of the phones, then, turned her attention to the child pornographers' computers.

She hated extracting and reviewing files that left mental scars on her just to see, but it was part of the job. She'd come up with some coping techniques to minimize the impact of the images she had to see, and they helped a little.

One of the write blockers she'd hooked up earlier dinged with completion of a hard drive copy of one of the pedophile's computers. She reconnected the copied hard drive to one of hers, and set the photos on low resolution for speed and lack of detail. She put her sunglasses on. This gave her enough of an idea of content to see what was in the files but by moving fast and buffering her vision, she kept herself from really absorbing what she saw.

Sunglasses in place, she put on headphones, filled her ears with Rachmaninoff, steeled herself, and dove into the unspeakable.

Chapter 10

Sophie's phone dinged with a breach alert, disrupting her review of the pornographers' files. She frowned and minimized her screen, pausing the classical music and scrolling through the phone's security alert.

Someone had tracked both her locations via her two workstations' IP addresses.

Sophie tore off her headphones and stood up in agitation. She walked to the water dispenser, pouring herself a glass of water to clear her head. She sipped it, staring out the great bank of windows in the corner of the lab where she liked to exercise.

How had this happened? She had any number of obscuring programs hiding both her work and home computer locations. She must have tripped something, digging into Security Solutions' network. Theirs was the only case she was currently working on that was sophisticated enough to have been able to apply a back trace.

The good thing was the trace could only go as far as the street address, not her actual apartment. Her apartment was in a fifteen-story building with over a hundred units. It was one thing to find her building, entirely another to find her actual location, and then find her in it. She had a lot of countermeasures she could deploy before that might happen.

She would begin by tracking the program that had found her.

Sophie set the empty cup down decisively. She walked back to her station, put her headphones on, and made a call.

"Hello, Jenns. This is Special Agent Sophie Ang." Jenns Rudinoff was her apartment building's security and maintenance manager, and she'd made sure she had his personal number on speed-dial when she moved in, and that he knew she was with the FBI and that her father was a diplomat. "I've had a security alert. Can you keep an extra eye out for any strangers coming into the building? Salesmen, repairmen, like that?"

"Of course, Sophie. I'm sorry to hear that." Sophie had brought Jenns and his family gifts and given him a bonus every Christmas, all to make sure he was loyal and took her security seriously. She was finally cashing in on the buildup of favors. "We don't have any outside repair or remodel projects on the books right now. I'll put out an alert to all our security guys and screen every repair call for legitimacy."

"Thanks, I know you'll keep me safe." Sophie hung up and, to the swelling emotion of a Beethoven concerto, dove back into the stream of data from Security Solutions.

Almost immediately she detected a break in the stream, a break that lasted over an hour. What could it be? Was her transmitter detected or turned off? She knew what she would do if someone had made a relay station out of one of her rigs—she'd set it up to send false data.

Sophie imported sections of the data into DAVID for analysis and comparison before and after the break in the data stream, and almost immediately DAVID confirmed that the data she was now receiving was outdated. Not only that, DAVID found a tracker program embedded in the data stream.

Someone at Security Solutions was onto her.

She sat back and frowned. This expert programmer was getting to be a real problem, and she didn't think it was Lee Chan. She hit her phone feature and called him, leaving a voicemail.

"Lee, I need to meet with your main programmer. Leave me a message at this number with the time he's available." She rattled off her office phone at the FBI building. "This is not a request."

That done, she extracted a signature from the bit of tracker code that had found her location and deleted it, sending one of her own hunter programs to follow its path back to the source. Of course, the source was obscured.

She deployed the prototype program that her friend had yet to patent and watched it work. It came up with two IP locations, one in the Security Solutions building, and the other to an address she matched to the ritzy Pendragon Arches building in Nuuanu, just a few blocks away from her own address.

She had the tracker's location.

But, like her own situation, having the building address wasn't the same as knowing what unit the originating computer was in. For that, she needed physical intel. She rubbed her hands together, anticipating tomorrow. All around, things were looking up. First she'd kissed Alika, and now there was a break in the Security Solutions situation that revealed she had a worthy opponent.

He could hide, but he couldn't run.

Sophie got up and hurried into Waxman's office. "Ben."

Waxman glanced up from a pile of reports. "Sophie. What's up?"

"I have a situation." Sophie shut his office door and told him what she'd found out and concluded. "I need authorization to penetrate the Pendragon Arches building where this unsub has his home computers, and deal with the threat."

Waxman sat back, the tips of his fingers together in a pyramid. "How did he find your locations again?"

She explained it as simply as she could. "And I know, by comparing the data stream from before and after the transmitter was found, that now he's trying to misdirect me by feeding me outdated data."

"And how did you discover the data was outdated?"

She opened her mouth. None of the FBI-sanctioned software she was authorized to use had those capabilities. "I have a program that ran it."

"DAVID?"

She couldn't lie, looking into those penetrating blue eyes. "Yes. And another off-the-books program I used to break into Security Solutions developed by an agent friend in New Mexico."

"Did I or did I not give you a direct order about DAVID?" Waxman's voice rose. "And did I or did I not give you a direct order about working on Bureau business at home?"

Sophie shut her mouth and felt her face go still. "Yes, sir, you did."

"So now what's happened?"

"The location of my personal home workstation has been compromised."

"Which is why Bureau business needs to be contained in Bureau locations where we have the full security and resources of the federal government available!" Waxman was shouting now. He depressed a button on his desk. "Bateman!" he bellowed into the intercom. Sophie had never seen him so agitated. "Go to Agent Ang's station. The central computer. Remove, erase, and wipe out every trace of the program called DAVID."

"Yes sir," Bateman's tinny young voice quavered. Waxman cut the connection.

"My God. You wouldn't."

"I just did. You are working on and using federal property and that program is ours to erase off of any Bureau computer at any time."

"I have a patent filed on DAVID," Sophie said. Yes, she'd called the lawyer her father had provided, but the process had only just begun. She had to bluff. "This is not the Bureau's software. It's mine."

"Possession is nine-tenths of the law, and I'm shutting it down," Waxman's voice was scratchy with anger. "You think you can outright defy me? Think again. You're getting written up for this, Agent Ang, and I'm sending Bateman to your home address to make sure you're shut down there too."

Sophie cast her eyes down, ticking through her list of choices. She needed Waxman on her side, backing her up. Appearing to comply was the best course.

"This programmer at Security Solutions might be dangerous to the Bureau or me personally. I know he, or someone working at Security Solutions, may be sabotaging their criminal clients. I don't like that he's tracked my location as close as my building. I agree with you, sir. I shouldn't have bent the rules. I'll take Bateman to my residence myself and extract DAVID. I've already debugged the tracking program from the Security Solutions data stream, of course."

Sophie's demure manner seemed to be reassuring her boss because she heard him shuffling papers and the low sound of his breathing as he reined in his temper. She kept her eyes down.

So much for calling him "Ben."

"That will be acceptable. And yes, let's identify and put out a Be On Look Out through HPD on this programmer of theirs if you don't get a call back from Chan with an interview time. You'll be happy to hear we are getting interest from our superiors on moving forward against Security Solutions."

"That's a good step. I'll keep you informed."

"Dismissed. Keep me up to speed on developments." His voice was cold.

"Yes, sir." She shut his office door softly.

Sophie went quickly to the women's room. She had to safeguard DAVID.

Using her smartphone, she shunted a copy of the DAVID software to her own secure cloud server location. She kept a copy of all the data from her investigation into Assan and the "simultaneous" cases in that secret file as well. Then, she initiated the process of deleting DAVID, and all her FBI programs, off her home computers.

Waxman was right about one thing. She didn't like having an unknown subject know where she lived.

Bateman was gone from her workstation by the time she returned to her cockpit of computers, leaving a post-it note with "I'm sorry" scrawled on it in the middle of her desk. She decided to take the young agent out to her apartment later, on her way home.

Lee Chan had left a message on her work phone. "Hi, Sophie. Our programmer, Todd Remarkian, is out of the country right now and is not available to speak to you in person. I've emailed you his itinerary to verify that he won't be back anytime soon, but you can reach him at this number." He rattled off a phone number.

Sophie jotted it down and immediately called, using her headphones and the Bureau phone line. A robust male voice with a slight Australian accent picked up. "G'day."

"Todd Remarkian? This is Special Agent Sophie Ang at the FBI. How are you today?"

"Well, it's sunny in Hong Kong, so that's something,"

Remarkian said. She ran a program on the phone to verify that's where he was. The trace ran in the corner of her screen, tracking his location. "What can I help you with?"

"I'm calling regarding some irregularities with your computer systems," Sophie said. "I need to speak with you and go over some trends I've discovered."

"Well, I'm on assignment here in Hong Kong, and I won't be back for several months," Remarkian said regretfully. The icon tracing the call pulsed, identifying the destination of the call as a cell phone in the New World Millennium Hotel in Hong Kong. Of course, it was always possible he had a location blocker enabled, but why?

"Perhaps we can videoconference later and I can let you know about our concerns." She wanted to get a look at this man.

"I just wouldn't feel right about talking about any confidential information over the phone or any of those apps," Remarkian said. "You never know who's listening. Especially around here." His voice sounded serious. "I do have an encrypted email account though. Perhaps you could send me some information, files to review?"

"And I don't like email. You've been identified as the mastermind behind Security Solutions' software division. Who can I speak with here in the States that you'd consider your next in command?"

"Well, I'm not, actually. The 'mastermind' is Sheldon Hamilton, our CEO. We developed the systems together, and he brought me in on the project. Lee Chan represents us right now since we're both in Hong Kong. I'm given to understand you've already met him."

"I have. We went to school together, actually. Lee it is then. Let me know the minute you're back in this country for any reason."

"Of course, Agent Ang. I confess I'm curious." Sophie heard a note of self-deprecating humor in his voice.

"Nothing I can discuss here and now." Sophie said. "I hope I can count on your full cooperation."

"Yes. We want the FBI happy with us," Remarkian said. "Not to mention the CIA, the NSA, and Homeland. So many federal agencies to keep happy." She heard steel in his voice.

"Okay, I'll call Lee then. Until we meet in person."

"G'day, then." Remarkian hung up decisively.

Sophie called Ken, brought him up-to-date and then called Lee asking to meet with him and Honing, vice president of the company, to discuss some "data irregularities" within the company.

"Can you tell me what this is about, Agent Ang? Confidentially?" She could hear the worry in Lee's voice. "I don't want my boss to be mad at me if I can help it."

She remembered his earnest face while studying with him. He'd been good, but a linear thinker. There was no way he had the brilliance needed to develop Security Solutions' software. She could see him being able to track her location, though.

"I'm sorry, Lee. I'll have to talk to you and the other VP in person."

It wasn't long before Sophie and Ken Yamada sat in the office of the Vice President of Security Solutions' client operations. Frank Honing, the VP, was a dark-haired man with a restless manner. He clicked and unclicked a stylus, with an electronic pad on his knee, as they sat down in a luxurious seating arrangement around a low coffee table. Lee Chan looked haggard, tilted dark eyes set in pouches of purplish flesh as if he hadn't slept in days. Sophie felt a stab of guilt, looking at him.

"So what's so urgent?" Honing asked. "First, we have an

unscheduled visit, now this meeting request. Should I call our legal department for this meeting?"

"No," Sophie said. "We're here to help you, actually." She had a folder on her lap. She hadn't wanted to give them any data to mine further so she'd printed out the texts from the various situations the saboteur had engineered. "I spoke to your programmer, Todd Remarkian, and verified he was out of the country. If your company's president is available, he should hear this, too. It's regarding some irregularities we've discovered within your company that intersect with criminal cases."

"Our Chief Executive Officer, Sheldon Hamilton, is out of the country, as well. They're both in Hong Kong," Honing barked. "I tried to get them on speaker at least, but they're in meetings right now. We're penetrating the Asian market and things are at a delicate stage of development. You can tell us anything you'd tell them."

Ken gave Sophie a nod. They'd got the go-ahead to disclose the information on the cases Sophie had gathered by verifying with Gundersohn and Waxman that the company, however shady it might turn out to be, deserved to have this information.

"This information came through my computer analysis and some detective work." Sophie took out three stapled stacks of paper. "Each of these is a transcript of extracted text messages from separate and unrelated crimes that may have been precipitated from within your company. In any case, Security Solutions is the only common factor in each of these seemingly coincidental setups."

Sophie handed each of them, and Yamada, one of the stacks of papers. It was ridiculously antiquated to disseminate information this way, but once something was in digital form there was no telling where it would go or how it could be manipulated. "I'll need to collect these printouts after this meeting. The upshot is this: we think you may have a saboteur within your company, someone who is using your clients' criminal enterprises against them."

She talked them through each of the cases: the gangsters killing each other, the SEC traders turning each other in, the kidnappers, the child porn ring. "We hope that by sharing this information with you, you can help us identify the saboteur within your company."

"I had no idea." Lee's face had gone the color of beeswax. "Clearly this person has some computer savvy, but we have a whole Internet security division. It could really be anyone with access to our clients and their phone contacts."

"Can you work up a list for us? We'll help you nail this guy," Ken said.

Lee glanced at Honing, who shook his head. "No. We don't want a joint investigation with the FBI. You appear to have some interesting intel. How did you even come up with this?" Honing pinned Sophie with sharp dark eyes.

"I ran an analysis on these cases." She shrugged as if it were both too simple and too complicated to explain. "It appears Security Solutions caters to the unsavory, and if someone is sabotaging your clients and helping them get busted by law enforcement, who are we to look a gift horse in the mouth?" It felt good to work the phrase into a sentence against this smug bureaucrat. "We've offered to help you, but fine. Clean up your own mess if you can. We'll continue with our inquiry. I warn you, though, so far, we're not impressed by the company you keep."

A dusky flush rose up Honing's neck. He tapped the tablet's screen and made a sweeping gesture with the stylus. "We appreciate the information you've just passed on, and assure you we will cooperate fully with the FBI. We will be in contact with

our management team for our next steps." He stood, six foot of
intimidating, forcing them to get up too.

"Let us know if you find the saboteur," Ken said. "On behalf
of law enforcement, we'll be hoping it takes a long time."

Sophie had to reach out and tug the printouts of the text
messages out of Honing's and Lee's hands. "We'll see ourselves
out. You'll hear from us if there's any further information that
comes to light."

* * *

The Ghost watched a video of the meeting between Honing,
Chan, and the federal agents. He zoomed in on Special Agent
Sophie Ang's face. Today she wore a pair of slim black pants
and a tailored button-down shirt that showcased a slender toned
body that reminded him of a human Doberman—and he was
partial to Dobermans.

He could see muscle definition in her forearms and he
glimpsed some sort of writing, tattoos, on the insides of her
arms. He loved the color of her bronze skin, smooth as
buttermilk. Her large dark eyes flashed with intelligence as she
sparred verbally with Frank Honing, and he was glad the
surveillance feed of the Vice President's office was both color
and audio wired as he noted every word and gesture.

He wondered what kind of program she was running to be
able to track the saboteur and draw these conclusions. He didn't
like what she was saying, of course. This was a major wrinkle.
One he was going to have to put some thought and planning into
addressing, but the fact that she'd gone to the company with her
findings earned his respect. *Gratitude, even.*

Sophie Ang wasn't just going to joust with him in the dark
alleys of the Internet, she was after him in the flesh. He liked

that, very much. He wondered if she was onto his countermeasures, but nothing in the video or conversation gave any hint.

The Ghost glanced down, annoyed, as his cell rang with a call from Lee. He'd known the tech would need reassurance, but he didn't want to deal with him right now. He wanted to get to know Sophie Ang better.

He replayed the video and watched it again, from the beginning.

Chapter 11

*B*ack at her office, Sophie told Ken she wanted to dig deeper into who was behind the kidnapping case by reviewing the whole file. It ate at her that whoever was behind Anna's kidnapping was still at large. She had about an hour before she needed to take Bateman to her house to verify DAVID was gone from her workstation and she was due to meet Alika. Her pulse picked up, thinking of their date. It was nice to have something to look forward to at the end of the day.

Sophie opened a file on Takeda Industries, the company that owned the apartment where Anna had been held, and began her digging. Even without DAVID, she could use the FBI's secure browser to gather deeper than usual data about the company. She identified a parent holding company, a board of directors with photos, a variety of ostensible enterprises that included rental units, used rental cars, even rental furniture.

Victims could be picked up in company rental cars, housed in company rental units, tended to by kidnappers lounging on company rental furniture. She curled her lip in disgust.

Or, the kidnappers had just bought information on the family, and all three were dead in the morgue. There was no way to tell which it was at this stage. Sophie shunted all she'd gathered to

Ken's computer for him and Gundersohn to review, and glanced at the clock. It was time to go.

* * *

Bateman glanced around Sophie's bedroom, avidly curious. Sophie keyed on her machines with the coded fob.

"Nice," Bateman said. "Wondering how you afford all this on the same salary I get." The podgy young agent had annoyed her with his fumbling advances in the past, and now she could add poorly hidden resentment of her family's wealth to her dislike of him.

Having him here, in her bedroom, was almost beyond bearing.

"Who said we're in the same pay grade? Just do what you came to do. Verify that DAVID has been removed from my home workstation."

Bateman sat in her office chair and accessed Ying's main drive. It didn't take long for him to scan through all three machines. "It's gone." He squinted at her. "But I'm sure it's not really gone."

"None of your business, Special Agent Bateman. Now get the hell out of my apartment."

He did, and she slammed and locked the door behind him. Ginger rubbed against her legs, whining as she sensed Sophie's distress. "Thank God I'm seeing Alika. That will take my mind off the kind of day this was."

Sophie showered and dressed in her best matching underwear, a pearl-colored satin set from a cousin who was a designer. She put on a whisk of mascara and a swish of scarlet lipstick and donned her favorite earrings, fat baroque pearls the size of cherries on little chains that swung when she turned her head. She dressed in black jeans and a tank top because that's what she usually wore. She didn't want him to think she was overly excited about their date.

She fed Ginger. She paced around.

Time went by. Alika didn't show. She texted him a half-hour after he was supposed to be there. *"Still going to sushi tonight?"*

No reply.

Sophie poured herself a glass of wine, sat in the chair that faced a view of glorious setting sun reflecting off a burnished metal ocean. She got up and paced some more, annoyed. Irritated that she was annoyed.

She missed DAVID and her FBI work on her computer with the sudden fierceness like an addict must feel, longing for the needle. Her oblivion was being 'wired in,' and without her work, she was aimless, floating. Unplugged.

Alika's no-show wasn't helping. She called his phone and it went immediately to voice mail.

"Hey, it's Alika. Leave a message."

"Hey, Alika. Sophie here. Thought we were getting together? Well, I guess it didn't work out. Give me a call when you get this." She tried to keep her tone free of anything but slight puzzlement.

She hung up. A sense of loss, strangling and disproportionately terrible, clenched her stomach. She wanted to cry. Angry and agitated, she got on her treadmill and walked just to move while she waited. Ginger watched anxiously.

Another hour went by. The sun was long gone and the phone still didn't ring.

Sophie took off her jeans, tank shirt and pretty underwear and put them away. She should never have let herself care about him.

She dressed in her running clothes, plugged headphones into her phone, and stuck it in the pocket of her running shorts along with keys and pepper spray. She broke into a jog on the sidewalk with Ginger trotting at her side. The lights of the city cast pools of amber on the sidewalk and familiar storefronts were rendered mysterious in the darkness. They ended up at Ala Moana Beach Park, much further than she'd intended to go.

It took that long running for Sophie to feel herself again after the blow of rejection. This was the first time Sophie really considered that she might need therapy, as Dr. LaSota had suggested.

A man hadn't come to pick her up for a date. It wasn't the end of anybody's world and shouldn't feel like it. That Alika could affect her that way frightened her. It was ridiculous, disproportional.

The run had also given her time to tick over all the information she'd gathered on the case. She came to the same conclusions about the saboteur and Security Solutions as she had earlier. For the short term, they could focus on finding the leak connection between Security Solutions and the kidnapping case, and as they did so, the FBI could build something long-term against Security Solutions, perhaps even use the company as a window to spy on their criminal clients.

It felt good to walk along the sand at the park and finally sit, gazing out at the ocean. Sophie watched the moon rise over the water and listened to the waves. The water smelled briny from nearby Ala Wai Canal, and the rigging of boats in the yacht harbor clanged in a melody accompanied by the rustling of palm fronds in the light breeze. Ginger flopped in the sand beside her, panting.

She was tired, too, but satisfied with all she'd done that day. It didn't matter so much about Alika. She'd be fine even if things didn't work out and he'd changed his mind about her.

Ginger suddenly sprang to her feet, panting with excitement.

A man was jogging toward them on the hard sand at the edge of the water, a dog on a leash at his side.

"Sit, Ginger!" Sophie exclaimed, but she'd let go of the leash while relaxing in the sand, and in the darkness, couldn't find it. The Lab leaped away and ran down the beach to greet the other dog with an indiscriminate display of friendliness.

Sophie ran after the lab and almost collided with the jogger as he tried to untangle his dog from Ginger's advances.

"Heel, Anubis!" His voice was sharp.

Sophie finally got a hold of Ginger's collar and wrestled her away from his dog. That animal stood like a statue, moonlight outlining a Doberman's sleek body shape and cropped, pointed ears.

"I'm so sorry," Sophie exclaimed. "She got away from me. She's a Lab—no sense of dignity whatsoever."

The man was as still as his dog. He topped her by several inches. She felt his gaze even in the dark, and somehow it made her wish she could see him. "You should be careful out here by yourself. There are all kinds of people here in the park."

"I can handle myself," she said, pepper spray and phone a reassuring weight in her pocket—not to mention her combat skills. "But thanks for the warning. And sorry for Ginger's bad manners."

He gave a brief nod, and she heard the clink of metal as he heeled his dog, and then, the man and the Doberman were jogging away down the beach, black shadows against silver sand and moon-dappled ocean.

Sophie frowned, wishing somehow they'd talked some more, that he hadn't just taken off. Something about him and the dog Anubis was magnetic. But she needed to get home and get to bed. Tomorrow was bound to come too soon, and be full of challenges.

Chapter 12

Sophie's phone woke her with Alika's Rocky ringtone. She reached over to the end table in the pitch-dark the blackout curtains guaranteed, and fumbled it up to her ear. "Hey." Her voice was husky with sleep.

"Sophie? Sophie Ang?"

It wasn't Alika's voice, but it was familiar.

"Marcus! Thought this was Alika. What time is it?" She squinted toward the red numbers of the clock by her computers.

"Four a.m." Kamuela's voice was grim. "I'm sorry to be calling you this way, but I saw your number was the last one Alika's phone received."

"What's happened?" Sophie could barely force the words out past the sudden constriction of her throat.

"We got a call. Someone beat up Alika. They found him outside his warehouse at the docks. He's..." Sophie could picture Kamuela's face and see the way the big Hawaiian detective pinched the bridge of his nose when he was troubled. "He's still alive."

"Oh my God," Sophie whispered. "Where?"

"Queen's Hospital."

"I'm on my way." Sophie hung up and turned on the light.

She sprang out of bed. Ginger leapt off, wagging her tail as if something exciting and fun was going to happen.

He's still alive, he's still alive he's still alive. Sophie hauled on her clothes, grabbed her weapon and creds, and drove to the hospital in a dawn so new it hadn't begun to stain the day. She hurried to meet fellow agent Marcella Scott and Marcus Kamuela in the waiting room. Marcella looked beautiful even in the dawn, her chocolate-brown curls caught up in a careless knot and her FBI outfit hugging a curvy figure. Marcella had known for over a year how she felt about Alika.

"Oh, girl. I'm so sorry this happened." Marcella hugged Sophie's stiff body tightly. Kamuela put a hand on Sophie's arm to get her attention.

"Alika's in a coma. Looks like it was a pretty systematic beating. He's got broken bones and probably some internal injuries, according to the doc I got a hold of. It wasn't anything like a fair fight—pipes and bats, and multiple aggressors. Most people would be dead right now."

Sophie swayed, and was grateful Marcella had a good hold on her. *He was fighting for his life while I was getting annoyed with him for forgetting our date.*

She felt disembodied. This was a dream. She just hadn't woken up yet. She wasn't really here, in this waiting room with its fluorescent lights, plastic palm, and dog-eared copies of *Highlights For Children.*

She'd grabbed the nearest clothes to put on, and realized that the black jeans and tank were what she'd been planning to wear on their date.

"He's going to be fine, right?" Sophie's eyes felt open too wide, but she couldn't seem to blink.

"They don't know. His family's on their way over from Kaua`i."

"Can I see him?"

"No one's seeing him."

That's when it finally sank in that it was really bad. *He might not make it.*

She reached behind her, groping with her hand, and eased down into a molded plastic waiting room chair. "What do you know?"

"He called and told me, yesterday afternoon, that you'd given him my number to talk to me about the harassment he was getting from the Boyz who control the Honolulu construction trade. I opened a case for him. I've been aware for a while that there was graft going on, but it's been too big and deep to do anything about, and I didn't have a case to dig into. I was glad to hear from him. I had someone who was ready to go up against the Boyz, testify, get them shut down." Kamuela pushed a hand through thick black hair, shook his head. "I'm sorry."

"I'm sorry too. He told me about it just a few days ago. Said things had been escalating, that he'd had some drug trace planted at his warehouse and the cops were looking at him for importing."

"I know. I found all that in a file on him. Opened by a detective I've got concerns about. But now we're thinking it's going to be a long haul. I hate to tell you this—he was set up pretty well. Initial search of the warehouse showed a lot of drug trace. So much I'm not going to be able to dismiss it. The scene was set up to appear that Alika was taken out by someone whose toes he stepped on importing drugs. You sure you know this guy?" Kamuela cocked his head, made eye contact with her. His gaze was all cop.

"I think so," Sophie whispered. "You can't let this happen. Please dig deeper."

"Don't worry," Marcella sat beside her and hooked an arm around her shoulder. "Marcus will do everything he can."

"We were just starting to date." Sophie looked down at her hands. "I mean, things were just getting going. I can't believe it."

"Shitty all around," Kamuela said. "Well, I'm going back to the scene. We've got a uniform here to make sure he's safe in ICU. So it's a waiting game right now."

"Marcella, can we open an FBI case? I mean, if there's corruption in HPD?" Sophie asked.

"We don't know that yet," Kamuela said sharply. Sophie didn't blame him for being defensive but she knew organized crime in something as big as the construction trade thrived through a system of kickbacks and payoffs across a number of levels. Alika Wolcott, a small fish developer from another island, was being made an example of.

He had a few friends those gangsters would have to contend with.

"Marcella." Sophie made eye contact with her friend. "Please."

Marcella tossed her head and the knot let go of her long chocolate hair. She scooped it up impatiently and re-knotted it. "Of course we'll get involved. Just as soon as local law enforcement asks for support from the FBI. You need our resources to battle corruption in the construction trade, right?" She poked Kamuela's broad chest with a scarlet-tipped finger.

He groaned. "This is damned awkward, woman. Let me get into the case first. I barely talked to Alika before the shit hit the fan."

"Clearly you need our resources. You're overwhelmed and there are concerns about leaks in the department," Marcella argued.

They were clustered together in the waiting room, their voices low and heads close together, when Sophie heard the sound of feet in the hall. She turned and saw a trio of people hurrying toward them. She shrank back in her chair at the sight of a regal Hawaiian woman, elegantly dressed in black slacks and a flowered blouse, leaning on a distinguished-looking Caucasian man's arm. This had to be Alika's mother and stepfather. An older woman in a dark muumuu followed, silver hair wound into a crown on her head.

"Where's the staff?" the man asked. "We're looking for where Alika Wolcott's room is."

"I'm Detective Marcus Kamuela—in charge of his case. And you are?" Kamuela stepped up to them, hand extended.

"His mother. Lehua Wolcott. My husband, Sean. And this is my mother, Esther Ka`awai," the woman answered as they shook.

Sophie had heard of this family, both from Alika and from her friend Lei, who had met them in cases on Kaua`i. Marcella stood up and joined the introductions.

"I remember you from Kaua`i," Marcella said to Alika's parents. "I'm sorry to see you again in such terrible circumstances. This is Special Agent Sophie Ang." She gestured to Sophie, still seated and trying to become invisible. "They were dating."

Three pairs of eyes fastened on Sophie. She stood awkwardly, surprised Marcella had introduced her that way—it made the relationship seem more serious than Sophie was ready for. "Hello."

Lehua Wolcott took two steps and embraced her. "He talked about you all the time." She let out a sob. Her husband drew her away and into his arms and Sophie was left looking into the deep, penetrating brown eyes of Esther Ka`awai. Sophie had heard of the famous Kaua`i wisewoman, known for psychic abilities and powerful connections in the Hawaiian community.

"I'm honored to meet you." She inclined her head respectfully.

"Alika says you are a talented fighter," Esther said.

"Not good enough to do anything to protect him." Sophie's eyes filled suddenly. The older woman embraced her, and Lehua broke into fresh tears. Sophie glimpsed Kamuela leaving, his athletic shoes squeaking as he strode down the hall. Eventually, she disentangled herself from Esther's arms and found a tissue beside the plastic couch and passed the box around.

"We haven't actually spoken to any staff about how he's doing," Sophie said, when Lehua, Esther and Alika's stepfather had pulled themselves together. "Since you're family you should be able to get more information."

"Absolutely." Sean Wolcott walked to the empty glass-fronted window and wiggled the slider, pushing it open. He stuck his head inside the nurse's station.

"Hello? Hello? We need some information out here," he boomed into the interior.

It wasn't long before one of the locked emergency doors opened. A doctor and nurse came toward them.

Their faces were grave, and Sophie found herself clutching Esther Ka`awai's arm as the Wolcotts pressed against each other. Marcella stood off to the side working her phone, but she pushed away from the wall to hear the news.

"I'm Dr. Kagawa." The doctor took in their names as they introduced themselves. He addressed his remarks to the Wolcotts. "I want to give you some preliminary findings. These next twenty-four hours are going to be critical. I just finished up with your son's surgery. He's in a coma right now, and that's a good thing. He has a fracture to the right side of his skull and a lot of swelling in his brain. Being unconscious is going to give the swelling time to go down. He has shattered ribs, a broken arm and a fractured tibia." Dr. Kagawa looked down at his clipboard at the sound of their gasps. "I also had to go in to repair some internal bleeding."

Alika's magnificent body had been beaten and broken almost to the point of death.

Sophie's stomach was so tight she found herself hunching over, as if trying to protect her own internal organs. "Is he going to live?"

"I can't say right now," Kagawa gave her a level gaze. "But I know he's a strong, healthy young man and he obviously has a lot to live for right here in this room."

Lehua broke into fresh sobs and Esther began praying, sitting down on one of the hard plastic chairs, her hands folded. Sean Wolcott held his wife and Marcella held Sophie close.

It was excruciatingly awkward to be here with the family in their extremity, when she didn't have words for the pain that twisted her stomach and strangled her breath. She hated emotion. She felt her face settling into that familiar opaque mask. Her eyes were dry.

"We'll let you know in the morning when he can receive visitors. You folks might as well go on home. We don't have accommodations here for you, and it's going to be hours before we know anything more." Dr. Kagawa and the nurse said goodbye and disappeared back into the off-limits area through the swinging doors.

"We're not going anywhere." Lehua sat down beside her mother on one of the hard chairs. "Sophie, we'll call you as soon as there is any news. What's your number?"

Sophie rattled it off automatically and got Lehua's as well. She said goodbye, and walked stiffly down the hall, arms wrapped around her waist. Marcella draped an arm over her shoulder.

"I'm already moving on this with Marcus," Marcella said as they went through the doors of the hospital into sunlight that felt shatteringly bright to Sophie. "I got the okay from Waxman."

"Good. I'll pick up the computer end."

"No. You're definitely not working this case. Waxman's orders. You have plenty to do on your own cases right now, without getting into something that's bound to be emotionally compromising."

Sophie spun toward her friend. "You're assuming this is such a big deal to me. In fact, I wish you hadn't introduced me the way you did to his family. He was my friend and my coach. We kissed a couple times, had one date."

Marcella didn't back down from Sophie's snarling tone. "You forget how well I know you. I told Waxman about your relationship with Alika because I know it's more than you're saying it is. I know how you feel about him and how long that's been going on. Yeah, it's awkward to be known as the girlfriend when you'd hardly had a date, but it was only a matter of time because you've both had feelings for a while. I know firsthand how cases can get messed up when emotions are high. You can't bullshit me."

Sophie balled her hands into fists. "You don't know anything." She spun and stomped away from her friend.

Sophie jumped into her SUV and drove to Fight Club, changed into her spare workout wear, and went to the heavy bag.

Everything, as she glanced around, reminded her of Alika. This was his place, his second home, as it was hers. She shook off tears as well as sweat as she worked combinations on the bag until she was too exhausted to think or feel.

Finally, in the gym's shower, she remembered she hadn't fed or let Ginger out. It seemed like a lifetime had passed since she got that call from Kamuela, but when she checked her phone it

was only 9:00 a.m. She dressed quickly and called her pet
service.

"Can you go in to my apartment this morning and let Ginger
out now as well as the usual noon time? I had an emergency very
early this morning and had to run."

"Sure." Lucy, Aloha Petsitters' coordinator, said. "Thought
I'd mention Sandra, who usually walks Ginger, is out sick today
so I'll send a sub. Ginger won't mind, will she?"

"She could lick your new walker to death. She's good
company but not much of a guard dog."

"Sounds good. Is the alarm code we have on file still good?"

"Yes. I'll call you with any changes." Duty done, Sophie
hung up and went out to her car. One thing Marcella had said
was true. She had her hands full with her own cases right now.
Hopefully, work would keep her mind off Alika lying in a coma
in a hospital bed. She felt a stab of pain in her chest at the
thought.

There were two new hard drives from other agents' cases to
mine at her computer bay, and she still needed to find out where
the unsub that had tracked her was actually located in the Arches
building. She sat down at her cockpit of computers. Her brain
felt spongy, her attention flickering in random bursts of
electricity that quickly short-circuited.

Thank God she had some tasks that didn't require her to
think. Sophie plugged in the write blockers to copy the new hard
drives, which would take a few hours. She put on her
headphones and stared at the screen with her work email on it,
but she couldn't focus enough to click on any of the icons even
with Beethoven in her ears.

Had Marcella called their mutual friend Lei Texeira on Maui
to let her know about Alika's attack? Lei had dated him in the
past and would want to know, even though they hadn't been an

item in years. Sophie knew she didn't have the words, or the energy, to tell anyone what had happened to Alika. She'd managed to write a note to other members of the gym that Alika was injured, and had taped it to his office door.

Was it too soon to call Marcella and Marcus to see what they'd come up with so far?

A hand on her shoulder made her jump and she whirled in her chair, whipping off the headphones.

SAC Ben Waxman was gazing down at her, hands on immaculate hips, blue-gray eyes troubled. "Understand you had some bad news this morning."

"Yes, sir. A good friend is in the hospital." Sophie's voice came out a whisper.

"I heard he was more than a good friend. I hope you understand why I couldn't authorize your working his case."

Sophie didn't answer. She still didn't know how to describe what she and Alika had. Talking about it with her boss didn't feel right.

"Anyway, I hope you're okay." Waxman jingled coins in his pocket.

"I am, sir, thanks." She could tell Waxman didn't like her calling him 'sir' again, but yesterday's confrontation over DAVID still rankled.

As if reading her mind he said, "I feel bad about DAVID. I've set up a priority review discussion with the higher-ups as we discussed. They aren't going to be in town for some weeks, but if you send me a report or a PowerPoint on DAVID's capabilities, I will present it on videoconferencing for this meeting. Hopefully we can get something to move ahead."

"Yes, sir," Sophie said woodenly. "When do you need it by?"

"The meeting is day after tomorrow."

"I will get it to you as soon as possible."

They stared at each other another long moment.

"I'm sorry about your friend." Waxman turned and walked out.

Things with Waxman were so strange. She wished they could get back to the collegial working relationship she was comfortable with.

Creating a presentation on DAVID was the perfect project to keep herself busy while she waited for news on Alika and didn't have anything breaking on her own case.

That reminded her that she'd told Todd Remarkian she'd talk to Lee again about the tech aspects of Security Solutions. While setting up a new presentation in slide software, she put her headphones back on and rang through to Security Solutions, identifying herself.

"I'm sorry, Lee Chan never came in today," the secretary said.

"Did he call in?" Sophie's brows snapped together in concern.

"No, ma'am. It's very unusual."

"Can I speak to Frank Honing, please?" The VP might know something.

"Yes, ma'am."

The transfer went through and Frank Honing's voice was brusque. "Yes?"

"This is Special Agent Sophie Ang. I'm wondering if you know where Lee Chan is. I urgently need to speak with him regarding the saboteur situation."

A pause. "He's not at work?"

"No. And his secretary said he hasn't called in. Does he have a personal cell?"

"I'll call him and get back to you." The phone banged down. Sophie blinked at the rudeness and frowned thoughtfully.

She went back to her presentation and composed several sections of description of DAVID's capabilities. She decided not to get too technical. She was filing a patent on DAVID; she didn't want to provide any of the agency's tech agents a way to replicate her program.

She still hadn't completed the patent application. This was as good a time as any, so she pulled up the online form for it. Developing that would help her with the description of DAVID, anyway. She was deep in pages of legalese and technical jargon when her phone rang.

"Special Agent Ang."

"Frank Honing at Security Solutions. I've sent a staffer to Lee's apartment. No answer at his door or cell. In fact, it's been twenty-four hours since anyone at the company has seen him, and he pretty much lives here at the company building. Agent Ang, I'm concerned."

"Well, you're a security company, so I'm sure you have ways of getting into his apartment and checking on his whereabouts that we can't legally perform without his being declared a missing person. Are you telling me you think he's missing?"

Honing harrumphed. "Yes. I had our security staff go into his apartment already, and it appears he cleared out in a hurry."

"Why would he run?" Sophie asked.

"He might be the saboteur," Honing said. "Other than our man in Hong Kong, Todd Remarkian, he's the workhorse behind all of our company's Internet security and no one is in a better position to manipulate our clients than he is."

Sophie frowned. This felt too easy. "Do you want us to try to find him? Or do you want to go through local PD?"

"We're already involved with the FBI, like it or not," Honing said tightly. "I'd rather not go through the rigmarole of bringing another bunch of cops up to speed. Here's Lee's cell number and address." Honing rattled them off and Sophie jotted them down.

"I'm sure you meant that statement as a compliment on the FBI's work," Sophie said. "I'll take this as your authorization to search for a valuable missing employee and go from there."

Sophie hung up on him as hard as he had on her. Using voice command, she called Ken Yamada.

"We need to find Chan." She filled him in on the tech's disappearance.

Ken swore. "I knew things were going to get thicker when we told them about the saboteur. I've been hard at work tracking the Takeda Industries situation. It's a shell corporation. There's no physical evidence of a real company, so it isn't going anywhere. I'll have to bring the team up to speed."

"I'm glad my intel was helpful." Sophie's brain, still overloaded from the situation with Alika, was having trouble remembering what Takeda Industries had to do with anything. "Want to go to Lee's apartment and see what we can pick up? I can at least bring in his home computer rigs. We should also send out a Be On Look Out through HPD on him."

"I'll let you call HPD because I know you'll want to check in with Marcus Kamuela about how Alika Wolcott is doing," Ken said. "I was sorry to hear he's in the hospital."

"Yes. I'll call Kamuela and meet you at the vehicle." Sophie didn't let any emotion into her voice. "Why don't you brief Waxman?" She wasn't in a hurry to speak to her erstwhile mentor again so soon.

Sophie backed out of her computer rigs, checking the time on the write blockers. They still needed a few hours. She strapped on her shoulder holster with the Glock 19, shrugged into her jacket and switched her headphones for a Bluetooth, calling Marcus Kamuela as she walked through the IT lab.

"Hi, Sophie. No updates on Alika's condition yet. We're just getting started down at his warehouse at the docks and I'm sorry to tell you it's really looking like he was shipping drugs," Kamuela said. "I'm in his office and I'm uncovering some irregularities in his shipments in addition to enough drug trace to make the dogs go nuts. I'm trying to believe you when you say Wolcott isn't dirty."

Sophie exited the lab and her athletic shoes squeaked down the shiny hallway toward the main entrance to the elevators as her thoughts whirled.

"It's got to be planted. Alika isn't that stupid. Please keep digging! Anyway, I called you about something else." Sophie rattled off the situation with Lee Chan. "We'll handle this as a direct request from Security Solutions to find their missing employee. Could your team post a BOLO on him?"

"Sure." She could tell Marcus was glad she wasn't grilling him more about Alika's investigation. "Gimme the details."

She told him. "I'll have Security Solutions fax a picture of Chan." Sophie got on the elevator, pushed the button for the ground floor garage.

"What else can you tell me about Wolcott?"

Sophie threw up her hands, frustrated, and remembered Kamuela couldn't see that gesture. "Just follow the evidence. Do what you have to do. But keep an open mind. Remember who this man's family is. Do they seem like a bunch of drug dealers with connections to organized crime?"

He blew out a breath. She could almost see him shaking his head. "My mom knows his grandma Esther Ka`awai, the *kahu*, and she's been calling me nonstop to help Alika and get the gangster sonsabitches that beat him. So I'm hearing it from all directions, believe me, and so far, Alika's looking like a Boy Scout if you don't count his heroin-sprinkled office and weird shipping receipts. I'll let you know what I find."

"That's all I ask. And call me if you hear of any change in his condition."

"Will do."

Sophie hung up with a flick of her finger to the device in her ear and broke into a jog to join Ken Yamada standing by the shining black hood of the Bureau's Acura SUV.

Chapter 13

Sophie and Ken Yamada pounded on Lee Chan's door at his modest apartment building on the outskirts of Honolulu. "Open up! FBI!" Ken barked.

When no one answered, Ken gestured to the building's manager. The stocky Filipino unlocked the door for them. Sophie and Ken kept weapons drawn in ready position per protocol as they entered.

A simple front room was decorated with a flat screen TV, a sleek lounger, and a coffee table. All was immaculate, the furniture black and the carpet and walls gray. Sophie had the impression that Lee had created his interior living space to feel like the inside of a computer: efficient, monochrome and dust-free.

They swept through the space and, as the VP had confirmed, empty hangers, missing clothes and sundries confirmed the tech was gone.

Sophie pulled Lee's desktop rig out from under the small modern desk in the bedroom and unplugged it. As she straightened up, with the computer in her arms, she felt a shifting inside the metal housing.

She set the computer back on the desk, pulled open a small

desk drawer and rooted around until she found a set of small graduated Phillips-head screwdrivers in a plastic case.

Ken returned. "Don't see anything that tells us where he went. What are you doing?"

"I have a sense Lee is pretty careful. If there is a clue to where he went, it's going to be on this computer, not lying around on the coffee table," Sophie said. "I'm checking inside. Thought I felt something shift around in here."

She applied the right sized driver to the screws on the back of the panel and opened it.

Inside were stacks of cash. She removed them and drew a sharp breath. Currency from China. Taiwan. Korea. Japan.

"Lee Chan could be anywhere," she murmured.

"That explains these minor digs." Ken gestured to the neatly made twin bed, impersonal as a motel. "He made plenty at Security Solutions. He was keeping a small footprint."

Sophie took an evidence bag out of the Kevlar vest she wore and dropped the money into it. "Maybe he is the saboteur after all. Though he didn't seem to have the nerve for something like that."

"Maybe he's being set up to look like it, though," Ken said. "He seemed smart enough when we met him."

"I don't know." Sophie picked up a black plastic comb from the drawer and lifted a hair with a root bulb from it, slipped it into an evidence bag. "It's time to dig deeper into Chan's life, for sure, but frankly, I hope he doesn't turn up floating in the Ala Wai Canal because he's someone's loose end."

Interviewing the building manager after the search, they got an idea of his habits. Lee left early for work, returned late, was quiet, had never been seen with anyone else in the apartment, was tidy, and paid rent on time. "The ideal tenant," the manager concluded.

In the elevator on the way down, Sophie mulled the situation over.

"Think he was the saboteur?" Ken asked, his arms around the computer. She'd planned to carry it but he had taken it from her with old-fashioned courtesy.

"Why else would he run?"

"Maybe he knew who it was? Was being threatened? Maybe he could tell Security Solutions was going to throw him under the bus in any case."

"It's true that Honing was quick to do that. Lee would make a handy person to blame," Sophie said. "But the Lee I went to school with in Hong Kong—he had an impulsive side. I once saw him delete a whole day's work because he'd made a mistake. Maybe this was like that."

"You mean, he got spooked and pulled the plug?" Ken was better with the colloquialisms.

"Exactly."

* * *

Sophie hooked up Lee's computer to one of the write blockers that had finished copying one of the previous hard drives. Ken had taken the DNA and fingerprint evidence as well as the cash to the lab for processing. Hopefully, they'd soon have more physical information on Lee, and in the meantime she had a lot of work to do.

Hours passed in wired-in oblivion as Sophie made headway on the analysis of the hard drives left on her desk, finished the presentation on DAVID, and sent that off to Waxman via encrypted email.

Sophie revisited the back trace that had tracked her computer to her building and looked at the two destinations: the Arches building, with a hundred and fifty units, and the building Security Solutions was housed in.

Most likely it was Lee who had tracked her. Did she feel threatened by him? No. He probably *was* the saboteur and his tracking of her was just necessary counterintelligence of someone who was trying to break into his system.

So who was Todd Remarkian and what was his role? He and Lee had to be connected if they'd worked closely on developing proprietary software like the surveillance monitoring program that was Security Solutions' crown jewel.

She began a file on Todd Remarkian and found it challenging to assemble. He seemed to have very little cyber presence. His credit card was issued by the company. His apartment was paid for by the company. He drove a car owned by the company. He had a squeaky-clean credit score and a phone issued by the company.

It was as if he'd been invented by Security Solutions.

She shivered. But she'd heard his voice, that light Aussie accent. He was real. On impulse she called him, clicking on the trace app for the number she'd dialed. A little skull spun in the corner of her monitor as the trace ran. The number rang.

Rang.

Rang.

"Special Agent Ang. G'day."

"You knew it was me."

"Who else would be calling from the FBI? Assume this is regarding Lee's disappearance."

"Yes. I was hoping you might have some more information for us."

"I'm sorry, I don't. I know he's missing because Frank Honing called the boss and me a few hours ago. We're worried he's made off with some of our customer information, if you must know."

The little spinning skull stopped. The location bubble appeared. HONG KONG pulsed in it.

Sophie relaxed. She didn't know what she'd been expecting. "I'm sorry to hear that. Tell me more." There was an art to interviewing a witness. One had to appear to be sympathetic and grateful for any information, while not revealing anything in return.

"Frank, Sheldon, and I suspect he's the saboteur. We think he's taking his chance to run now that we're onto him. We've sent one of our private investigation teams after him. No offense, but we thought you might appreciate the help."

"None taken. Your company has its own private army and it's true that there are only two of us on your case," Sophie said. "But we expect to be apprised as soon as you find him. He hasn't done anything that we can charge him with yet."

"Except steal our information and sabotage our customers." Remarkian's tone was silky and deadly at the same time. "But of course. We'll let you know the minute we find him."

A silence. She could hear Remarkian breathing, which was amazing considering he was halfway around the world in Hong Kong.

"Anything else?" she asked. "Anything at all?"

"Yes. Lee isn't all he appears. Dig into his financials." Abruptly, Remarkian hung up.

Sophie immediately revisited Lee's identity file. She'd been able to crack into his employee file at Security Solutions through her backdoor into the company's server, and saw there was a direct deposit for his paychecks.

It was a simple matter to follow that to locate his account at Bank of Hawaii. A few phone calls later, the email alert on one of her rigs beeped with the receipt of faxed copies of his bank statements.

Sophie set one of her smaller analysis programs to weed through the reams of information to find any payments or extraordinary data, and quickly identified a pattern of nine thousand, nine hundred ninety-nine dollar payments twice a month in cash, payments that wouldn't trip the federal reporting laws designed to track drug traffickers.

She printed up the anomalies and further wire transfers out of his bank to another account in the Cayman Islands. Lee had been stockpiling. Perhaps for this move. His current balance was zero. Her phone rang in her headphones, jarring her out of hypnotic analysis mode.

"Special Agent Sophie Ang."

"Sophie? This is Alika Wolcott's mother, Lehua. The doctor has allowed Alika to have visitors. We've just been in sitting with him and I thought you might want to stop by."

Sophie's heart began pounding. "Is he okay? Any change?"

"No." Her voice came out on a sigh of released sorrow. "But no change for the worse, either. Come down and we'll update you more fully."

Sophie glanced at the clock on the wall. It was well past the dinner hour and she'd done enough today. "See you soon."

On the drive to the hospital, she ticked over Alika's situation. It was frustrating not to be able to do anything for his investigation. She mulled over the similarities between what Alika was being investigated for and what she suspected her ex, Assan Ang, of actually doing.

She'd heard about the investigation against Alika that her friend Lei had initiated on Kaua`i, the murder of a young woman involved with the drug trade. He'd been completely exonerated, but the fact remained that he'd been associated with those accusations and it had left a stain, made him vulnerable.

Sophie didn't believe Alika was a drug smuggler because it

went against everything he believed in as an athlete and a mentor to so many. But Assan was a different story. The only thing he loved more than power was money. For him, they went hand in hand.

Assan had an operation that shipped into Honolulu. Perhaps he had ties to the Boyz. She had to remember to ask Kamuela to look into it.

A uniformed police officer was seated outside Alika's room when Sophie arrived just as Lehua was coming out. The older woman's rich brown skin looked gray with fatigue and stress, and her sleek black bun was unraveling. Still, she forced a smile and took Sophie's cold hands.

"He's stable," she said. "Try not to be too shocked when you see him. The doctors say the coma is the best thing for him right now because of the swelling in his brain."

Sophie bit her lip. "I'm so sorry, Mrs. Wolcott. I'm just sick about this."

"My boy is strong. He wants to live. My mother, Esther, has been communicating with him in the gray place between and she says he has every intention of coming back. It's not his time yet, and we're all supporting him with prayer." Lehua's large brown eyes shone with conviction.

Sophie couldn't find a response to a statement so far outside of her world's operational framework. Her mother had been a Buddhist, and she and her father were agnostic. She knew Alika practiced hula with his grandmother's *halau* for special occasions, but she wasn't familiar enough with Hawaiian tradition and spiritual practice to do anything but nod in agreement.

"I hope the prayer helps," she said carefully.

Lehua squeezed her hands one more time. "They're only allowing two people in the room at a time, and I'm meeting the family in the cafeteria for dinner. So you have him all to yourself for a little while. They say to talk to him. He may be able to hear you."

Lehua let go of Sophie's hands, patted her arm, and walked away. Sophie smelled a hint of gardenia perfume in Lehua's wake. Sophie squared her shoulders and pushed down the door handle, stepping inside.

She'd tried to prepare herself. She'd told herself it would be bad, and she'd seen what people looked like after a fight many times. But there was no way to brace herself emotionally for what lay on the bed.

Alika's was a body she'd studied from every angle as a coach and an opponent, someone she'd known so well she could predict his moves in the ring. Someone she'd dreamed about, whose heavily muscled, lithe body she'd craved to know in a different way, and whose kindness, intelligence, and business savvy she'd admired.

Someone whose friendship and passion she'd only begun to explore.

He was propped at an angle, his head swathed in bandages. An oxygen mask covered his nose and mouth, but every bit of skin on his face was discolored, swollen, and unrecognizable. His arms lay stiffly on top of the covers, one of them in a cast, his hands bandaged. One whole leg was encased in plaster and hung from an overhead pulley. Sophie could barely see any skin that wasn't empurpled with bruising.

He was breathing on his own, she noted. That was something.

Her legs collapsed and she dropped into a hard plastic chair beside the bed. The room was filled with a chorus of tiny beeps and blips, and she could see his various functions tracking on a monitor.

Talk to him.

"Hi Alika. It's me, Sophie." Her voice sounded thready and her lips felt numb. She tried to imagine where he was, somewhere in the "gray between" as Lehua had said, and what might help him come back.

A storm of emotions engulfed her in a toxic welter that made her breathe hard, eyes prickling. Grief and rage at his brokenness. Compassion. And something like shame. She hadn't been able to protect or help him, and she'd been angry with him while he was being attacked and fighting for his life.

None of that matters right now.

All that mattered was that he get better, and come back from this. The rest would sort itself out.

She leaned forward to touch the one uncovered spot of skin she could find, the bulge of his shoulder muscle. It was patterned with a curving tribal tattoo of interlocked triangles that followed to a dent where the cap of deltoid muscle met his biceps.

Sophie scooted as close as the IV stand, dangling dripping bags of liquid, would let her. She traced the tattoo gently with her fingertips, then leaned forward and placed her lips on it in a soft kiss.

"I'm so sorry this happened to you. I want you to know I'm here, and I'm going to help with your case as much as I can. I don't know what we are to each other yet, but I care. A lot. More than is comfortable." She stroked the small patch of golden brown skin with the black triangles on it. It felt hard and cold as marble, as if he were already dead. "I know you're in there. And you can relax, and leave this to us. Marcella and Marcus are working it hard, and no matter what they uncover, we're all fighting for you."

She leaned forward and rested her forehead on his thigh under the white blanket, feeling her eyes sting with unshed tears, her hand still on his shoulder.

The door opened with a snick and she sat up abruptly, blinking.

Marcella had slipped inside the room. She sucked in a breath and covered her mouth with a hand at the sight of Alika, big brown eyes wide.

"I know. There's just no way to be prepared for how bad..." Sophie didn't want to finish her sentence in case Alika could hear her, somewhere in the dim place where he was. "They say to talk to him."

"Hi Alika." Marcella came around to sit on the chair opposite Sophie. "You look like hell, man, like you've gone ten rounds with Mike Tyson and his six cousins, which I guess in a way you did. And they had bats and a pipe." She nodded to Sophie. "We found one of the weapons used in his assault. The piece of pipe was thrown into the bushes beside his warehouse at the docks. We've gotten some DNA evidence off it. I've put a rush on the trace. He had some skin under his fingernails too. The lab thinks we might have something we can use to check for matches in ViCAP and AFIS by tomorrow."

"That's good news. Hear that, Alika? The attackers were careless." Sophie stroked the tattooed dent on Alika's shoulder, her eyes still on Marcella. "You might as well update us, Marcella. He should know what's going on, too. We have no idea what he's hearing or understanding, but you have to tell me anyway."

"Okay. Well, initially it's looking bad. Marcus and the forensic team found heroin trace all through Alika's office and the warehouse. However, the crime techs think it has an odd pattern, more like someone took a packet of horse and sprinkled it around randomly than something that would have come about in the course of a package breaking open or something. In addition, as Marcus said he told you earlier, there were odd bills of lading in the files that have coded entries. And then, there was the cash."

"What cash?" Sophie frowned.

"Ten thousand in his office safe."

"That's nothing. Pocket change for a business like his."

"True. But we had to log it in. There was also opposing gang graffiti on the back of the building, as if the Triad had claimed it and then the Boyz came back and laid their signature across. It's all circumstantial, but it's systematic and multi-layered. Someone's done a good enough number on him that we're really going to have to dig for what was going on and who's behind it."

Sophie hissed a breath between her teeth, and turning to the still form on the bed, squeezed the bare spot on Alika's arm.

"Bateman's deep in his computers and we've done a search at his house. So far nothing there of note," Marcella finished.

Sophie kept stroking Alika's shoulder. She imagined the skin was warming under her touch and wasn't quite so rigid and unresponsive. "Good."

A soft knock came at the door and Sean Wolcott's head turned around the jamb. "We're back from dinner if you're done visiting."

"Sure." Marcella stood. "I was just updating Sophie on progress on Alika's case. Thought we'd let him hear it too. Let me bring you up to speed on what we've found out about his attack."

She slipped out the door.

Sophie wanted to hug Alika goodbye, but that was impossible with all the cords and IVs and strapping on his chest. Instead, she rested her head on his chest and turned her ear against his heart. She could hear a slow, methodical thud, a metronome echoed on the monitor across from them.

"Just rest and heal." Sophie stood and studied Alika carefully for any sign of change. There was none. He lay there like a broken mummy, just the way he'd been when she came in.

Chapter 14

Sophie settled in front of her computers at home, her short hair damp from the shower. Ginger, still panting from the hard run they'd done upon Sophie's return, flopped at her feet and heaved a sigh of exhausted happiness. Sophie dug a toe into the dog's side, idly scratching as the home workstation booted up. The dog's leg twitched and tail thumped.

Sophie had made a few decisions on that run, and as Ying came up to power, she put one of them into action. Accessing her coded cloud account, she downloaded DAVID once more back onto the computer's hard drive.

She wasn't going to be able to help Alika's investigation without it, and she actually had a lot to do to catch up to where she would have been if Waxman hadn't shut her down.

She consulted the checkbox task list she'd developed back at the office. Alika's battered face was what filled her vision and demanded focus. She easily hacked into Marcella's case on Alika in the FBI database and downloaded all the details to DAVID. She also re-activated her investigation into Assan Ang's drug trafficking operation, the one she'd considered stalled. Maybe there was some commonality there too.

She set DAVID to mine for more information on Alika and

Assan's cases and then turned her attention to the worrisome situation with Lee Chan's disappearance and whoever's computer in the Arches building had tracked her.

Perhaps that was where Lee was hiding. Maybe he, or Security Solutions, kept some sort of presence there. It was worth checking out.

She accessed the Security Solutions database through her backdoor and scanned for any addresses or information regarding the Arches building.

It didn't take long for an apartment number to come up: 9C.

That could be the location of the probe's origin that had tracked her. Lee might be there. But wasn't Security Solutions sending their own team looking for him? Who was the main user of the apartment? She scanned some more, but no renter's name was listed on the lease but that of Security Solutions.

Lee wouldn't hide on company property, would he?

Sophie glanced at the clock. It was 9:00 p.m., really too late to call Ken Yamada with something that wasn't an emergency. It could wait until morning. She switched back to Ying as the DAVID prompt dinged with new inputs.

The DNA from two of Alika Wolcott's attackers had been uploaded by the lab. It sat there, glaring at her from his case file.

Should she access ViCAP and AFIS from this workstation and run the DNA, in spite of being clearly directed not to, and it not being her case? Marcella and Marcus were probably home in bed, and it would take hours for the database to sort through all the DNA on file for any possible matches. Her friends would not thank her for pushing in on their case and violating her boss's orders just because of her own impatience.

Tomorrow was going to have to be soon enough for that, too.

Sophie blew out a breath in annoyance. She was exhausted but too wired and upset to sleep. She dimmed the lights and slid out of her dragon-patterned robe. But instead of going to bed, she padded naked through her apartment to her home gym in the corner of the living room, and, in front of the wall of windows overlooking the jeweled city and moonlit ocean, she began a series of yoga poses.

Peace eventually came from the meditative, deep movements and controlled breathing, and eventually, Sophie sat in the lotus position, empty and calm, moonlight bathing her.

* * *

The Ghost realized he'd been holding his breath when it whooshed out in a whisper, loosening the burning sensation in his chest. He hadn't noticed because he was so intently watching Sophie Ang, beautifully, perfectly naked, doing yoga in the moonlight.

He'd never seen anything like the sculptured perfection of her controlled movements. The light flitted over her skin in the grainy feed in a gorgeous striptease so that she appeared and disappeared in the black and white video.

He'd never meant to spy on her, stealing the dignity of a worthy opponent this way. That's why, when he'd unlocked her apartment and fended off the ecstatic greetings of Ginger, he'd carefully pointed the camera in her bedroom at her computers so he could monitor what she was doing there.

He was no prurient peeping Tom. He was doing necessary surveillance.

He'd put another webcam in the kitchen where she might talk on the phone while doing chores, and a third in the living room, pointed toward the corner where her exercise equipment was stowed alongside a sleek desk with a phone on it. He'd placed the camera to catch her on business or phone calls.

He'd never dreamed she had such a habit of walking around her apartment naked. The sight was pure visual poetry, and made him want to play violin while she moved to create a worthy background.

He'd wired for audio too, in case she let slip confidential information germane to his situation. Tonight he saw she'd reloaded that program she wasn't supposed to have, and she was on some sort of mission. By zooming in on her computer, he'd been able to grab screenshots of what she was doing, and it bore close watching.

She was trying to find the origin of the computer trace that had found her location. He'd beaten her in this particular move of their virtual battle, but he couldn't let her find him. He had to set up an alternative identity, move out of the corner she was trying to box him into.

He could hear the slow, deep sounds of her breathing as she sat perfectly still, her legs folded and hands on her knees. Her spine was a supple wand, her profile as pure and beautiful as the ancient Egyptian head of Nefertiti sculpture he'd liked enough to buy in bronze for his bookshelf.

The moonlight flowed in an unbroken mercury line from her throat down her small, round, pointed breasts, along her contoured stomach, and over the curved lines of her thighs and buttocks.

The Ghost's whole body was rigid as if electrified. The fine hairs of his arms stood on end, and his heavy, painful erection seemed to throb with the beating of his heart.

Sophie Ang was perfection. Everything he'd ever wanted or dreamed of in a woman. She was his physical, intellectual, and emotional equal. Even her lonely habits echoed his.

She was his female counterpart.

He'd never had such a violent attraction before. He prided

himself on independence, easy to maintain because women were tiresomely emotional and talkative. They were always trying to attach to him like remoras to a shark. He had no use for them and his sex life had been, until now, a series of one-night stands with willing partners who wanted more from him than he'd ever give.

She was different.

He continued to watch her and finally got out of his chair, sitting on the floor and assuming her posture. He synchronized his breathing with hers. He entered the same quiet peace she occupied.

When she finally stood up and walked back to her bedroom, his hard-on throbbed painfully. He made no move to deal with it. She wasn't responsible for what she'd done to him, and he wasn't going to sully thoughts of her with mere masturbation. He sighed with the loss as she went into the inner sanctum of her bedroom with that silly dog of hers, and total blackness stole his view of her.

"Good night, Sophie," he whispered. He got up and went into his bathroom to take a cold shower.

Chapter 15

Sophie woke the next morning with the cottony headache of an emotional hangover. She turned the lights on and threw off the covers. She never had gotten into her pajamas last night. Everything was too heavy and abrasive on her sensitized skin, even her silky sleep tee.

Ginger was on her bed again, and this time she patted the coverlet beside her and the lab crawled up beside her sheepishly. "I liked having you with me last night," she murmured as she hugged the dog around her sturdy neck. "I needed someone cozy and hairy to snuggle with."

Ginger thumped her tail in agreement with this plan.

"Okay, time to get moving. Got a lot of things to get done today." She hopped out of bed, slipping into the discarded dragon robe. She keyed on her computers with the fob and while they booted up, she started the teapot and got in the shower.

The homey and routine tasks helped her wake up and get underway, shucking off the last of a bad night. She'd tossed and turned, tormented by fragmented, feverish dreams of Alika in his hospital bed, Alika being beaten, Alika being arrested for drug trafficking.

She set strong morning tea to steeping and called Lehua's cell phone. The older woman picked up right away.

"Any change?" she asked after greetings.

"No. The doctor's going to meet with us today after they do another follow up CAT scan of his brain," the older woman said. Her voice sounded rough, snagging on the words.

"Please let me know what's happening. I'll come by today," Sophie said.

"I will. Are you helping with his investigation?"

"Informally." Sophie bit her lip. She hoped Lehua made no mention of that to Marcella or Marcus.

"Well, we're doing our own thing to protect him as his *ohana*. We've put the word out in the Hawaiian community to ask for any information on who might have been a part of beating him. Not just that." Lehua's husky voice firmed. "Anyone who might be a part of this ridiculous drug trafficking scenario they've set him up for."

"I hope it works," Sophie said. "Can you call me after his CAT scan?"

"I'll try."

Sophie's next call was to Ken Yamada, made from the kitchen as she sipped her tea.

"Glad you called me," he said immediately. "HPD just notified me that they spotted Lee at the airport in the United area."

"Did they catch him?" Sophie hurried to the bedroom now and began throwing on her FBI work clothes.

"I think he's giving them a run for their money. Slippery little dude."

"We should go help them. He's going to be traveling under another identity and we at least know what he looks like. I'll meet you at the airport." Sophie grabbed her shoulder holster and

Kevlar vest, standard for chasing a suspect in the field. "I called you because I found an apartment in the Arches building that Security Solutions rents. No lessee listed, but I want to go check it out and see who's in there. I think I'll call the VP first, see what they use it for, but I wanted you to know I plan to take a little field trip over there."

"Okay, but later. We're early enough to beat traffic and I'll see you at the airport."

Sophie threw some puppy pads down in the corner of the foyer and gave Ginger a pat.

"So sorry girl, I don't have time to take you out. I'll call the service and have them give you an extra long run."

The dog's soulful brown eyes were accusing as she shut the door and locked it, running to the stairs and getting some cardio on the way to the garage.

She parked in a loading aisle at the airport and put her FBI placard up in the window, hopping out of the vehicle and running into the departure area. She met Ken and they approached one of the TSA uniforms, showed badges, and asked to get access to the security headquarters. It wasn't long before they were sitting in a cockpit-like area surrounded by monitors. Cameras pointed at all the key traffic flow points were filled with people moving to and fro.

"Do you have any facial recognition software?" Sophie asked. She had a photo of Lee on her phone taken the day he'd given them the tour of the facility at Security Solutions. She often used her phone camera to unobtrusively photograph the witnesses she met in the field, and had found this practice invaluable many times.

Now she faxed the photo via phone to the Homeland Security computer and got the facial recognition software up and running, her fingers flying.

She and Ken Yamada visually scanned the computers along with a Homeland officer holding Lee Chan's employee mug shot. Finally, it was the facial recognition software that found the diminutive tech, lighting up one of the cameras with a ding.

Sophie recognized him once the software had identified him. He was definitely in disguise, wearing a fedora, a goatee, and had completely changed his style by dressing in a three-piece suit and carrying a shiny leather briefcase.

"Appears he's waiting for United Flight 730," the Homeland officer said. "I'll radio the desk."

"Don't alert him that we're onto him." Sophie could see Lee's anxiously darting eyes under the fedora. "Just delay the boarding of the plane. Agent Yamada and I will take him with some of your officers."

The TSA man called for backup. Soon they were jogging through the long shiny halls and open concrete work bridges with gorgeous mature plumeria trees between the buildings that were trademarks of the Honolulu Airport.

Lee saw them coming and made a run for it, throwing his briefcase into a man who stumbled into their path. Adrenaline surged as Sophie yelled, "Stop! FBI!"

She bolted after Chan, Ken right behind, dodging screaming travelers who crashed into each other trying to get out of the way. Sophie hit him with her shoulder in the center of his back. Lee flew forward and crashed to the ground. She held him down with a knee, pulled up his arms and slapped cuffs on him. She leaned down to whisper in his ear. "I can't wait to find out what's really going on at Security Solutions. I'm on your side."

He seemed startled, his eyes wide, but Ken and the TSA agents reached them, pushing back the staring crowds. Chan was frog-marched out to the curb by Ken. HPD had a secure vehicle, so he was driven to the FBI headquarters in the back of a Crown Victoria as Ken and Sophie followed.

They took custody of Chan from the police at the Prince Kuhio Federal Building. He'd been patted down and had his phone removed at the airport. They put him in Conference Room A, with its stark interior, steel bolted down table and chairs, and mirrored observation wall.

"I want my lawyer," Lee said clearly, the minute they were in the room. "I know you're recording me, and I want legal counsel."

"We aren't arresting you," Ken said soothingly.

"I don't care! You just heard me request legal representation." He glanced at his watch. "I requested representation at 9:37 a.m."

"Who can we get a hold of for you?" Ken asked.

"Bennie Fernandez."

Sophie groaned inwardly. They all knew the Santa-like little defense lawyer. Charming, relentless, and deadly were adjectives that came to mind. "We'll call him for you."

She and Ken briefed Waxman, who'd come to watch the interview. They all waited in the observation room, a small side area equipped with audio and video monitors, until the defense lawyer showed up.

Bennie Fernandez played up his Santa appearance today in a red aloha shirt with green leis scattered over it. His pink-cheeked face trimmed in white beard was almost a caricature, but his shrewd blue eyes never warmed. "Where's my client? I will need thirty minutes of confidential consult time."

Ken took him into the conference room. Sophie, alone with Waxman, shut off the monitors. She sighed and chewed her lip, wondering what was happening with Alika and his case.

"You look like you have a lot on your mind," Waxman said.

"I received your presentation and skimmed it. I'd like a little more on how DAVID is able to penetrate law enforcement databases and read-only through their files. I think that's one of the biggest concerns Headquarters has. Can the files be altered by DAVID? And the exact mechanisms of how it's able to penetrate law enforcement firewalls."

Sophie frowned. "I cannot disclose proprietary details that could make the program replicable."

Waxman snorted. "We have the program. It's work product. We just need you to explain it to us."

"I told you before and I'll say it again: its proprietary software. You were using it with my cooperation and participation, which I'm considering rescinding." Sophie felt her cheeks heat as she glared at her boss.

"All right now. We're not going to settle this here." Waxman appeared regretful, his eyes sincere and mouth pulled down. Sophie decided it must be because he'd just tipped his hand as to his real attitude about her work, and her temper spiked further. "Why don't you just explain a little more, and leave it at that."

Sophie spun on her heel, yanked open the observation room door, and stalked down the hall. Her skin felt flushed and gritty from chasing Lee. She'd already been stressed from what she'd been working on the night before and the visit to Alika. Annoyance with her boss and the FBI's high-handed treatment of her program ratcheted her temper higher.

"First, they had me begging to use it, then they took it away, and now they want to take it over," she muttered angrily. "*Misbegotten poxy swine.*"

Back in her office she booted up her workstation and pulled up the presentation. She added a few general paragraphs of explanation but was careful to hold back essential details. At least she'd finally finished the patent application and sent that off during her work binge last night.

That reminded her of poor Ginger, shut up in the apartment.

She called the pet service and asked for an extra long walk for Ginger. "She's a sweet girl," the coordinator said. "Our sub didn't have any trouble with her. He said she's just an angel."

"He?" Sophie went still. Something about it being a male staffer who'd walked her dog put her on alert. "Who is the sub? Is he going there today?"

"No, Sandra's back at work. His name was Fernando. Very handsome, too." She giggled.

Sophie frowned. "What sort of background do you do on your people? My apartment has to be secure." She didn't want to get into why, but it couldn't hurt to put a little fear into the flippant coordinator. "I'm an FBI agent."

"Oh, I had no idea! Of course, we do the usual background check." She named a company that for twenty-five dollars, checked for major legal trespasses. It was the barest bones, and Sophie was suddenly chilled. Ginger made her vulnerable in a lot of ways, not least of which was strangers having access to her home.

"First and last name," Sophie rapped out.

"Oh. Well, I told you there was going to be a sub and you didn't object then."

"Things have changed since then." Sophie remembered that phone call. She'd still been in shock about Alika, hadn't processed the threat to her security. "First and last name, please."

"Fernando Llamas."

"What did he look like?"

"Mid-thirties, maybe. Dark hair and eyes. Um—nice body." The coordinator's voice had gone small.

"Height, weight?"

"Maybe six foot? Not fat, that's for sure."

Sophie typed the name and physical description into the FBI's much more in-depth background check program. "Please advise me any time there's going to be a sub, and I will check them out myself."

"Of course. I'm sorry if you were alarmed."

Sophie hung up and searched the name. The little skull spun and stopped.

The man had no record, but then the name came back to an Argentine actor popular in the fifties deceased in the 1980s.

She hacked into Aloha Petsitters employee database and consulted Fernando Llamas's resume, which included being a vet tech and "sales." He did not fit the usual profile of a dog walker, whose demographic she'd already assessed as college students or housewives whose kids were in school.

Someone had been in her apartment. Someone who didn't feel right.

Her phone rang. "Interview is starting." Ken's voice.

"Be right there."

Sophie needed help with this security breach. Not later, but *now*.

First priority was to scan her computers. She started a spyware removal program remotely to sweep her home rigs, and walked to Bateman's workstation.

"I have to go into an interview, but I suspect someone's been in my apartment. Can you go out and do a bug sweep?"

Bateman blinked pale eyes. Their last encounter had been so hostile she could tell he was surprised she was asking him for help.

"Please," she added, though it pained her to do so. She dug in her pocket and handed him her keys. "Next to me you're the best at detecting unauthorized tech."

"Okay, since you put it so flatteringly." Bateman took her

keys and she handed him a slip of paper with her alarm code jotted down.

"Watch out Ginger doesn't knock you over."

"I'll be careful." He grinned. "You owe me now."

Sophie rolled her eyes. "Oh, God."

"When you least expect it, I'll want a favor."

"Whatever. Just make sure my apartment's bug-free." She hurried out the door and down the hall.

Sophie slid into a seat beside Waxman in front of the observation window. Her boss had adjusted the cameras so they also had back and side views of the people in the room. Gundersohn and Ken Yamada were on one side of the table, Lee Chan and his lawyer on the other, and things were already underway.

"I've advised my client that he is not under arrest, but he is choosing to cooperate with the investigation into Security Solutions because of his own concerns about the company."

"Very good." Ken smoothed his tie. "We appreciate that, Mr. Chan. We only came after you because of the concerns of your employer, Security Solutions. They were concerned it appeared you'd gone missing."

"I no longer felt safe," Chan said, with a glance at Fernandez, who nodded. "I'm in possession of valuable information and I'm worried for my life."

"What information would that be?" Ken was deliberately keeping his voice casual. From Gundersohn's folded arms and intimidating stare Sophie could tell the looming Swede had adopted the "bad cop" role. "As you know from our previous interview, a connection on one of our cases led to a probe into Security Solutions' internal operations. In the course of that, we've found some patterns that have piqued our interest. So why don't you add to that picture and tell us your concerns."

"I need protection. And immunity."

"We have to know more before we can make any such deals," Gundersohn rumbled.

Sophie felt rather than saw Waxman nod beside her.

"My client can give you a thumbnail sketch but nothing more without agreements in writing," Bennie Fernandez said.

"I'll contact the District Attorney to alert him," Waxman said into an intercom mic from beside Sophie. His voice echoed tinnily inside the room next to them. "Proceed."

Waxman began working his phone while Lee leaned forward. "I was a part of developing the automated surveillance software that's proprietary and our best selling point as a company. But then, I began noticing that many of our clients, who are not the most savory of characters, began having bad things happen to them. Blackmail, things like that. There's a client information leak. And now the FBI is aware of this."

"Yes," Ken said. "We came to you to alert you that you had some sort of saboteur within the company."

"Well, I agree that we do. And I'm being framed as that saboteur. But it's not just that. Our client information is being leaked to someone." Lee rubbed his chin with a shaking hand. "I think that person will kill to shut me up."

"It does seem like one possible scenario is that you're being set up," Ken agreed. "But running away only strengthened the impression people had of you being the culprit. What makes you think that your life is in danger?"

"Well, our CEO, Sheldon Hamilton, seems to have disappeared. He's supposed to be in Hong Kong, but when I called him to update him, apprise him of what's happening, he was gone. He can't be located anywhere. I trust Sheldon, I felt he should know what's going on. But when I couldn't reach him, I knew it was time to disappear. This person wants to set me up."

"Why wouldn't someone at Security Solutions have alerted us to Hamilton's disappearance?" Ken said.

"Because—they want you to think I had something to do with it!" Lee's eyes were wild.

"So what about..." Ken consulted his notes. "Todd Remarkian? He's the other tech guy."

"I talked to Todd. He was the one who told me he can't find Sheldon anywhere. He's contacted the Hong Kong authorities. You can verify this." Lee looked down at his fingers and picked at a bleeding cuticle. There was a long pause.

"I'm still not hearing anything worth disturbing the District Attorney about. Your company seems bizarre and badly run, but that's not a federal offense. Nor a killing one," Gundersohn said.

"But Sheldon Hamilton's gone. And it's Sheldon who has the patent on the automated surveillance software. It's his product. And someone has had him killed. Hong Kong is not a safe place." Lee's voice vibrated with fright. Sophie could tell by his blanched skin and trembling hands he wasn't faking it.

Waxman's phone toned beside Sophie. He stood up and went to a far corner to take it, talking in a low voice.

"Tell us more that shows you are in real danger," Gundersohn said. "And evidence that Sheldon Hamilton hasn't just skipped for his own reasons."

"Someone broke into my apartment."

"That was Security Solutions under orders from Frank Honing," Ken said. "And then we searched it too, at their request. They were concerned that you were missing. While searching for you, we found a computer with bundles of multi-national cash hidden in it, which kind of undermines your claim." Ken smiled, made a deprecating hand gesture. "Not to mention all the cash deposits you've been routing to the Cayman Islands. Just wondering what you could tell us about that."

Lee turned staring eyes to Bennie Fernandez. "I don't have any extra cash! I don't have any Cayman accounts!"

Bennie patted the young man's shoulder as Waxman returned and addressed the people in the interview room through the intercom. "I've described the situation to the District Attorney. He says there's no case here that involves us until there's some evidence of a crime. So we're going to hold you for twenty-four hours while we check out your claims. If we find anything, we'll reconvene. If not, you'll be released pending whatever charges Security Solutions decides to bring against you."

Lee's mouth opened and closed. Bennie patted his shoulder again. "Don't tell them anything more," the lawyer said. "Just think of this as a spa day. Rest and recuperate. You're safe in custody."

Sophie couldn't help smiling as she caught Waxman's eye—jail as a spa day? The lawyer got up and went out with Lee and Gundersohn as Ken radioed for HPD to take him to the local jail for holding.

They exited the observation room and met Ken in the hall.

"I'm going to try to locate Todd Remarkian and see what he has to say. I have his number back at the lab," Sophie said.

Ken nodded. "You do that. Start phone and online tracking of Sheldon Hamilton. After we get Lee situated, Gundersohn and I will go search Hamilton's offices at Security Solutions. And his home, if we have time."

"Lee Chan seems really frightened, but I'm not convinced anyone in this scenario is homicidal," Waxman said. "Corporate espionage, internal blackmail of clients, maybe even catering to criminals—but killers? Not convinced Chan's on the right track there."

"But what about the saboteur?" Sophie argued. "That person's responsible for at least six deaths if you count up the bodies from the gang leaders shooting each other, and those are only the ones we know about."

"Didn't pull the trigger, though, did he?" Ken said. "Did us all a favor there."

"That's what's interesting about all the saboteur's work, and it doesn't change the fact that someone's taking advantage of Security Solutions' intel to play God," Waxman said. "Which speaks of deadly intent to me. I think Lee knows something, and that's information worth protecting as long as possible. Move fast. We only have him for twenty-four hours."

Chapter 16

Back at her work bay, Sophie called Todd Remarkian's number.

"Yes." This time the affable Aussie's voice was clipped. "What can I do for the FBI today?"

"We have located and interviewed Lee Chan, whom we apprehended at the airport," Sophie said.

"I should return to the States," Remarkian said. "But I can't, with Sheldon missing. And I'd take a good long time deciding to believe Lee. Someone's selling our client information, and it could well be him." Frustration tightened his voice.

"What do you mean? He seems scared for his life." Sophie thought it was safe to say that much.

"He's blowing smoke to cover his ass, because Sheldon and I, before he disappeared, had verified that someone was stealing and selling client information."

"The saboteur?"

"Not necessarily. The saboteur seems to be focusing on manipulating our criminal clients. This is a genuine breach. We found some of our data on some digital forums for sale—access codes to houses, like that."

"Could that be what happened to the Addams child? The kidnapping case that brought us to you?"

"Possibly."

"Considering that you're a security firm, these are really serious issues," Sophie said. "Now tell me what you know about Sheldon Hamilton going missing."

"We had a meeting with some future clients in the morning. We're trying to set up a satellite office here in Hong Kong, and it went well. We sold several big players' security packages and were doing some interviews for key staff members for the office we're putting together. But Sheldon seemed distracted. He was working his phone, really agitated, told me right after the meeting he had some things to do. I said g'bye, and off he went."

Sophie frowned, glancing at the little skull spinning. It was having trouble tracing the call today. "And that was the last you saw of him?"

"Yes. We were supposed to meet this morning, go over the game plan for the day."

Just then Sophie's phone dinged with a text message. Bateman's number appeared on her phone. *"Found three cameras in your place."*

Sophie's stomach dropped with a breathless sensation of horror.

"Where? Check again, make sure you got them all" she texted back, fingers moving jerkily. She glanced up. The trace still hadn't connected.

Remarkian's voice continued in her ear. "Sheldon didn't show, didn't call. I went by his hotel room and pounded. No one there. Had the management unlock it and he'd packed up his stuff, no signs of violence. I called hotel security and Hong Kong police anyway, because I know we aren't wanted here by several firms in the city."

Sophie focused with difficulty on the conversation. "So you have concerns about violence from your competition?" she asked.

"It's been known to happen."

"Well, who else has secure, top level access to your company's computers and their data? We need to make a list of who the saboteur could be."

"Sheldon. Frank Honing. Lee Chan. Myself. Only we have total access to client information and the computer mainframe. Everyone else just has enough for their functions."

"Anyone else really knowledgeable about your automated nanny-cam software?"

"No one comes to mind. We run separate divisions. Lee, Sheldon and I developed the software. Frank is in charge of client operations and human resources. The rest of our core people are just technicians, not programmers."

Sophie stroked the surface of her phone, waiting for the next text message, trying to concentrate on what he was saying. "Lee said Sheldon owns the software."

"Yes. But I'm on as a co-developer and co-owner. Lee wasn't listed."

"So you inherit the program if Sheldon's gone?"

A long silence. "I don't like where this is going," Remarkian said.

"Just asking."

"Technically, yes. But we license the software to Security Solutions. Exclusively."

"Interesting way to run a company."

Todd Remarkian didn't reply. Once again Sophie had the sense that he was right beside her, breathing in her ear. It was unnerving.

"Well, is there anything else you think I should know right now?"

"I hope you look hard at Lee as the saboteur. I told you to check his financials, right?"

"You did. And they're suspicious, but not criminally actionable."

The phone in her hand lit up again. *"There were only three cameras. Locations in kitchen, bedroom and living room. Locking up now. The dog is cute."*

Sophie's head swam. Someone could have been watching her as she walked around naked. How long had those cameras been there? The dog walker situation might have tipped her off to look for something, but there was no telling how long she'd actually been bugged.

"Well, listen, Mr. Remarkian, I have to go. Why don't you try to return to the United States as soon as you can? I'd like to speak with you in person about exactly how a saboteur could use the software, and your boss's disappearance."

"All righty then," the chipper voice said, and hung up briskly. She took off the headphones and planted them on the charger.

Her priorities had just shifted from the Security Solutions case to her own personal nightmare. Three cameras in her home, broadcasting her naked. On the phone. Working top security cases on her computers.

They'd probably been able to stream video of the work session last night. She wanted to vomit with the stress of it. Waxman was right. She should never have taken any FBI work off-site.

She stared blankly at the monitor in front of her, trying to make sense of what had happened. How had her security been breached? Through a back trace to her computer's IP? Then, probably it was a simple matter to ID which FBI agents were working the Security Solutions case. They would have tracked her to the Makanani Building and found out she had a dog, and the rest was history.

Even though the Bureau did everything possible to obscure their agents' home locations, this was no ordinary unsub.

This was someone as good, maybe better, than she was. He knew where she lived. What she ate. What she was doing on her computer. And that she liked to walk around naked in her home.

Sophie found herself hyperventilating. She got up and fetched her weighted jump rope, going to the corner of the room.

As the rhythm of the rope's spinning steadied her pulse and respiration, she considered.

It didn't have to be the pet sitter service that provided an in. She remembered the unknown workman in the elevator the night she and Alika were taking a walk, with his duffel. She would have paid more attention to a stranger like that on the elevator with her if she hadn't been so bemused by her date with Alika.

In fact, the whole thing with Alika had been a tremendous distraction. She'd missed key pieces of information because her mind and emotions were tangled up with what had happened to him. She'd been distracted and gotten sloppy.

What if Alika's attack was supposed to do that to her? What if he'd been attacked because of her?

Sophie shook her head and jumped faster, the rope whistling through the air and striking the floor with a sound like a scythe cutting corn.

"No," she whispered aloud. The cases couldn't be connected.

But maybe it was Assan, going after Alika—because Sophie cared about Alika. Because they'd kissed in public, on the street, and he'd seen it.

She flashed back to Hong Kong.

She was lying on her back across the black marble island in that showplace kitchen she seldom cooked in, her skirt up around her waist, panties pinioning her ankles. Assan was choking her as he raped her.

He'd come home from some work meeting dark-browed and furious, and her effort to soothe and distract hadn't worked. The bottle of Grand Marnier she'd been pouring had shattered on the tile floor beside them and filled the room with a sickeningly sweet smell of orange.

She slowly came back to consciousness, her diaphragm reflexively heaving to bring in air, the black she'd disappeared into ebbing to gray, receding in and out with her intermittent air supply. He was still banging away at her, grunting above her. The gray parted, black spots receded, and she gasped for air— but a part of her longed to stay in that black forever. Then she wouldn't have to keep coming back to the hell that was her life.

Eventually, with a final heave, he finished. Her whole body was numb but she knew every second of this assault, and that it was going to hurt later.

Assan still had one hand clamped around her throat, depressing the nerves, veins and air supply that could so quickly snuff her out. His face, congested with the blood of his recent arousal, was inches from hers. His breath smelled of Grand Marnier, because now he was sipping from the bowl-like glass she'd poured him an endless half hour ago.

"You'll never be with anyone else. You're mine, until I'm done with you."

He'd said it many times. She'd chosen not to remember. Five years of lonely celibacy since she escaped hadn't put that promise to the test.

Until now—she'd finally found someone she cared about, and she'd kissed him on the street.

In the womblike corner of her beloved IT lab, her stomach lurched with remembered horror. She jumped faster. The rope thwacked down like a whipping. She'd had those, too.

Could Assan have something to do with what Alika had been going through?

"No!" she cried aloud. The rope slammed down and tangled in her legs. She fell forward, hitting the heavy glass window and welcoming the pain.

No one saw in the empty lab. No one knew the terror and grief that constricted her chest.

Assan had to go.

Even if he wasn't behind the attack on Alika, she couldn't allow him to continue living—in her mind, in her memories, in this world—and in Hong Kong, torturing a new young bride.

He might even be the one spying on her in her house.

She had to find a way to stop him. Sophie walked around the lab, cooling down, trying to form a plan. If only she could deal with Assan the way that clever saboteur at Security Solutions had dealt with the criminals he had access to.

DAVID was how she'd find a way if there was one. She could cross check the information on the shipping companies Alika dealt with and she might find something tying Assan and Alika together. The world of heroin smugglers couldn't be that big.

The pneumatic doors slid open and Bateman came in, carrying a little duffel bag and puffing from exertion, his watery eyes bright.

"You have a serious breach going on." He tossed her the apartment keys. As she caught them, she realized that the pet company had copies, and that weird dog walker could have made his own. She had to get the locks changed and upgrade the security system.

Ginger was going to have to be dealt with some other way than daily incursions by strangers into her apartment. Maybe she should find Ginger a new home. She immediately felt queasy.

"Show me the surveillance units you found," Sophie demanded.

"Let's dust them down for prints. We might get lucky."

She followed Bateman to the print and trace lab and he took three tiny cameras, each the size of a tack, out of an evidence bag. "Nice stuff, here. Got a remote transmitter, totally wireless, tiny renewable battery. State of the art." Bateman told her things she already knew as soon as she saw the cameras.

He dusted them with fingerprint powder, then hit them with a light. "No dice."

"No way to tell what location they were transmitting to, is there?" Sophie asked, for form's sake. She already knew the answer to that.

"Nope."

"You sure you got them all?"

"Went through three times. These blipped right away." They used a consistently reliable portable handheld device for bug sweeps. "Any idea how he found you and got in?"

"Yes. But I'm not discussing it."

"Want me to open a case for you?"

"No. I'm dealing with the breach." Sophie scooped up the cameras and slid them into a plastic evidence bag. "I'd appreciate you keeping this quiet for the moment. I'll handle it."

"One day." Bateman firmed his jaw. "I'll stay quiet one day. I know Waxman's on your ass and he'd want to know about this."

"One day. Then I'll tell him myself."

Sophie walked back out of the lab with the little cameras in her pocket. She had a way to communicate now. She had to get home, run everything through DAVID to see what she could put together. But she couldn't leave without first trying to find the head of Security Solutions.

Back at her work bay, she ran searches on Sheldon Hamilton

and began assembling a dossier. His basic information first: Single. Thirty-eight years old. Interests in classical music and computers. MIT graduate with degrees in software engineering and business. Started company with venture capital he raised. Clips from magazines of articles and news items, anything that would help. She noticed his address was listed as the Pendragon Arches building. She dragged and dropped items, more in a hurry to leave than ever—until she came to a photo.

The CEO leaned against a Corinthian column in a doorway, wearing a well-cut suit. He had expressive brown eyes behind fashionable glasses. Chiseled features. Short dark hair. Broad shoulders. Height was around six feet.

He could easily be Fernando Llamas, the dog walker.

Chapter 17

Sophie's need to get home throbbed in the pulse points of her neck, where she'd been so recently reminded of her vulnerability by reliving those moments with Assan. She shut down her workstation and headed for the door.

"You'll be okay?" Bateman called from his work bay, blue eyes earnest. For once she didn't resent his intrusiveness.

"Fine. I'm getting the locks changed right now." Sophie waved as she went through the doors of the lab.

"Sophie! I was just going to call you!" Marcella's voice was cheerful as she emerged from her office, pinning an errant curl back into the French roll she called the "FBI Twist." Sophie blew out a breath in surprise and relief to see her friend. "Marcus and I caught a break. We've brought in two of the thugs that assaulted Alika. They're willing to roll on their bosses in the construction trade and it's looking good that we won't only get the Boyz who attacked Alika, we'll get some bigger fish, too."

"Great news! Need my help for anything?" Sophie could have hugged Marcella, it was so good to hear something positive.

"Nope, we've got it rolling. They're down at HPD station singing like canaries. I just came back to pick up recording equipment."

"Have you heard anything about Alika's condition today?"

"No. I've been too busy running around like a chicken with its head cut off, trying to get some traction on the case and bring those Boyz in."

"Okay, I'll call Alika's mother. In the meantime, I've had some developments I'm really worried about." Sophie filled her friend in on the situation.

"What the hell? How could this guy be in Hong Kong and at your apartment at the same time? And why?" Marcella threw her hands up in a classic Italian gesture.

"Exactly. I'm wondering if Security Solutions isn't a whole lot more worried about us following their case than they're letting on. So Hamilton comes back and goes and puts cameras in my place himself? I mean, it's too strange." Sophie found herself breathing too fast and put a hand on her diaphragm to calm herself. "I had the cameras removed but I think I'm going to call him out, try to set up a meet and find out what his game is."

"Sounds risky."

"He's supposedly in Hong Kong, and missing, but I suspect he's right here in town. Do you have a better idea?"

"Just don't meet him alone. Call me. Are you getting your place secure again?"

"Yes. Better late than never." Sophie shivered, and Marcella put a hand on her shoulder and squeezed.

"How long were the cameras up?" her friend asked.

"I don't know."

"Oh God. I'm sorry. At least you caught it early, if it was when the pet sitter went in, which seems the logical breach."

"Right." Sophie straightened, adjusted the backpack she carried. "Anyway, I just had to get this off my chest. Thanks so much for the good news on Alika's case. Now if he just wakes up and starts getting better…"

"Exactly. Gotta keep positive," Marcella said. "At least we've got the rat bastards that did it."

"Thanks for telling me. Keep in touch." Sophie headed down the hall.

Still walking, she put in her Bluetooth and called Jenns Rudinoff, head of security at her building, alerting him. "Someone's been in my apartment and planted surveillance equipment. I've removed it, but I need a locksmith, someone absolutely trustworthy."

She cut short Rudinoff's apologies, got the name, and called in a rush order on a change of locks after doing a quick check on the company via her phone.

Her next call, weaving home through the heavy downtown commute traffic, blind to the sunset and waving palms, was to the alarm company for a full system reset and change of codes. "I'd also like a video surveillance unit put in outside the door with a remote feed to my phone," she ordered.

The third call was to the dog walking service.

"Aloha Petsitters."

"Hi. I'm revoking consent to access my apartment," Sophie said. "Get me your manager."

Sophie was very controlled as she described to the manager how the company had been used to get into her place. "In view of damages to my security which have necessitated changing my locks and alarms and untold stress because your dog walker substitute was an impostor, I'd like your company to pay for and provide me with a secure location where I can board my dog during the day."

The manager didn't argue, instead arranging for Ginger to be a regular at Doggie Daycare, a location with a big fenced yard where Ginger could socialize with other dogs and staffers during the day.

Sophie's tight chest had begun to loosen by the time she was pulling into her parking place at her building. She probably should have taken Ginger somewhere like that in the first place.

The doors of the elevator slid open in the garage and she entered. She leaned against the wall as it ascended. She had a flash of memory: leaning against Alika in the elevator. *Happy. Relaxed.*

It seemed like a year ago and it'd only been a few days.

The elevator doors slid open in front of her penthouse apartment. She got out and stood looking at the shiny red lacquered door. Her feelings about coming home had changed now that she'd had a hostile in her place. She could hear Ginger whining and the clatter of her toenails on the other side of the door.

"*Son of a snake with two penises,*" she muttered in Thai. "Everything is fine. I'm handling it." Sophie unlocked the beautiful door.

All was normal. Inside, the apartment was pristinely clean and looked exactly the way she'd left it that morning, so long ago. Sunset was beginning, and the dying day blazed in the bank of windows, bisected by the iconic silhouette of Diamond Head and the necklace of skyscrapers along Waikiki.

"Hi, girl," she greeted Ginger, rubbing the dog's chest and behind her ears. Ginger wriggled in an ecstasy of happiness.

The locksmith was on his way, so she turned a chair and propped it under the door handle after relocking it. She took the bug-detection wand out of her backpack. Ignoring Ginger's bids for attention, she walked methodically through the apartment and swept for any new devices.

It was clean.

Sophie went into the bedroom. Her rigs were on, but locked

down. She'd programmed them remotely that way, and now she activated the screens with her fob.

The spyware scan showed No Threats. Finally, some good news.

Sophie sat down at her rigs. Her fingers rattled on the keys as she pulled the file she'd started on Sheldon Hamilton into DAVID and expanded the background search on him. She then pulled down the file on Assan that she'd started and re-hacked into Alika's FBI/HPD case. She set DAVID to searching for commonalities in companies and contacts between the two.

That was enough for the computer to chew on for a while. Ginger was trotting in little circles by the door, clearly needing to go out and not wanting to use the puppy pads.

Sophie changed quickly into her running clothes and put her Bluetooth in, loading her pepper spray, keys and phone into her pockets. She wanted to take her weapon too, but didn't want to deal with the holster and windbreaker for keeping it covered up. She put it away in the bedside drawer.

Sophie waited until she was on the sidewalk and Ginger was blissfully piddling on a scrap of lawn to call Lehua Wolcott.

"I thought I might see you here at the hospital today," Alika's mother said without preamble.

Sophie pushed past a stab of guilt. "I'm sorry, I couldn't make it. A lot was happening at work today, and, it turns out, on Alika's case. But first, how's he doing?"

"No change." Lehua's voice sounded leaden with something like hopelessness. "They say the swelling's going down in his brain but he still isn't waking up. Nothing but the most basic reflexes." She rallied with an effort. "We just have to keep praying. We've all been taking turns reading to him. I wondered if you were coming."

"I don't think I can." Sophie had to distance herself. *Can't afford to care too much, become too entangled with this family.* "I just thought I'd check in, and let you know there have been some positive developments with Alika's case. You can check with Detective Kamuela for more information. I'll be in touch." And she hung up, softly, but firmly.

Until she knew who was really behind the attack on Alika, it was best if she kept her distance. She wasn't safe. For him, or anyone. Maybe when Assan was dealt with, and she'd laid a few more demons to rest.

Sophie broke into a jog and took Ginger all the way to the beach again. On the way back, she bought a *laulau* for herself and one for the dog from a sidewalk vendor. As she was crumpling the wrapper and dropping it in a corner trashcan, her phone rang.

Her heart sank a little when she saw it was her father. *More guilt.*

"Hello Dad." She walked rapidly, her eyes scanning the street as the Bluetooth piped in his deep reassuring voice. She never held her phone to her ear when walking; it was too much of a distraction when in the open and vulnerable. She wondered at all the people who seemed to think their phones made a cone of oblivion around them, when the opposite was true. Phones made them vulnerable: to theft, assault, or worse.

"Sophie. You never called to check on your mother."

"There's been a lot going on. We had a security breach in the apartment. I've had to change the locks and codes. I'm still sorting it out. And a good friend was attacked."

"What's going on?"

She sketched the basics, not wanting to alarm him. "I'm taking care of it all, but I've been seriously distracted."

"Well, then." He harrumphed. "Perhaps I should put off my visit. I'm coming in next week."

Sophie's mind zipped through the various scenarios. Her

father didn't have his own Secret Service agent, but he was under their protection and jurisdiction as needed. Perhaps an extra security layer was a good idea right now.

"No, Dad, come. Keep your plans. I'd welcome the company." She got his travel details and then asked for the number of the agent assigned to monitor him. "I want to bring him up to speed."

"It's a she," he said with a grin in his voice. "Ellie Smith. Official badass."

"Dad. You sound like you like her." Over the years, he'd done nothing but grumble about the Secret Service and his intermittent support from them overseas. "Babysitters and nosy as hell," he used to say.

"Ellie doesn't take my crap. And she's good at what she does. I'm supposed to call her when I get something fishy like a threat or something. I'll tell you when I get there, some of the stuff she's gotten me out of." He rattled off her number. Sophie memorized it.

"See you soon, Dad. I hope things will have settled down a little around here by then or you won't be seeing much of me—but Ginger will enjoy having a human around. I have to take her to a doggie daycare now." She filled him in on how the pet sitter service had contributed to the breach.

"She's going to love daycare," he said. "Maybe you can find one for me, too. With ladies in bikinis."

Sophie laughed, but her eyes were still scanning the busy street, the dark corners. Ginger glanced up at the sound, and lolled a doggy grin.

"See you soon, Dad." Sophie hung up and focused on getting home. She lengthened her stride. She felt better having talked to him. Stronger. Not so alone. She wasn't as good at being alone as she used to be.

Chapter 18

Sophie let the locksmith in. The alarm company operative was already outside her unit, up on a ladder, installing a surveillance cam in the ceiling outside the door.

She had run backgrounds on the companies and the employees, including calling in separately to check that the person who showed up at her door was really the one who'd been sent by the company, verifying with signatures, IDs and photos.

"Can't be too careful these days," she said to the locksmith, a grizzled Portuguese man who knit his brows in annoyance at her verification process. "I've had security problems."

"No wonder, pretty girl like you." The locksmith displayed a mouthful of tobacco stained teeth.

If only it were that simple.

She kept an eye on them through the open door of her bedroom as she called Ellie Smith.

"Special Agent Ellie Smith." The Secret Service agent answered on the second ring. Her voice was brisk but warm.

"This is Special Agent Sophie Ang, Ambassador Francis Smithson's daughter," Sophie said. "I'm calling to alert you to a recent security breach at our residence in Honolulu, since the Ambassador is visiting in another week."

"Thank you for advising me, Agent Ang. Yes, I'm aware of his trip and your position. What can you tell me about the breach?"

Sophie filled her in on the basic details: that her investigation into Security Solutions had led to a trace back finding the location of her computers. She outlined the steps she was taking to rectify the damage.

"Seems like work and home should be separate locations," Smith said mildly. "Especially given your father's sensitive position. And yours, too."

"I assumed too much," Sophie found herself admitting. "I'm taking every precaution now."

"Well, we'll need to monitor the situation. Maybe there's something we can do here."

"I'm not sure what that would be, but I'll keep you apprised." Sophie dragged and dropped the info of her alarm company, building, and Security Solutions via secure cloud site for the other agent to access.

"We'll be in touch before your father's visit." Ellie Smith hung up.

Sophie was relieved not to be solely responsible for her father's safety when he arrived. She turned her attention back to DAVID's caches. The file on Sheldon Hamilton was not getting any bigger since he'd started the company with his then partner, Todd Remarkian.

She had more luck with the cross check on Assan and Alika's shared interests. Assan's company used the same shipping outfit that Alika used, and the same storage facilities here in Honolulu.

That could be nothing, or it could be something.

She needed to find more on Assan. If that led to finding more on Alika, it was better to know now than later.

After she'd been briefed on her enhanced alarm features and

the extra front door deadbolt "rated to withstand 2000 pounds of pressure" and the security services left, she sat down, put on her headphones, and called Marcus Kamuela.

He answered on the third ring. "I'm off duty, at home with Marcella. This better be good."

"I'm sorry to bother you. But I ran a cross check on Alika's business contacts and the ones of a suspected drug shipper, and I came up with a couple of mutual contacts. Might be worth a drop by search with dogs."

A short silence. "Don't recall asking you to work this case. In fact, I recall that you were specifically excluded. And what's this cross check program? Not that rogue software, was it?"

Sophie chewed her lip. "*Boils on the devil's backside,*" she muttered.

"What was that?"

"Just a little Thai. I'm keeping in practice. Can you put Marcella on?"

"No." Marcus was no softie, and that bite she'd come to know was in his voice. "If you recall, this is my case. The FBI is just providing support as appropriate. And this doesn't seem appropriate."

"I'm sorry." She realized that made two apologies so she restrained herself from a third. "I just thought you might like to check out this lead. It could be something, expose a part of the smuggling ring."

"I need probable cause," Kamuela said.

"I can't help you with that part."

"Okay then. Lay it on me."

She told him the company names, addresses. "There's one for shipping, one for storage."

"Who's this known drug dealer?"

This was where it got really challenging, because she didn't actually know Assan was smuggling. Maybe she should go to the docks and search herself.

"You know what? Never mind," she said. "Forget I called."

"No. Spill. Tell me who."

"No, I'll just go check it out myself."

"Just tell me, for God's sake."

"Assan Ang."

A long pause. "Relative?"

"My ex."

"Oh. Crap." Marcus's voice held a combination of sympathy and chagrin.

Sophie swallowed, and finally spoke. "The thing is, I don't know for sure he's smuggling. But I strongly suspect it. He had unsavory characters over to our place in Hong Kong all the time, and really too much money for just a medium sized import-export business. I wonder if there's any way to go...you know, just look around?" She bit her lip.

Another long pause. "You mean an illegal search?"

"I bet you could come up with a legitimate reason to be on the docks, with Alika's case and all. And if you find anything, you could call in a raid."

"This is pretty thin."

Sophie heard Marcella's voice in the background. "Let me talk to her."

"No. She called me." Marcus had a note of satisfaction in his voice. "Sophie, at least, knows who's in charge here." Sophie heard a smacking sound and knew that Marcella had slapped the big detective's shoulder.

"Assan needs to be stopped." Sophie was in no mood for joking around. "He's an abusive sadist and likely a drug wholesaler."

"Well, I'll take all this under advisement and get back to you.

Now, here's Marcella." He handed the phone over to Marcella.

"Girlfriend. What shit pot are you stirring now with that program of yours?"

"I think this is a real lead." Sophie repeated the crossover information. "Just promise you'll take me if you guys go investigate."

"I'll promise no such thing. Your presence could taint any case we might have, involved as you are with both the suspects," Marcella said.

"Please. I don't need to be anywhere around when you make arrests."

"Marcus is on the phone right now with the vice task force that has the K-9 drug dogs. Wait, and we'll call you back."

Sophie hung up and, too nervous to settle, dressed in her FBI clothes and athletic shoes. Putting the second part of her idea into motion, she took out one of the surveillance cameras and turned it on by depressing a tiny button on the back. She pointed the camera at her face.

"This is Special Agent Sophie Ang. You violated my privacy by planting surveillance equipment in my apartment. I suspect you're involved with Security Solutions and I want to speak with you. I'm going to give you a secure encrypted email address. Send me a link to a chat room of your choice and a time to be there, and let's talk. I respect your abilities." She gave a flirty smile, batted her eyes—but not too much, it couldn't be overplayed. "It's not often I'm outmaneuvered at my own game. No risk to you, just a chat. You pick the location. Here's my secure email." She rattled off the email address. "Hope I hear from you."

She turned the camera off, with a feeling like she'd just pointed a radio signal at outer space with little hope that an answer would come back.

She was stowing the evidence-bagged cameras in her small safe when her phone rang.

"We're going down to the docks with dogs," Marcus Kamuela said. "Meet us at Pier 28. Wear Kevlar and a helmet if you have one, so no one recognizes you. And you owe me. Big time."

"I owe you. Yes." Her heart gave a welcome bump of excitement and dread. "That's fine. I'll see you there."

Chapter 19

The Drug Enforcement Agency personnel, with three working dogs, had spread out along the warehouses of the dilapidated docks of Honolulu's industrial shipping area. Marcella, gorgeous even dressed in FBI black body armor, strode toward Sophie, who gave her friend a shoulder bump in greeting.

"I know you're responsible for Marcus letting me come. Thank you."

"You owe me," Marcella said.

"I'm getting used to that. What's the plan?"

"The dogs are just working around the company's buildings you put us on to. This is all perfectly legal. We're hoping to get some probable cause, and then we can go in for a full search."

As if on cue, one of the dogs, a huge German Shepherd, let out a short, sharp bark in front of one of the steel-fronted doors. The other handlers brought their dogs, and when all three signaled, the agents brought a door cannon and three blows later, the DEA team and Marcus were flowing into the darkened warehouse.

"You know this could end up implicating Alika," Marcella whispered as they moved along the edge of the building toward the dark well of the door.

"Better to know," Sophie said. "No matter what we find."

Marcella gave a nod, and they stepped inside, weapons in ready position.

Bright lights exploded in their retinas.

Sophie crouched against the wall, blinking. The lights coming on had been so overwhelming it felt like an explosion—but they were just huge overhead arc lights in the cavernous building, glaring down in hot bowls of radiance on stacks of crates and piles of storage. Marcus Kamuela was nearby on his phone. The dog handlers and DEA agents had spread out through the warehouse.

"So this is one of the companies Alika uses?" Marcella asked.

"Yes. And my ex, Assan."

"That piece of shit. You'll pardon me if I'm hoping it's him we get."

"That's why I'm here." Sophie grinned at her friend behind her helmet, but Marcella couldn't see it, too busy tracking the action as the team searched the warehouse, pulling out random cartons and boxes and letting the dogs sniff them.

Suddenly, the German Shepherd sounded at a big steel container. One of the agents brought a pair of bolt cutters and in moments the lock was off and the door was opened. Rows and rows of decorative ceramic boxes filled the container, padded with bubble wrap. One of the agents, gloved hands moving fast and expert, unwrapped one of the boxes and took the lid off.

A bag of powder fell out with a faint thud onto the floor.

"We got 'em!" he yelled. The shepherd sat, looking proud, its ears pricked.

"Who's that container registered to?" Sophie hustled forward, snatching the clipboard with the inventory on it and running a gloved finger down until she came to the numbered steel container.

"Ang Enterprises," she read aloud, with satisfaction.

The search went on. Now that they'd found something, the agents went through every box, crate, pallet, and barrel in the warehouse and came back with several more containers full of drugs, some even nested inside bags of scented potpourri, which had been the most difficult for the dogs to detect.

Marcus Kamuela clapped Sophie on the shoulder. "Nice lead, Agent Ang. Glad you had it in for your ex." He grinned broadly.

"It's not a laughing matter," Sophie said, with dignity.

He wiped the smile off his face. "You're right. That was out of line. But the good news is, we haven't found anything tracing back to Alika Wolcott. Working with this storage company could be how he ran into the Boyz, though—if he didn't want to play with them in this sandbox, they didn't want him around."

"I'm glad we haven't found anything from Alika's company." Marcella joined them. "I wonder what's going to happen to it with him in the hospital."

Sophie stayed silent. She didn't want to get involved any further. "What's going to happen about Assan?"

"DEA is going to move on this with HPD support. We'll seize all his assets here in the States and try to extradite him for trial—but he's in Hong Kong, and likely to stay there. We have trouble getting criminals over here for trial. So likely, the best we can hope for is to shut him down in the U.S. and send his case to Interpol, see if they can keep him boxed up elsewhere."

"It's a start." Sophie was still thinking of Assan's new young bride. She had to find a way to get that girl out. And on the way home, she thought of little girls trapped in closets.

Chapter 20

*I*t was very late when Sophie finally got home. Unlocking the door, she deactivated the alarm, and once inside, reviewed the new security camera footage of the front door area and swept the apartment for bugs. This would be her new routine every time she entered.

Once she was sure the apartment was clear, Sophie stripped by the washer as was her habit, and dropped everything down to the skin into the basket. She sponged the Kevlar vest and helmet and hung them to dry on a rack.

Her body was stiff and exhausted, though she'd done nothing more than observe the raid. It was the adrenaline overload, she decided, and realized she hadn't gone to the gym since that first day after Alika's attack.

She was avoiding Fight Club. Too many reminders of Alika. And now she wasn't getting enough exercise to feel on top of her game, or to keep her depression under control.

Alika's family must think she'd dropped him when he was down. It was too bad if they did. Staying away from him was the safest choice she could make until she knew Assan was out of the way.

It would be great if the Security Solutions saboteur could

hack into Assan's operation and set him up to be taken out by one of his dealers, Sophie couldn't help thinking a second time as she sat down to her computers.

She was already pretty close to being inappropriate by bringing the team down on Assan with nothing more than intuition.

Intuition which had been right.

Maybe she and the saboteur had more in common than she'd ever imagined. If she had the software and access he did, she didn't think she'd be able to resist the temptation to make sure something permanent happened to Assan. Shutting down his drug operation in the U.S. was going to be a blow, but it was probably only a temporary one that he'd not only recover from, but take out on his new child bride. Sophie was all too familiar with how Assan would experience some setback at work, and come home to displace his aggression.

She struggled to suppress a sense of futility. Nothing she did was really going to touch him.

Sophie clicked on the secure email address she used for Bureau business. A short message with a link attached was waiting from an unlisted source.

Could this be from the unsub who'd planted the cameras?

Sophie's pulse picked up. She clicked on the message.

"Got your video message. Yes, let's talk. Meet me at this chat room at 9:00 a.m. tomorrow."

Her appeal had worked. She could scarcely believe it. She saved the chat room address, one of those "old school" chat sites where paradoxically, older software used to run them protected users' anonymity.

Nothing more to be done on this until 9:00 a.m. tomorrow. It was time to find out what was happening on the Security Solutions and kidnapping case, no matter the hour. She put on her headphones and called Ken Yamada.

"Yes." Ken sounded alert and irritable.

"Hi, Ken. Wondering what's been happening with the Security Solutions and kidnapping cases? I've had a bit of a personal crisis I've been dealing with, but I didn't want to go to bed without checking in with you."

"Yes. We searched Sheldon Hamilton's house and office. Didn't come up with much. We got some DNA samples; running those as standard procedure but not really expecting it to match anything in the system. What's most remarkable is how little real presence the man had. His apartment was pristine, a showplace. Apparently has a maid that comes once a month, and she said nothing much changes between her scheduled cleans. She's never seen Hamilton. Which isn't in itself unusual; the man is constantly traveling according to Honing, the VP. Still, we found very few personal effects in the apartment or office. Gundersohn and I think we should have found more and had more of a sense of who this man is. I know you were running the online stuff, did you do any better?"

Sophie clicked open the file on Sheldon Hamilton. "Same thing here. Most everything he has is in the company's name or given to him as perks. He's the owner and CEO and effectively uses the company to provide a front and take care of all his personal expenses. I couldn't find any assets but one bank account in his name where he apparently receives payment or wages. I didn't want to get into that until we're sure he's a missing person; then I'll take a look at his financials."

"Go ahead and access the finances. He's missing all right. We had another call from Todd Remarkian; he's returning from Hong Kong after doing all he can to find his boss. Apparently, the Hong Kong police have no leads."

A silence as they considered. Sophie had three screens going, each working on something else, but she minimized Amara's current project and pulled up Sheldon Hamilton's bank and went to work drilling into their mainframe. She could get an injunction granting access to Hamilton's accounts, but that would take more time.

"Well, I'm still not sure what case we can make against this company," Sophie finally said. "Certainly there are gray area activities going on, but are they illegal?"

"The saboteur is illegal of course, but proving what he's doing is going to be next to impossible. And we know Security Solutions caters to criminals, but are they responsible for their clientele's actions? Again, hard to bring a case here."

"Did you have to cut him loose?"

"We did. He didn't want to go, if that tells you anything. Begged us to charge him with something. He's afraid of someone."

"Was he willing to tell who the saboteur was?"

"Said it was his only bargaining chip. I told him we weren't interested enough to make him a deal for Witness Protection with no real threat identified. He wasn't happy, but also not miserable enough to spill."

"Where's he at now?"

"His apartment."

Sophie remembered that impersonal little shoebox of a place. "I'm betting he tries to disappear again."

"Without something more, we have nothing to hold him on and nothing to offer him. So I wouldn't be surprised if that was the last we saw of Lee Chan. He has a lot of money stashed in the Caymans."

"So what's the latest on the kidnap case?"

"Every time we try to get something hard on Takeda Industries, we come up dry. We thought we found an office address but when Gundersohn and I went by, it was a vacant lot."

"So who's collecting the rents on that apartment building where Anna was held?"

Ken sighed. "You want the truth? I haven't had time to track that. But I'm beginning to think this isn't some big operation."

"I agree." The back of Sophie's neck prickled with her conviction. "But Remarkian told me that he and Sheldon had found evidence their client information was being peddled online. So maybe our kidnappers in the morgue bought the Addams family information and used it."

"Speaking of. I did run down their case file at Security Solutions, and it seems that someone had the access code to deactivate 'Helen,' the nanny-cam software and alarm system. That's how they were able to take Anna from her bedroom."

"So that confirms it as a leak from inside Security Solutions?"

"It seems that way. The house staff had the code to turn the alarm on and off, but only Belle and her husband had the code for Helen. It must have been a terrible moment when they realized she'd been taken."

"Just think how Anna felt," Sophie said, her skin going cold with remembered trauma. She'd been snatched in the marketplace, an ether-soaked rag held over her nose and mouth until she passed out.

"Yes, well." Ken cleared his throat. "Back to work." He hung up.

Sophie opened her file on Takeda Industries. It couldn't hurt to follow up with the building manager, since Ken hadn't had time to. She texted Ken that she was going on a field trip to interview the building manager tomorrow morning, just as Sophie's software broke into Sheldon Hamilton's bank accounts.

Immediately she leaned in, scanning through the data. Twice-monthly wages were deposited and then immediately diverted, to a numbered account with its location masked.

His salary, as founder and CEO, was an eye-popping amount. Why was he diverting and hiding it? Had Sheldon Hamilton planned his own disappearance?

Sophie set down her headset, leaned back in her chair, stretching. She was too wound up for bed. Doing one more sweep of the apartment for bugs, she hung up the detection wand by the door and, wearing her silky sleep tee, went through her yoga routine in the icy silver moonlight, finally ending with meditation.

Breathing, resting upright in the lotus position, she let her mind float free. Suddenly, she was sure she knew who the saboteur was. The hard part was going to be proving it.

Chapter 21

Sophie held up her creds wallet. The manager of the apartment building where Anna had been held was a stocky Filipina woman named Florence Torres, wearing a big plastic gardenia pinned to a tight bun. Shiny dark eyes flashed as she checked the ID. "I thought you cops were done with that apartment."

"Can you keep this conversation confidential?" Sophie subtly imitated the woman's posture, her legs slightly spread and arms open, a way of helping create rapport she remembered from her Academy training. She waited until Florence, curiosity evident in her narrowed eyes, gave a brisk nod. "We've had some information that this kidnapping might not be a one time thing. So is there anything you can tell me about Takeda Industries, about how the apartments are rented, that might help us prevent another situation happening in your building?"

They were standing in the doorway of the manager's office, and the woman gestured for Sophie to come in.

"Sit." She shut the door and pointed to one of the plastic chairs positioned in front of a battered metal desk. "I saw the pictures of that little girl. So sad. And, as you may know, we have a kidnapping problem in the Philippines, too."

"I'd heard that," Sophie said.

"Well, I don't want to be a part of anything like that. So, I'll tell you I have some worries. But this can't get back to me." She pointed a stubby brown finger at Sophie, the petals of the gardenia in her bun quivering with suppressed emotion.

"Of course not." Sophie hoped she didn't have to call Torres in as a witness.

"Apartments on the fourteenth floor are kept open for short term rental. Last month, I got a call to hold the apartment the kidnapping took place in, as I told the other investigators. But what I didn't tell the other investigators, was that this happens every four or five months. Always from the same number. I didn't realize something bad was happening on that floor until now." She dug in the desk, fished out a file labeled CASH TRANSACTIONS. "I run it through the usual billing, but I don't get a name, and I don't get anything but an envelope of cash stuck through the door." She pointed to the slot.

"Didn't you have concerns about this before?" Sophie asked.

"It's a good job," Torres said. "I want to keep it. The number is all I have to give you. But Takeda Industries, the parent company, is the one that directed me to keep all those apartments on that floor open, in case they need them."

"Thanks. I hope it will be enough. And this will remain between us." Sophie stood.

"I just don't want to think of any other little children stuck in a closet. I hope that helps get whoever's behind it—if it's more than just the one time."

Sophie looked down at the Post-it in her hand. "This is more than we've had to go on so far. Thank you. But I'm afraid it will just be a burner phone. Would you be willing to call me the next time one of the rooms is reserved?"

The woman pursed her lips, looked Sophie up and down. "Yes. Give me your direct number."

Sophie handed her a card and handwrote her own cell number on it. "I will do my best to answer, day or night."

Outside, the wind of early morning soft as a caress, Sophie checked the time. She had to get back to her apartment for an important online chat.

* * *

At her home workstation, Sophie set a trace to working on Torres' phone number and logged into the chat room at 9:00 a.m. The old-fashioned blank screen of the DOS chat room field felt like stepping into a black room, blindfolded.

"I'm here," she typed. Her screen name was MMA Fighter, one of her favorite monikers, not least because people usually assumed she was male and it was interesting to see how they reacted to her differently because of it.

The letters glowed green on the black background. Of course, she had a tracker program queued up for when the unsub arrived, but for a long moment the cursor pulsed gently and slowly, highlighting how alone she was.

She wondered if it would always be this way. Sophie, alone, reaching out with a little, tentative *"I'm here."*

And no one responding.

The phone number for the possible kidnapper connection came back. *NO REGISTERED USER.* Of course it was a burner. She'd just have to hope Florence Torres called to tip her off the next time the apartment was used.

Depression she'd been beating back with the stress of the case and nonstop activity rolled over her in a fog. A sense of leaden heaviness filled her bones. The sludgy meaninglessness of it all rolled across her mind and slowed everything down to pointless effort.

Nothing good ever lasted. Alika, just a possibility of something wonderful, lay broken and unconscious for the fourth—or was it fifth—day. Her mother was in a psych hospital, suicidal. Her father's safety was at risk because of her. Her program, probably confiscated, was doomed to be unused. She'd compromised her home and endangered Bureau assets and intel with her actions. But Sophie knew it wouldn't have mattered if everything had been going great in her life right now.

The depression was there, some hereditary sickness of the brain, and it swamped her like quicksand whenever it wanted to.

Ginger glanced up from Sophie's feet as if sensing something wrong. The lab sat up and whined, expressive brown eyes intent on Sophie's face. She pawed at Sophie's leg. Sophie couldn't bring herself to touch the distressed animal.

It reminded her of so many days when she knelt by her mother's low bedside with fragrant morning tea, and those huge, sad dark eyes just stared, and nothing she did could bring a response or a smile.

She'd finally come to understand her mother. Deep inside, she was afraid the void would pull her into darkness, too.

But she'd go down fighting. Literally. That was something different between them.

Sophie had called the office to let them know she was coming in a little later, and heard that Waxman had a team meeting to review the Security Solutions case scheduled for 10:30 a.m. She didn't have much longer to sit around waiting in the chat room.

It was a good thing, too. She was in no mental shape for the acuity needed for this encounter.

"You there?" she typed. The question mark at the end of the sentence seemed to mock her, pulsing green in the black screen.

It made her feel needy and vulnerable. She was angry that this unsub had hooked her emotions.

Another five minutes, then she would leave.

The depression was so bad she wanted to crawl to her bed and pull the covers up over her head and disappear into that darkness, so much like the blank screen of the computer that stared at her now like a void she could fall into…and keep on falling.

"Sorry to be late. Delayed." An answer appeared at the speed he was typing it, unspooling in green letters like a rope thrown to a drowning victim.

She focused with an effort and typed back.

"Thanks for responding. I don't appreciate the cameras in my apartment. I asked for this chat to compare agendas and see if we can come to an agreement."

A pause, then his answer blipped across her screen. *"Sorry about the surveillance. I needed to stay ahead of what was catching up to me."*

"What do you mean?"

"You know what I mean."

"Security Solutions? I take it you're with them."

"You could say that."

"That's enigmatic." Sophie tried the word, since it most closely matched her sense of this unsub.

"Amorphous. Inscrutable. A ghost in the machine." He was showing off a little now, demonstrating his vocabulary. *"All true."*

"I see your handle is Ghost. Is that what you are?"

"Among other things. I also make a mean omelet and love dogs."

She smiled involuntarily. Was he flirting with her?

"I think you know I'm a dog lover, too. Hope Ginger didn't lick you too much when you broke in."

"She's a sweet girl. Listen, you don't have to worry about me being in your place. No hostile intent there. It was a one-time thing. Unless you invite me back."

Sophie smiled again. The depression receded a tiny bit. This dialogue was stimulating.

"I can't see any way that would ever be appropriate," she typed. *"Still, I have to give you credit. Not too many people in the world can beat me at this game and you found my place first."*

"That's the part I like, too. It's a game. No one gets hurt when I play but those who deserve it. And I can tell you're close to finding where I tracked you from. I'm keeping an eye out for you—but I warn you, I won't be easy to find."

"What are you saying?"

"I'm saying I won't be anywhere you can find me."

"That's too bad. It might be fun to meet in person." Might as well exploit the flirty thing to see if she could lure him into the open.

"I plan on it. In fact, we've already talked."

Now the tiny hairs rose on the back of Sophie's neck. *"I think I would remember."*

"Oh, you would. If you knew who I was."

Sophie was getting uncomfortable. It was time to put him on the defensive. *"I think I figured out who the saboteur at Security Solutions is."*

Sophie waited for his response. Her mouth tugged up in a smile. She liked this dance they were doing. It had dispelled some of the fog of depression, though she could still feel the dark wings of it beating around the back of her mind.

"Do tell."

"What do you have to trade?"

"Got some good stuff on Lee Chan."

"I think we found all that already, and I don't think he's the main man."

"Ah. What makes you think he isn't?"

"Show me yours, and I'll show you mine." She was flirting again.

"You forget. I've seen yours. And may I say, it was nothing short of breathtaking."

Sophie winced. He had, indeed, seen hers. *"A gentleman doesn't spy on women."*

"If you checked the angle of the cameras, it was all business," came back almost sharply. *"I've never been called a gentleman but I do have certain codes. Spying on you wasn't intended."*

She paused, chewing her lip, then typed rapidly. *"Nuff of this. I'm going to find you."*

"I expect no less and I'll enjoy that. In the meantime, if you ever need any help, send me a note at this address." An email address appeared.

He was saying goodbye. She didn't like it, wasn't ready to say goodbye. *"Pox ridden obese pig farmer afflicted with ringworm,"* Sophie muttered.

"Don't go" she typed, and blew out a breath.

The cursor blinked. She shut her eyes. The depression reached out to clamp onto her brain.

"Why not? What do we have to say to each other?"

Sophie leaned forward, typing rapidly. *"I'd like to know what you're trying to achieve. What your agenda is. You tracked me, you know who I am, but while we've been able to find out a little about who you are, I don't understand what could possibly motivate you. What's your game?"*

A long pause.

"I can't tell you more because you might be able to use what

I say to find me. What you can trust is that I'm not trying to hurt you, or anyone. In fact, I'm trying to help."

"So you're the saboteur?" It seemed like he was confirming that, like he'd admitted it earlier, when he said only those who deserved it got hurt.

"I'm saying I'm on your side. In every way I can be. In fact, you should consider me a friend. To you, and to law enforcement."

Sophie stared at the screen, waiting for something more to appear, but it didn't.

"Are you the saboteur?" she typed, pushing for that confirmation. *"Are you Frank Honing? Sheldon Hamilton? Lee Chan? Or Todd Remarkian?"*

"None of the above."

He was probably lying.

"I could use help with something," she found herself typing. *"Prove you're a friend."*

"I'm listening."

"A man named Assan Ang, in Hong Kong, has a new young wife. He does unspeakable things to his wives. Can you get her out?" Sophie bit her lip, her breath coming in short, hard pants. She couldn't believe what she'd just asked. On the other hand, she had nothing to lose. Assan was outside her reach, and his child bride, even more so.

The question mark at the end of the sentence pulsed to the beat of her pounding heart.

"I'll look into it. And then you'll owe me. Goodbye, Sophie."

The cursor beside his moniker disappeared. The Ghost was gone.

"I'm getting used to owing people," she murmured aloud as she saved the email address he'd given her mechanically and, moving very deliberately, shut down her rigs. She had a meeting to go to about the saboteur. She was pretty sure she'd just met him, and he'd offered to help her. He might be able to help Assan's bride. If so, the chance she'd just taken would be worth it.

The soundproof room had come with the Hong Kong apartment as a "safe room." It was outfitted with rings, hooks, an armoire of props and devices, and a bed. She didn't think of the sex he acted out on her in that room as something she'd participated in. No, she'd done her best to be somewhere mentally far away.

There were no windows in that room. When he turned the lights off, it was so dark inside that she couldn't see her hand in front of her face. She'd come to dread being imprisoned in that room more than any of his carefully concealed beatings—Sophie could take a beating. Those didn't get to her like that room did, with its darkness and isolation. She'd eventually taught herself to go to sleep whenever he locked her in there.

Now she needed silence and blackout drapes to sleep at all.

That he had another victim in that room could not be allowed, no matter the cost to herself. No matter what it cost her to owe the Ghost.

Sophie had escaped through careful planning. During one of her tech classes at the university, she'd met an FBI recruiter who was impressed with her skills and the three languages she spoke. After securing a job offer, she'd waited until her ticket to a U.S. interview was available. She'd taken carefully hoarded household budget money she'd amassed over months and years, and fled one day with just the clothes on her back.

Sophie remembered walking calmly out of the sumptuous lobby with her heart pounding and body aching from Assan's choking assault of the night before. The doorman, on Assan's payroll, bowed respectfully even as he took note of her clothing, suitable for her computer class. Her modest leather computer satchel contained the passport she'd broken into Assan's safe to take, along with her jewelry.

She'd ditched her cell phone at the corner and taken a taxi like she always did, but this time she directed it to the airport.

She'd made it out, and her new life had provided a powerful layer of protection. But she'd never been entirely sure that she'd made it beyond Assan's reach. She thought of Alika in his hospital bed.

God forbid she'd been the cause of his attack.

How was the Ghost going to get a young girl, probably much less prepared than she'd been, out of that fortress of a building?

Yes. If the Ghost could help that girl, it would be worth what she'd owe him.

Chapter 22

Sophie sipped an extra strong mug of tea as she sat down at the team meeting in the conference room at the FBI building. Waxman was already seated beneath the shiny FBI logo on the wall at the head of the table, and he'd asked Ken to take notes on the white boards as they reviewed the case.

"So where are we with this kidnapping case, exactly?" Waxman asked. "It seems like we've gotten diverted down a rabbit hole with this Security Solutions lead."

"Sir, I met with the building manager this morning." Sophie described the meeting. "I ran the number she gave me, and it came back to a burner phone, which I'd expected. But someone is renting the rooms on the fourteenth floor of that building on a regular basis."

"That seems like something we can stake out and follow up on. Keep us posted if you hear anything from Torres," Waxman said.

"Yes, sir. Does anyone have any new ideas about the disappearance of Sheldon Hamilton at Security Solutions?" Sophie asked.

No one answered that. Finally, Gundersohn said, "I think at this point we need to assume that the suspect with the means and opportunity to be the saboteur/information seller is Lee Chan."

"And I take it he isn't talking." Waxman made a pyramid with his fingertips.

"I think I know who the saboteur is. It's not the same person selling the confidential client information." Sophie had taken a caffeine pill along with a deep sip of her tea, hoping the stimulant would counteract the lethargy of depression still plaguing her and give her the energy to disclose everything that had happened. "I have a lot to fill you in on, sir." She got up, went around the table, and took the erasable marker from Ken Yamada.

"Yesterday I detected a security breach in my apartment." She drew circles on the board and labeled them: Honing, Chan, Hamilton, Remarkian, Saboteur, Data Leaker.

"I'm pretty sure the saboteur is the one who got into my apartment and wired cameras to monitor me." She described the situation she'd gone through yesterday and the steps she'd taken to correct it.

"I used one of the cameras Bateman retrieved after he swept my apartment to send the unsub a message. He responded, and this morning I talked to him in an untraceable chat room. He called himself a friend of law enforcement."

Sophie explained that her apartment had been broken into by someone similar in appearance to the missing Sheldon Hamilton. She suspected that he had returned from Hong Kong and set up surveillance on her to keep ahead of her investigation into Security Solutions.

Waxman's blue eyes were steely slits fixed on her face over his steepled fingertips. "So you think he's the saboteur?"

"It's my best guess." She swallowed, looked down. "I don't think we have any idea what his motives are. I asked him, but he wouldn't say. Denied being any of the four main players at Security Solutions. But I think when we find Sheldon Hamilton, we'll know more."

"You haven't presented any evidence that Hamilton is anything but missing and possibly the one that broke into your apartment," Waxman said. "For all you know, it could have been Lee Chan in that chat room. Or Remarkian or Honing."

"Well, all we have to do is see what each of our suspects was doing at nine a.m.," Gundersohn said. "The one that was chatting online was the one who broke into Agent Ang's apartment. That's all we can say for sure, not who that person was or whether or not he was the saboteur. And it wasn't the saboteur Lee Chan was so afraid of, it's whoever is selling secrets. Got any ideas about that, Agent Ang?"

"No. There are still too many possibilities." Sophie frowned, hands on her hips. "Working up my background on the CEO, I broke into Hamilton's financials. He's been rerouting all his money to a numbered account for two years. Whatever he's doing now, he's planned for a long time."

"None of this makes any sense," Waxman said impatiently. "Why would Hamilton build up this company only to abandon it to Honing and Remarkian, even if he did siphon off some cash? This company is worth a lot. And who's Lee Chan afraid of, or is he faking all that to throw us off?" Waxman smacked his hands down with a sound like a rifle shot and stood. "You know what? Let's do a raid on Security Solutions and gather up whomever we can and put them in interrogation and grill them about an alibi for 9:00 a.m. See what we can shake loose. Yamada and Gundersohn, get some local PD muscle to go with you, and find Lee Chan while you're at it."

Sophie stood with the men.

"No, not you, Agent Ang. I want to talk a little more about the security breach in your apartment," Waxman said, his eyes the color of steel.

Sophie sat back down, apprehension tightening her throat.

Chapter 23

Sophie sat beside Waxman as the other team members left the room, already working their phones. She wished she'd eaten something that morning because now the caffeine pill was making her queasy. It was too much to hope that Waxman wouldn't be angry about the security breach. But at least he didn't know that DAVID and her FBI workstation were back up and running on her home computer lab.

"You're on administrative leave without pay. Two days. And a disciplinary note is going in your file," Waxman's eyes were on his computer monitor.

Sophie felt the blood drain out of her face. She'd never had a consequence like this before in her life. Her insubordination note from the DAVID usage was the first time she'd ever had anything but commendations added to her record.

She bit her lip and gazed down at her hands in her lap, schooling her face into the mask that hid her emotions.

"I can contest this with my union representative," she said at last. "Any agent's residence could be discovered and broken into by a skilled enough unsub."

"You chose to withhold vital information germane to your case from a superior," Waxman said. Sophie glanced up and could see patches of red on his cheeks, though his eyes were still on his monitor and his voice, icy. "You chose to use department resources, namely Agent Bateman, to cover your situation without going through proper chain of command."

"I decided speed was the best course and the minute I knew my apartment had been breached, I took action. I had Bateman sweep my apartment for surveillance equipment because we were going into a meeting and I didn't want to slow anything down by doing it myself. He knew where it was, and knew Ginger, my dog." She took a long, shuddering breath and let it out on the remembered stress. "My building security was advised. I called in a change of codes for my alarm system, changed the locks, and had a surveillance cam installed at the doorway, which is the single egress point. Ran full security scans on my rigs. I even notified the Secret Service, because it's actually my father's apartment and he's coming next week. I dealt with it. And yes, the unsub found me through a back trace on the Security Solutions data stream I'd diverted. The programmer behind their systems is good. As good as, or better than, I am."

"What makes you think the saboteur's Sheldon Hamilton?" Waxman finally looked at her and now she knew why her friends Marcella and Lei had complained about being in his crosshairs— she felt like an insect under his withering stare.

"Deductive reasoning. Todd Remarkian said he and Sheldon Hamilton developed the software together, so I know Sheldon has the skills. Lee appears to be the saboteur, but I don't like him for it because I don't think he's smart enough, or ruthless enough. Same reason why I don't think he's the information peddler." She twisted her fingers in her lap, keeping her eyes down. "I know programmers and hackers. Lee's a tool—an implementer, not an innovator. I don't think he has the genius to be the man behind the remote surveillance software that is

Software Solutions' main asset. That software is verging on being artificially intelligent. It analyzes patterns, takes countermeasures, and alerts the people it decides need to know about something going on within its parameters." She took a breath, glanced up. Waxman was still intently listening.

"I think Sheldon was in Hong Kong and heard that the saboteur was detected after our meeting with the top brass at Security Solutions. He disappeared, taking his software and assets, leaving Lee set up to appear guilty." Sophie paused again and Waxman made a 'go on' gesture. She continued. "I think Hamilton's the one because, while I don't think Lee's smart enough to be the saboteur, I also don't think he's stupid enough to load his computer full of cash and run money through a personal, traceable account in the Caymans."

"Why don't you think Remarkian is the saboteur?"

"Remarkian could be the saboteur, it's true. But it's Sheldon Hamilton who may have imitated a dog walker and broke into my apartment, by his physical description, and I verified Remarkian's location as Hong Kong during our calls."

"So do you know what Remarkian looks like?"

"Roughly the same height and weight as Sheldon, but blond and blue-eyed. Has an Australian accent."

"Well. More will be revealed, and for you, that will be in two days. Give me your creds and weapon."

Sophie pulled her gun, badge and wallet and smacked them down on the table. She stood, feeling anger waft over her in an energizing wave.

"You're making a mistake. *Ben.*" She spat his name like it tasted bad, spun on her heel, and left.

* * *

Sophie went where she'd always gone when life was hard. When cases were complex. When hated emotions took over her brain. Where she went when the depression was bad, when it was gone entirely, where she'd gone in every range of need she'd had since she escaped Assan Ang and made Honolulu and the Bureau her home five years ago.

Fight Club.

After working the heavy bag long enough, the talons of depression's hold finally began to uncurl.

Sophie looked around to find the gym going on as usual even with Alika in his hospital bed. Pairs of fighters were sparring in the warm up ring. The gleaming bodies of athletes worked exercise bikes, treadmills and ellipticals against one wall. The weight area clanked with the grind of metal on metal and the grunts of heaving lifters. The smell of leather, rubber, metal, and sweat was a familiar perfume that lifted her spirits.

Done warming up, Sophie climbed into the empty main ring, gloves on, and raised her arms in the air.

"Anybody up for a workout besides me? Bring it on!"

A ragged cheer rose from her gym mates. Minutes later Sophie was completely immersed in a fight with a Japanese jiu-jitsu champion with the attitude that women weren't real competition. It took six hard rounds to disabuse him of that opinion, though she lost in the end.

Showering in the locker room, watching blood from her mouth and nose drain into the shower between her feet, Sophie decided the gym was what she'd been missing lately. And that it was way past time she visited Alika in the hospital.

Her eye swollen shut and her lip split, Sophie hid the rest of the damage under a concealing hoodie for her visit to Queen's Hospital. She didn't call first, but she stopped at the gift shop to pick up a bouquet of daisies. She held them up in front of her battered face to deflect questions on her appearance, and was surprised to be redirected when she reached the ICU.

"He's stable now, so he's been moved to a convalescent floor," the nurse on duty said, peering suspiciously at Sophie's face between the daisies. "Do you need some first aid yourself, Miss?"

"No thanks. I'm a fighter. MMA. Hazards of the sport." Sophie's smile hurt and didn't seem to reassure the nurse.

"Well, okay. He's on the fourth floor. Room 427."

Sophie took the elevator back down, realizing she was a little lightheaded. She never had eaten anything that day, but at least the depression was back in its box.

There was still an officer outside Alika's door, which she was relieved to see. Though she'd given Waxman her creds wallet, she still had a departmental ID badge, which she showed.

"Anyone with him?" Sophie asked, avoiding the officer's curious eyes on her face.

"Not right now. The parents said they had to take care of some errands and business."

His parents probably still had to work, might even have to leave the island soon. She felt a pang of worry and pushed the door handle down, bracing herself.

Alika seemed better. He was still prone and unmoving on the bed, but the swathes of gauze covering his head were down to one big bandage. The only tubes running into him were an IV and a catheter, tactfully concealed by bedclothes. His broken leg was lowered now, and his bruises had gone down, leaving his face recognizable, if still discolored.

Sophie sat in the chair beside him. "Hi Alika. It's Sophie."

She wriggled a bit, gazing at him, wondering if they were still supposed to talk to him, wondering if he was even in a coma anymore since it had been a while since her last update. Curious, she got up and tried to read the chart hanging on the wall, but there were no clues in the little boxes filled with squiggles and code.

"I don't know anything about how you're doing, but I want to tell you I'm looking pretty bad right now, too. Took a bit of a pounding this afternoon from that Japanese fighter. You remember him, right? They call him The Breaker. Well, he didn't break me, but I lost, that's for sure." She fingered her swollen, split lip. "I was in the mood to take on a whole football team today. Work has been really challenging, and I needed to fight or go down. Whichever. Didn't matter. I know you understand."

Sophie gazed at him, still hoping for some response. There was none. She let herself really take in the sight of him.

His eyes, shut, sunken in pouches of bruised flesh left from his beating. Chest rising and falling evenly. Skin sallow and multicolored with bruising. Heart monitor blipping in the corner. He'd shrunk in mass, the muscular body seeming to melt away. It was going to be a long road for him back to health and fitness when he finally woke up.

She reached over and traced the triangle tattoo on his slack shoulder muscle.

"I can't tell you about my case and work even if you're in a coma, but let's just say it's been even more stressful than usual, and now I'm off on admin leave for the next two days. So I was in the mood to really go at it, and kudos to The Breaker. He made me work hard, and I know I gave him more of a run than he was expecting from a woman, if his insults were anything to go by." She picked up Alika's limp hand, brought it to her cheek. "Feel this. Got a nice contusion here on the cheekbone, and on my eye. Looks worse than yours right now."

His hand felt clammy and limp. It made her sad to press it

against her own wounded face. She set it down among the bedclothes, still holding it.

"Anyway, I haven't been here to visit because I'm worried about my ex, Assan. He used to make threats when I was with him, tell me what he'd do to anyone I ever tried to be with. It was five years ago, and I'd put it all behind me because after we divorced I never heard anything from him. But I never gave him cause to act on any of his jealous threats until…until you." She hung her head, still holding his hand. "I can't take the chance that he had something to do with your attack. We're going after his business and I feel confident we're going to shut it down in the States, but I don't know how to get him locked up. From so far away, I don't know how to get him put away where he can't hurt anyone. And until I do, I don't want to take a chance of adding to whatever's going on with you. I hope you understand."

She gazed over at Alika. No change in his face. His chest rose and fell like a metronome. He seemed peaceful, at least.

She felt the prickle of tears and used a bit of sheet to dab them away, careful of her blackened eye. "Well, this is harder than I imagined. I brought you flowers. You'd probably hate them, but here they are." She set the wrapped bouquet on the blanket in front of him. "I should get going. I have to put some ice on these bruises before they get really bad. And get on with finding Assan again, my admin leave project. Then, maybe someday we can be together." She picked up his hand, kissed the battered knuckles, and set it down.

She went to the door, pushed down the handle, and glanced out into the hall.

No one was there.

Even the officer guarding the room was gone.

Chapter 24

*E*ven the police officer's plastic chair was gone. Sophie tensed as she looked up and down the empty hall.

This could be nothing, or it could be the beginning of something very bad.

She withdrew back into the room and checked for some way to lock the door, but there was none. She grabbed one of the plastic chairs and propped it under the handle of the door. She pulled a pillowcase off one of the pillows wedged beside Alika's head and, ripping off a bit of surgical tape from the roll inside the wall-mounted rack of supplies, hung it over the window into the hall so no one could see through the safety glass insert into the room. Then she hurried to the phone and called the nurses' station.

The phone rang and rang and rang.

Maybe there was a major emergency that had called all the personnel away.

Maybe the officer had left his station for a bathroom break, knowing she was a Federal cop visiting the victim.

But she'd turned in her badge, creds and weapon, and even though she had her own gun, it was at home in a safe where it could do exactly no good.

"Always better to assume the worst in a combat situation," she told Alika, glancing around for something to use as a weapon even as she dialed 911 on her cell phone. "You told me that."

No Signal.

She'd experienced the notoriously bad reception in the hospital before, but the timing didn't seem coincidental.

Sophie went back to Alika's bed and hit the Call Nurse button on the cord beside his hand. A light went on at the back of his bed, and she suddenly wondered who saw those lights in the nurses' station, and whether alerting a possible unsub that she was aware of a problem was worth the risk.

Too late now.

She grabbed the wall phone and instead of dialing 0 for the desk, tried an external line and called 911 again.

The phone was dead too, the absence of a dial tone as deafening as a siren in her ear.

Sophie lifted the makeshift curtain she'd made off the window and peeked out. Unfortunately, now she had only a limited range of view, but she still saw no one. She wondered if she had time to try to move Alika somewhere else, decided it was too risky to try to wheel him into the hall.

But she could try to shelter him from the line of fire through the door. And she needed a weapon.

Moving fast, she unhooked all the various bags of liquid from the tall steel IV pole beside Alika's bed and set them on the bed beside him. It was wheeled, so she unplugged all the electrical units on the bed from the wall. This set off an alarm from the cardiac monitor, a high-pitched beeping that she hoped was going somewhere else in the hospital to bring help. She pulled the brake lever, and, grunting with the effort of moving the heavy, unwieldy bed, hauled it over out of range of the window and door. Anyone trying to get a bead on the bed would have to come inside the room and turn to do so. She wasn't going to let that happen.

Sophie picked up the steel pole, hefted it.

It was solid, with clunky wheels on one end a T-shaped crossbar at the top. She unscrewed the wheel unit from the bottom and took up a position beside the door to wait, the pole raised.

She didn't have to wait long.

The door handle jiggled against the plastic back of the chair propped under it. Jiggled again. Jiggled a third time.

What if it was hospital staff? She had done all she could to alert the medical team to a problem in the room.

The glass of the door's window shattering was her answer as something blew it out. The pillowcase she'd put up deflected the heavy glass to tinkle onto the floor beside her. The rest of the glass was knocked out of the window. She glimpsed the red metal of a fire axe.

No one called out. Medical personnel wouldn't enter a room that way. The unsub was trying to get a look inside, see what was happening in the room and where the target was.

A hand appeared in the window's opening, holding the silver gleam of a Sig Sauer with its barrel lengthened by a silencer. The gun's muzzle lifted the pillowcase, questing for the bed. She was very glad she'd wheeled Alika off to the side against the wall with the bed's back to the door.

Sophie brought the steel pole down like a guillotine on the wrist protruding into the room. There was a gratifying crack of snapping bone, a scream, and the Sig dropped at her feet. Sophie scooped up the weapon, and, staying beside the door, stuck her hand out the small window and fired blind into the hall.

The silencer made a sound like spitting watermelon seeds. Sophie hoped like hell she didn't hit some innocent nurse coming to help.

Gunfire erupted from the other side of the door.

Sophie dove to the ground beside Alika's bed. Shards of wood and metal blew out as the unsub unloaded another weapon on the door. There was no silencer on this one, and she covered her ears, head ringing from the blasts in the enclosed space. She tried to count the shots but they were coming too fast. *A semi-automatic?* Even so, she could feel the vibration of running feet through the floor as the unsub ran away when he'd emptied his clip.

Sophie scrambled up and looked at the door. Light shone through forty or fifty holes and the wall opposite the door was peppered with embedded ammo.

"It was a good thing I moved your bed," she said to Alika.

The Sig in ready position, she depressed the handle and pushed open the battered door, peering into the hall.

Several people in white coats were running toward her, led by the officer who had been on duty.

She held the gun up in the air above her head along with her other hand, so they didn't think she was the attacker. "Got this weapon off the shooter and moved the patient. He's okay. But I think we're going to need another room."

* * *

Sophie didn't leave Alika's side all through his transfer, vigilant beside the staffers as they wheeled him, bed and all, to another room.

She called Waxman on her cell when he'd been moved and re-hooked up to all his support systems. She was finally sitting down, waiting to give her statement to Marcus and Marcella, who were on their way. The HPD crime lab team was currently picking bullets out of the wall two floors below her.

"I was visiting my friend Alika Wolcott in the hospital when someone tried to kill him," Sophie said to Waxman. She turned the Sig over and over in her hands. It was evidence. And it was a nice weapon, the weapon of a professional, right down to the silencer screwed into the barrel. "Probably not related to any of my cases."

"What?" Waxman said. "Say that again."

"Just wanted to let my superior know an occurrence happened to me in the field while on administrative leave. I'm sure there's a form I need to fill out or something." She knew she sounded sarcastic.

"Are you okay?" Waxman's voice sounded blank with shock. "Were you injured?"

"I'm fine." She glanced down, noticed a long sliver of wood from the door protruding from her forearm. "Well, mostly fine. Few bumps and bruises, but I had those going in." She set the Sig down and tugged out the sliver. Blood welled in its wake.

The door opened and she grabbed the Sig and spun toward the threat. It was Marcus Kamuela, scowling. Sophie didn't ever want to be someone he was coming after.

"The officer investigating this has just arrived. I have to go, but I wanted to take a moment to apprise my superior." Sophie hung up the phone and set the weapon down. "Better late than never," she said to Marcus. "I hope you talked to that officer that was supposed to be guarding the door."

"Sure did. He said he was called away on his walkie-talkie by someone claiming to be a fellow officer spotting someone suspicious in the stairway. When he got there, the unsub clocked him. Good thing you were inside and took steps to protect Wolcott. Let me get your statement." He took out a voice recorder.

Sophie stood up and a whirlpool of black dots danced in front of her eyes. "I'm not feeling so well."

She came to a minute or two later, lying on the floor next to Alika's bed, feet elevated on a spare pillow. Marcella knelt beside her, covering her in a thin blanket, and she had an IV in her hand. A nurse was hanging a bag of clear liquid on the same IV pole as Alika's.

"Just some glucose and water," the nurse said. "You were in shock and severely dehydrated. Take it easy. You'll be fine in a little while."

Marcella knelt by Sophie, tucking the blanket around her. "Looks like you had an encounter today before the gunfight," she said, touching Sophie's cheek lightly.

"You'll do anything to avoid giving a statement," Kamuela said, with weak humor. He seemed rattled by her fainting. "You look like hell, Sophie. Who gave you the beat down?"

"So embarrassing." Sophie shut her eyes. "I didn't eat all day and had a bout at Fight Club, then the attack...guess it got the best of me." She sat up slowly. She was already feeling better, the IV working to rehydrate and energize her. "Sometimes I get so caught up in my head I forget to take care of the body."

"Lie back down and tell us the series of events." Kamuela pressed Record on his device.

Sophie went through the attack and how she'd ended up with the Sig. Marcella bagged the deadly looking weapon. "Hopefully, the rounds from the wall tell us something and so does this."

"So someone came with intent to kill Wolcott. Or were you the target?" Marcus asked.

"Don't see how they came for me," Sophie said. "No one knew I was coming here and I've been staying away on purpose." She told them her worries about Assan.

"So then we don't really know who this shooter was going after."

"I think it's safe to assume the target was Alika." Sophie got up slowly from the floor and sat down on a handy chair beside Alika, glancing over at him.

Alika was gazing back at her. His golden-brown eyes were circled in pouches of old bruising, but clear and conscious.

"Who are you?" He articulated each word clearly. "And what am I doing here?"

Chapter 25

Sophie unlocked her apartment, feeling a thousand years old. Marcella was right behind her as she went in, deactivated the alarm and greeted excited Ginger, who badly needed to go out. That was the first thing the two women did, walking the dog out of the building and standing close together against the wall, still sun-warmed though evening was casting purple shadows on the patch of lawn trimmed in hibiscus hedge beside the building. The lab nosed around the grass and did her business

"They say amnesia is common with a head injury like he has," Marcella said.

"That's the third time you've said that and the fourth time I've heard it, if you include the doctor who told me the first time." Sophie cleaned up after the dog and tossed the bag in a nearby garbage can. "Let's go to that little noodle place on the corner. I need to move. My muscles are stiffening up."

Marcella was subdued, and Sophie couldn't think of what to say either, reduced by exhaustion and trauma to a zombie-like state as they proceeded down the sidewalk to the noodle shop where she and Ginger sometimes got meals.

"His parents were so happy to see him awake, but he didn't

recognize them either." Marcella was obviously still bothered for Sophie's sake.

"Marcella, it's okay. I'm just glad he's alive and going to get better. As long as we can stop whoever's going after him," Sophie really believed that right now. The relief of seeing Alika awake had more than made up for the blow of his amnesia. She'd taken comfort from the fact that the forgetfulness seemed global. He hadn't just mentally deleted her in particular. Ginger flopped down when Sophie secured her leash and they went inside, sitting at the long communal counter.

They earned a few curious glances from the various patrons of the restaurant, but the owner recognized Sophie.

"Hope you gave back some of the same." He made a gesture that took in her battered appearance as he served her a huge bowl of *saimin*.

"I made him work for it." Sophie scooped up fragrant broth with the deep square spoon. "But I didn't win this time."

They talked about the MMA scene as the proprietor served Marcella, and finally moved off to wait on other customers.

"So I might as well catch you up on Alika's case. We've got the gang members who beat him in custody, and we're following leads from their testimony." Marcella slurped a mouthful of noodles and chased a slice of egg around in the broth. "Things are promising with prosecuting your ex. We can't find any link between Alika and Ang, besides using the same shipper and storage facility. I don't think this attack is personal, or about you having a relationship with Alika like you've been worried about. Everything we're uncovering seems to point to him running afoul of the Boyz who control the construction trade. They set him up to appear like a wholesale drug shipper and then used him to send a message to other noncompliant developers. But we may not get anyone higher on the food chain for a while. Marcus is digging in for a long investigation into the activity in the construction trade. For now, I'm glad we brought in the hoods who beat him up. They were probably supposed to kill him, and the Boyz sent someone to finish the job at the hospital. Hopefully, we can put enough heat on them so they leave him alone now."

Sophie set her spoon down, turned to her friend. "He should probably go home to Kaua`i and recover, get off their radar for a while. And what about shutting down Assan's operation?"

"That's going well so far. We've got the injunction approved to seize everything we can locate that he owns in the United States. I've been enjoying that." Marcella grinned the toothy, triumphant smile she reserved for evildoers getting what they deserved. "Even if we can't extradite him, we can put a serious dent in his business, and that's going to hurt."

"Not enough. And it won't do anything for his new bride." Sophie said. "He needs to be stopped. Permanently."

"One step at a time." Marcella picked up her bowl and drank the broth straight from the rim. They both finished, and Sophie took a twenty out of her pocket and set it on the counter. "I think you can be confident we've at least shut him down in the United States."

"It's a start. Keep the change," Sophie told the owner, and got a head nod and the flash of a gold tooth in reply.

"Win next time." He shook the bill at her. "I'm planning to bet more than twenty on you someday."

Sophie smiled, and it hurt her split lip. They untied Ginger and headed back toward her building.

"So you know I'm on admin leave, right?" Sophie said as they walked down the sidewalk. Her full belly had brought on immediate sleepiness, and now all she could think about was getting to bed. "Waxman is disciplining me for not telling him about the break-in at my apartment."

Marcella gave an exaggerated shudder. "I'm way too familiar with being on his shit list. I don't envy you right now. Yeah, I heard in the staff briefing—he used your breach as an example of 'the wrong kind of independent action.'" She made air quotes. "I'm sorry. But you need some time off anyway. You can visit Alika tomorrow, take that dog to the park. Get a pedicure." Marcella dimpled at Sophie.

"Right. I finally have time to do a pedicure. Ow. Mouth hurts when I smile." They'd arrived at her building.

"I'll call you tomorrow. Make sure you're okay. And brace yourself. I think Waxman's sending Dr. LaSota to make a house call on you." Marcella gave Sophie a hug.

"Thanks for the warning. I don't care for that woman."

"I don't know anyone who does."

"She told me I should have therapy—because of Assan. I didn't want to hear it at the time, but..." Sophie raised her shoulders, dropped them. "She might be right."

"Well, you don't have to do therapy with her. Dr. Wilson is a much better choice." Marcella named the petite blond psychologist that worked for the state police department and did contracting work for the FBI.

"Maybe I can head off Dr. LaSota by already having an appointment with Dr. Wilson," Sophie said. "Worth a try."

"I'll text you Dr. Wilson's number. See you."

Sophie waved at her friend and tugged Ginger away from a dead toad on the sidewalk. "No, girl." The brown, warty amphibians came out everywhere in Hawaii after a rain, and this one had been flattened by a car. Ginger loved nothing better than to roll on a dead toad, and the strong reek was hard to get out of her thick fur.

Up in the apartment, Sophie did her new security routine: relock door once inside, activate alarm, review security footage from the day on fast forward, and sweep the apartment for bugs. Only when all that was done did she open a can of food for Ginger.

"Wish you were a better guard dog," she told the lab, giving her an affectionate pat. "But that's okay. You're good company, and that's enough for me."

She turned on her computer rigs with the fob, stripped out of her dirty clothes, and got into the shower. Under the warm flow of water, she reviewed the day.

She and Alika were both lucky to be alive. Sophie decided what she'd do tomorrow morning. There were still some loose ends she could run down, some unfinished business she could take care of, even on admin leave.

Wrapped in the dragon robe, she called the number Marcella had given for Dr. Wilson, and left a message requesting at least a phone or Skype appointment "to discuss a case and do a post-shoot debrief."

Done with necessary reaching out, she blinked blearily at the multiple screens, and realized that, exhausted as she was, she was still lonely. Sheldon Hamilton, wherever he was, must sometimes feel that way. He had to be so alone, hiding from everyone.

She clicked on the email address she'd saved from the Ghost, and sent him a message.

"I had a hard day. I told my boss about your getting into my apartment, and he didn't like how I handled the situation and put me on admin leave for a couple of days. Then, I went to the gym and lost my bout. Haven't taken such a beating in the ring in a long time, and it was just fine because I was so angry. It made me feel better, but then I visited a friend who's in the hospital, and someone tried to shoot him. We barely got out alive. I hope your day was even a tiny bit better than mine. Why don't you tell

me why you disappeared? What does that accomplish? I'm curious. I just really want to know."

The cursor blinked, and Sophie stared at it, realizing that was the truth. Sheldon Hamilton's disappearance just didn't make a whole lot of sense. Maybe her conclusion yesterday was wrong. The Ghost wasn't Hamilton after all.

Chapter 26

The Ghost's phone beeped with an alert to his secure email address. He was in the middle of a difficult section of a Bach concerto, and he ignored the tiny beep. But even as he held a note vibrating at the top end of the scale, then ripped through an arpeggio, he wanted to check it.

Only a handful of people had that email.

One of them was Sophie Ang.

The Ghost faced the windows overlooking the moonlit ocean, the music stand open in front of him. He'd been working out before practice, and just wore the silk boxers he liked for bed, a swatch of silk protecting the violin from the skin of his shoulder. He enjoyed the easy movement of his muscles, the warmed up feel of his fingers, the sensation of air on his skin and the feeling of the music coming to life under his fingers, moving through his body.

When he got to the end of the piece, he lowered the violin and bowed to Anubis. The dog's alert eyes watched him from a graceful pose.

"I want to get that email," he told Anubis. "That means I need to play the piece again. Delayed gratification is what makes life sweet."

Anubis twitched his ears and blinked.

The Ghost started the piece again, and shut his eyes, giving himself over fully to the music, his mind completely silent for once as every sense and nerve ending engaged with playing it perfectly. But not just perfectly. *With passion.*

At the end, Anubis sat up and inclined his head.

"You're a king among dogs." The Ghost set the violin in its case and tossed Anubis a treat. Anubis only provided that acknowledgement when the Ghost had played perfectly.

He delayed gratification further by taking a shower. Under the stream of water he mentally reviewed his earlier live chat with Sophie Ang. He didn't think he'd given her any clues, and he'd tried to allay her justifiable anger at being under surveillance. He hoped he'd succeeded. He'd meant it when he said he hadn't planned to spy on her.

But now, he missed seeing her. Knowing what she was doing. Still, he knew the next overture had to come from her.

Finally, dressed for bed in a fresh pair of boxers and a thin tee, he sat down at his workstation and opened the email.

He finished reading Sophie's note and savored the fact that she had told him about her day, even though it had obviously been harrowing.

Using a search program, he tracked everything he could find about the attack at the hospital. He blanched at the sight of the bullet-riddled wall of the hospital room where "an intrepid off-duty FBI agent moved quickly to save the life of a friend."

No details about who it was or why they were attacked.

But he knew. Alika Wolcott was her MMA coach and "friend." His name had been kept out of mainstream news articles and features, but he'd followed the blog of one of the gym members at Fight Club who was speculating on Alika's beating and the case against him.

The Ghost suspected Alika and Sophie were dating, though he hadn't been able to confirm it. He didn't like having competition for her, but he wasn't going to exploit his superior position against someone who didn't deserve it. For now, it appeared Alika wasn't in need of anything but the hospital.

He hunched forward over his keyboard, nimble fingers flying.

* * *

Sophie drove to Queen's Hospital and entered the cool underground garage the next morning. "You should be okay here for a half hour or so," she told Ginger, cracking the windows and filling the water bowl on the back seat. She locked the car and glanced around in the dim acres of parked cars, wondering if there was a security guard she could ask to keep an eye on her dog. Parking garages were not safe environments, and she hated to leave Ginger. But the place was deserted, echoing with the sounds of faraway traffic and smelling of gas and rubber.

She'd put on her spare weapon. It was a comforting weight in its holster under her left armpit beneath the lightweight FBI-gray jacket. In the elevator, on the way up to Alika's floor, she rehearsed what she'd say, how she'd explain to him who she was. There hadn't been an opportunity for that last night.

She was met at the door of Alika's room by Lehua Wolcott, looking radiant in a short fitted muumuu, glossy hair wound into a roll pierced by *koa* chopsticks, brown eyes sparkling.

"He's much better today." She hugged Sophie's stiff body. "He remembered us! Remembered his name, remembered he grew up on Kauai. Just can't remember anything about the attack." Distress puckered her face. "I told him that you saved him. I'll give you two some privacy. Maybe when you talk, it will help."

The officer was back at the door, Sophie was relieved to see. He gave her a little salute of recognition. "I'm not leaving no matter who calls me." He was wearing Kevlar over his uniform.

"Good." She followed Lehua into Alika's room.

"Son, this is Sophie. I hope you remember her," Lehua said. Alika was sitting upright this time, wearing a buttoned aloha shirt over his bandaged chest. It gave him a look as if any minute he'd get up and walk out, but the casted leg, back in traction, gave lie to that.

"I remember Sophie," Alika said impatiently. "Thanks, Mom. Give us some space, will you?"

Lehua rolled her eyes at Sophie, still smiling. Sophie could tell that she was so happy to have Alika awake she didn't care that he seemed irritable. She shut the door gently behind her.

"Hello." Sophie approached, sat in a plastic chair beside his bed, still tentative even though he'd said he remembered her. How much did he remember?

"Hi." He studied her intently. "What's with the bruises? Did you get those during the attack yesterday?" Alika's voice was so clear, so familiar and energetic that she smiled, and winced again, touching her sore lip.

"No. Had a bout with The Breaker at Fight Club before I came to visit you yesterday."

"Hell no, you didn't! Man's got a fist like a hammer!"

Sophie smiled, her lip cracking at this evidence that he remembered more recent events. "I probably shouldn't have taken him on, but I was in a mood. I made him work for it. Six rounds with a woman. I suspect it is some kind of record, somewhere."

"That's my girl." His familiar grin brought up the less-swollen side of his face. He remembered—if not their date, at least that he was her coach.

She reached out a hand and touched his arm lightly, that tattooed spot she'd made friends with. "I'm glad I was here yesterday."

"Me too." His good hand, bandaged, but at least not in a cast, came to pat hers briefly where it rested on his arm. "I have to go back to Kauai for awhile. Do rehab and physical therapy. Can you help out at the gym for me? Maybe run things in the evenings?"

She glanced up into his golden-brown eyes, looked away again. "Sure. You're going to hire a manager, then?"

"I have to. Don't know when I'll be able to come back." He coughed, and his whole body constricted around the obvious pain. Sophie weathered it with him and he finally went on. "My dad is going to stay back and try to get things set up at the gym and my business for me, but HPD wants my parents to get me out of here as soon as I'm safe to transport. For my safety, and they want their man back. They're thinking tomorrow."

"That's soon." Sophie felt her face settling into that expression that hid her emotions. "Of course I'll help in the evenings at the gym. I go there anyway."

Did he remember their date, their emerging feelings? There was no indication of anything but the collegial friendship they'd had before in his face or demeanor. This was her opportunity to cut their connection—*for his safety, and for hers.* Until she knew Assan wasn't part of the equation. She drew in a quick breath and steeled herself.

"This is awkward. I get the feeling your mom might have said the wrong thing about what we were to each other. We were friends. You trained me, and I recently graduated from having you coach me. And we went on one date. We were…" Sophie fumbled for the right words. "We were exploring if we might be more than friends. But it was just one date."

"I remember everything about it. We both know it was a lot more than just one date." Alika's golden brown eyes were intense as he looked at her. "But I don't want to drag you into this situation. So for now we're just friends, and I don't expect you to wait for me, for all the time it's going to take for me to heal. For things to be different for me on Oahu. For someday."

Sophie let out the breath she didn't know she'd been holding.

"Things could change." It was ironic that they were ending their relationship because she was worried about Assan being a threat to him, while he was afraid the Boyz were a threat to her.

"Kiss me goodbye," he whispered.

Sophie leaned over and set her bruised mouth on his bruised mouth. The kiss tasted of blood, pain, and the saltiness of tears. It was unbelievably sweet and tender and hungry.

She sat back up, stood. Wiped her eyes with the heels of her hands. "I'll keep an eye on the gym. Have your dad call me and we'll get organized."

"Thank you. Be safe." He looked away, out the window.

"And you get well."

Sophie turned and walked out, face in that familiar immobile mask that hid her feelings and kept her moving. She said goodbye to Lehua, telling her she was in a hurry, a work thing had come up. She fled at a trot down the hall and didn't cry until she was in the Lexus with Ginger in her arms.

Chapter 27

Sophie was waiting in a drive-through line to grab something to eat when her phone toned. She glanced down and put on the brakes when she saw FLORENCE TORRES in the little identification window.

"I had one of those calls." Florence's voice was a hoarse whisper. "Apartment 14C. It's down the hall from the other one. Someone's moving in today."

"Thank you," Sophie said, but the woman had hung up already.

Someone honked behind her and she pulled forward, putting in her Bluetooth and calling Ken. "Before I get into what I called to tell you, what happened with the raid Waxman ordered on Security Solutions?"

Ken made a disgusted noise. "A whole lot of nothing. Honing and his underlings were all we could grab and they all lawyered up. It was a waste of time like I knew it would be."

"Well, I just got a call from Torres at the kidnapping building." She filled him in on what she knew. "Can I assist? Come in and work the surveillance, something?"

"I'll call Waxman. We're going to want to move in to see what's going on in there."

"We are still going to need to get who's behind this," Sophie said. "If Waxman won't let me come in, I'll keep working on the tech angle."

"Sounds good."

Sophie got a salad to go and took Ginger to the dog park as she'd planned to—there was no point to moving on the situation until she knew more. But she didn't have a tech angle to work, she thought in frustration, stabbing her salad with a flimsy plastic fork as she sat down on the park bench. She'd followed every lead she had on Takeda Industries but she still didn't know who was behind the apartment rental. She didn't think the kidnapping went beyond the three dead men in the morgue.

Her phone rang again. "Waxman says no to your participating in the raid," Ken said.

"*Demon spawn of triple-horned goats,*" Sophie said.

"What?"

"Nothing. I'm just disappointed."

"We're going to stake out that floor and see what comes in. I'll let you know what happens."

"Dammit," Sophie said.

"I understood that one," Ken laughed, and hung up.

Sophie finished her salad while Ginger romped with a pug and a Chihuahua. Around the fenced area of the dog park, the colorful tents and beach umbrellas of the homeless village that inhabited Ala Moana Park created a peaceful, ragtag enclave, in spite of repeated attempts to dislodge them. She watched the denizens playing cards and sharing an anonymous brown-bagged bottle in the shade of a spreading monkeypod tree.

Her cell phone rang again. Sophie answered when she saw that it was Dr. Wilson, the psychologist, returning her call.

"Thanks so much for getting back to me," Sophie said. "Is there a time we could meet or talk?"

"I'm one step ahead of you." The psychologist's voice had a smile in it. "I called your SAC, Waxman, and told him you had requested me. He approved it and canceled Dr. LaSota's home visit scheduled for this afternoon. Unfortunately, we can't meet in person because I'm on the Big Island, but we can talk on the phone. Is this a good time?"

"I guess. I'm at the dog park with Ginger. She's enjoying a little socialization."

"Well, can you speak freely there?"

Sophie glanced around. The other two dog owners were chatting on a bench a good distance away, and there was no one anywhere nearby. "Yes."

"I got a copy of your employee file faxed to me, and Dr. LaSota entered a few notes, concerned about your social life. So where do you want to begin?"

"I just left the hospital. Alika and I broke up before anything even got started." A thickness in her throat threatened to choke off her words.

"Why don't you start by telling me about the attack."

"That was really intense." Even though the scene flashed before her eyes as she described what had happened, it was still less stressful to tell about how she'd responded to the attempt on Alika's life, minute by terrifying minute, than it was to tell about how the tiny bud of their relationship had died.

But of course, one thing led to another, and she finally ended her sad tale with her worry about Assan's involvement in the attempts on Alika's life.

"Is there any evidence of that?"

"No." Sophie shut her eyes on horrible memories of Assan and his threats. Ginger reappeared at her knee, reaching up to lick Sophie's hand.

"I think you should stop torturing yourself with guilt that you somehow brought this on Alika, when everything appears to be pointing to him bringing it on himself. Unjustly, but nothing to do with you." Dr. Wilson blew out a breath. "You were a victim of domestic violence. Your husband was your first sexual partner, and he did his best to break you down, ruin you for any future healthy relationship, even if you got away from him. That's part of *his* pathology. It's important for you to remember it was done deliberately. If you let him keep you from ever trying to be with someone else, he's won."

"It's a hard thing to live with. I can't think about it for long or I just want to find a way to kill him." Sophie bit down on her lip, fondling Ginger's ears. "Until now, just having escaped was enough. Finding a way to rebuild my life. Achieving all I have in the FBI and the fight scene so no one could make me a victim again. But then, I began to want more. A relationship. I was even attracted to a female friend at one time. But I knew I wanted Alika. From the time I first met him. It's been five years, and something was finally happening. Then, bam."

"Life's not fair, is it?" Dr. Wilson's voice was so soft, so sympathetic, that Sophie shut her eyes and let the fat tears collecting under her lids slide out and roll down her cheeks.

"No, it isn't."

"Focus on the good things. Alika woke up. He's going to recover, even if it takes a while. And if Detective Kamuela can get some traction on the Boyz in Honolulu, it's possible you two could move forward."

"I don't think I want to anymore. I don't want to take the chance. Not until I know Assan isn't going to be a problem, ever again. It's been forty-five minutes. Are we done?"

"I don't know. Are we?"

Sophie gazed around the park. The other dog owners had left. It was early afternoon, and Ginger sprawled at her feet. High white clouds scudded by in a deep blue sky, and a soft wind shushed in the high branches of the trees overhead. Off to the left, Diamond Head cut the sky with its jagged, iconic silhouette, and on the right, the homeless people had laid down their cards and were napping on beach towels.

Just another day in paradise.

"I have a confusing case. Can I tell you about that?"

"Total confidentiality means total confidentiality," Dr. Wilson replied. "There are no case notes on this session except documentation that it occurred. Did you ever see that old TV show Get Smart?" She chuckled. "Consider me your Cone of Silence."

"No, I grew up overseas, without TV. So, there's this security company." Sophie described Security Solutions and the various events within the company, which still weren't producing anything that the FBI could act on besides searching for the missing CEO, Sheldon Hamilton. She described why she believed he was the one who'd breached her apartment.

"I have begun a dialogue with him. I'm going to try to lure him into view," she concluded. "I think he's a vigilante of sorts. Used the company to draw in criminals and then set them up against each other."

"Fascinating." Dr. Wilson sounded sincere. "What an interesting criminal."

The word "criminal" didn't seem right to describe Security Solutions' saboteur.

"Brilliant is what he is. Obviously has his own code of ethics. He's living and operating under a different set of rules." Sophie couldn't quite bring herself to describe the flirty dynamic that had arisen between them, the favor she'd asked of him. "It's a deep game he's playing, and my sense is that no one is going to find him until he wants to be found. What I wonder is why he let

Lee Chan get away. If Chan knew who was selling the company's information gathered by the nanny-cam, AI, and other records, then he'd be a real threat."

"So criminal *is* a good word if you suspect this vigilante or saboteur is capable of murder."

"Oh, certainly capable. If you count all the bodies he's incited to kill each other, it's quite a mountain. But as far as I've been able to tell, he's never actually killed anyone himself."

"So, you don't think it's murder. What he does."

Sophie squirmed on the bench. She felt a chill breeze waft over her. "Not exactly, no. It's not always killing, either. Sometimes the perpetrators turn each other in. It's a kind of justice."

A long-distance crackle as Sophie waited.

"Sounds like rationalization to me," Dr. Wilson said.

"Anyway." Sophie didn't want to discuss that further. "The only other thing I feel kind of at a loose end about is the little girl, Anna Addams." She filled Dr. Wilson in on the kidnapping operation, and the lack of answers. "I've been wanting to visit her, return the rabbit she gave me."

"That's a great thing to do," Dr. Wilson said. "She probably needs to see you as much as you need to see her."

"Okay, I'll visit her." Sophie said. "And I have a couple of other places to stop by, too." She ended the call. She needed to get home and look under the Takeda Industries shell corporation, and she wanted to get into that mysterious apartment in the Pendragon Arches building, 9C. No one seemed to know who lived there or what it was used for. Could that be Sheldon's hideout? And she wanted to swing by Lee Chan's apartment. It was worth one last try to find him, warn him.

That reminded her to check her messages.

The Ghost had responded to her email. Her heart hammered as she clicked on the message box.

"I am working on a plan to get the target out. Do you want me to get rid of Assan, too?"

Sophie blinked. That casually, the Ghost was asking if she wanted to participate in murder. She clicked Reply.

"Let me know if there is any information I can give to assist in her escape. I know, for instance, that Assan pays the building staff to report his wife's activities to him. He also has a locked safe room where she may be held prisoner. You probably have one chance to get her out." Sweat beaded on Sophie's forehead and under her arms as she remembered the ways Assan had punished her own early attempts to flee. *"But leave Assan alone. He's mine to deal with."*

She pressed Send.

Chapter 28

Sophie rested a hand on the glossy brass rail inside the rosewood-lined elevator of the Pendragon Arches building as it rose. She had a funny feeling in her gut, the kind of tingling that told her something was close to breaking on a case. After an hour of digging under the Takeda Industries shell corporation, she'd finally unearthed a physical address—and it was 9C Pendragon Arches, the suite she'd already been planning to visit.

What did it mean? There was no way to tell until she saw inside.

The doors whisked open and Sophie stepped out into a long, expensively carpeted hallway. The lighting was subdued with ceiling spots highlighting art prints on the walls. She looked for the direction of the alphabet, and walked down to where a pair of heavy brass urns flanked the glossy black door of 9C.

The building's doorman had let her go up after she'd shown her ID. "Not official business, just interviewing one of your residents for a background check," she'd said, and it had been enough.

Sophie found herself tight with nerves, wishing she'd at least called Ken Yamada to let him know what she was doing, but he was busy with the stakeout of the kidnapping apartment building, anyway. She smoothed her black pants and straightened the plain white button-down she wore, with her spare weapon and a gray linen jacket over it.

Glancing around, she spotted the shiny recessed dome of a mirrored security camera.

Her visit was not going to go unnoticed.

"Blighted offspring of a split-tongued serpent," she muttered, and pushed the doorbell.

No one answered.

She pushed it again.

Still nothing.

"Cursed twin typhoon devils." She hadn't packed her lock picks.

It was severely anticlimactic to go back down on the elevator. At the help desk, she asked for the building manager. She was led to his tiny office, identified herself again, and then inquired as to the inhabitants of 9C.

"I'm investigating on behalf of Security Solutions, who leases that apartment. There's been some confusion and changes in the company, and they've lost track of which employee is actually living there."

"Interesting that they had to send an FBI agent to find out who's in their apartment," the rotund building manager said, squinting skeptically at her. "Especially since they're a security company."

"It's part of a bigger investigation. Confidential." Sophie held her neutral expression. She wished she had some of the quick glibness that Ken and Marcella demonstrated in the field.

"Well, okay." The manager activated his computer console and tapped a few buttons. "I can't let you in without their permission or a warrant, though. Residents are listed as the upper management team of Security Solutions: Frank Honing, Lee

Chan, Todd Remarkian and Sheldon Hamilton. I don't think any of them live there. It's a job perk kind of thing. They use it here and there when they want to."

"Thank you." Sophie considered leaving a message for Todd Remarkian, who must be returning from Hong Kong soon. But no, it might be better not to. "Do you happen to keep any video footage of the hallway?"

"We do."

"Well, I'd like to review that, if you wouldn't mind." She deployed her smile. "It would save a lot of time and back and forth with other agents if you're just able to give me a copy of the hallway surveillance footage."

She was able to get him to make a copy of last week's footage on a quickly burned CD. Back in the Lexus, Sophie cued up the CD on her laptop, curious to see who, if anyone, was using the place.

The first sign she saw of anyone approaching the door happened several days prior. A messenger service dropped off a package, sliding it through the elegant little slot at the bottom of the door.

She froze the image and zoomed in on the package.

It wasn't large, just a white cardboard envelope. There was no name on it, just the address.

She fast-forwarded, but frowned and paused the video as a man appeared within the hour of dropoff. The man in the video wore a white belted robe and a baseball cap. He kept his face angled away from the camera, obviously well aware it was there, and unlocked the apartment door. He retrieved the package, relocked it, and walked away.

The man could not be Todd Remarkian, who was in Hong Kong at the time. She checked the datebook feature on her phone. The time and date stamped on the recording was the day she'd started streaming data from the Security Solutions transmitter she'd planted in their building.

The robe the man wore at first looked like a bathrobe. Could this be some other resident in the building? Perhaps someone authorized by Todd to pick up mail? She froze the image of the man, door open, reaching inside to pick up the package.

Sophie took hasty notes in a text box on the side of the screen as she tried to gather every detail she could.

She blew up the still photo from the video and studied it. All she could see was a hard jawline in the shadow of the ball cap. Skin was consistent with Caucasian ancestry. Hair was hidden by the cap but appeared to be a medium shade in the black and white video, either dark blond or light brown, and short. Height was around six feet. Build, athletic.

The man was wearing white pajama-style pants that matched the robe and simple rubber slippers, common Hawaii wear. She blew up the image more. The weave of the robe was the rough cotton of a martial arts *gi*, and what had at first appeared a bathrobe tie was, in fact, a black fabric belt tied martial arts style. While not the dishabille at first indicated in the video, the outfit was not the kind of thing people wore walking around on the street.

This unsub did martial arts, lived somewhere in the building, had a key to the apartment and was authorized to pick up mail. She was quite possibly looking at the man who, called himself the Ghost.

It couldn't be Todd Remarkian or Sheldon Hamilton. They'd been in Hong Kong at the time date-stamped on the video. But this person could be whoever had tracked her computer's location, because as she traced back her own movements, she realized that package could contain the transmitter from Security Solutions that had resulted in her breach.

She had one more apartment to visit before the day was over. She couldn't shake a sense of urgency about finding Lee Chan.

Sophie got into the Lexus after dropping off Ginger at the apartment. The Bluetooth in her ear toned, and she checked her phone—it was Marcus Kamuela.

"Hello, Marcus. Got some news about Alika's case?"

"That's why I'm calling. He got discharged from the hospital this morning and his parents took him back to Kaua`i for his own protection and his recovery. He seemed fine with going."

"Oh." Sophie's hand had been on the key to turn on the Lexus. Now it fell limply into her lap. *Getting hit by a truck must feel like this.* She leaned her forehead on the steering wheel and shut her eyes, suddenly feeling the effects of the bout with The Breaker. "I'm sure that's best, especially when he's got so much rehab ahead."

"Well," Marcus cleared his throat. "I didn't want you to try to go visit or something and find out that way. And more good news on that front. We've closed our investigation into Alika's business. He's clear."

"Great," Sophie made herself sit up and put some enthusiasm in her voice. "I always knew he was clean."

"Can't say the same for your ex. Marcella told me she filled you in yesterday on how things were progressing against him. We shut down everything he has in the States and put in a case on him with Interpol, but chances of extradition seem slim to none."

"I expected as much."

"That's why it's interesting that Interpol let us know that his new wife has come forward as a witness to the drug trafficking. She is pressing charges against him with the Hong Kong police for domestic violence, too."

"What?" Sophie sat back so hard that she hit the headrest. "What did you say?"

"She got out. And she's trying to take him down."

Relief felt like joy. "I can't believe it. How'd she do it?"

"More like a commando team did it. Full frontal break-in to Ang's apartment in Hong Kong, and extraction under guard. A crack team of mercenaries for hire pulled it off. They dropped her off at the police station and disappeared."

"Security Solutions has commandos," Sophie said.

"I guess it's possible it was them. The Interpol guy didn't have any more information than that they'd rescued her, she was safe, and she was prepared to press charges on Assan Ang."

"Good. I hope they're providing protection."

"Her family's doing that. They have plenty of money. Anyway, I just thought you'd want to know," Marcus said.

"Thanks for the news. I really appreciate knowing this. I'll follow up and see if there's anything I can do to assist. What's the contact information for Ang's Interpol case?"

He gave it to her.

"Thanks again for calling. You do good work." The words felt stilted but she knew from the warmth that came into his tone that he appreciated them.

"Takes one to know one," he said. "You do some nice work yourself."

"Takes one to know one," she murmured, unsure of the phrase. Marcus took her repetition as acknowledgement.

"Well, I'm sure I'll see you soon."

"Indeed you will." She hung up, touching the Bluetooth at her ear.

The Ghost had fulfilled the favor she'd asked. And now she owed him.

It was worth it.

She turned the Lexus's key with a definite movement and punched on the air conditioning, pulled out her laptop and opened it up, finding her email.

She checked to see if the Ghost had replied to her earlier note. He had.

"Mission accomplished. Sorry you didn't think it was a good time for Assan to go to hell where he belongs, but I bow to the greater debt he owes you. Until next time. ~ the Ghost."

Sophie typed rapidly.

"Thanks for what you did for that young woman. She deserves to have a life. But just because I owe you doesn't mean I'm going to let you go. I'm going to find you. Count on it."

Prick his vanity. Provoke him, and lure him into the open.

Sophie put the vehicle in gear. She needed to talk to Lee Chan.

* * *

In the surveillance video, Sophie Ang glanced up and down the hall, her tawny golden-brown skin reduced to a medium gray, the white of her shirt crisp in the grainy tones of the recording. For one long second her unforgettable face, still distorted with bruising, gazed directly at the camera.

She rang the bell. Muttered something. Rang the bell. Muttered again. Looked up and down the hall, annoyance clear in her body language. Finally, she walked back to the elevator.

The Ghost amplified the audio feature. Played her muttered comments. They sounded like something in a foreign language. He frowned, clipped the section out of the audio and fed it into a translation program.

Sophie's inventive swearing in Thai played back to him in the tinny, perfectly flat, automated voice of the translator. He tipped his head back and laughed, feeling the release of genuine humor.

"My God, this woman," he said aloud to Anubis. "Just when I think I'm getting to know what she's about, she surprises me again."

That moment of humor gave him the energy to launch into the preparations for what he needed to do next. It was time for his final play.

"Check, and mate." He got up and left his workstation.

Chapter 29

The familiar beige hallway outside Lee Chan's apartment was deserted. Her own team had not expended much effort to find the tech after he'd been cut loose the first time because his claims were so vague, and her search of his work and home computer had come up empty. That meant exactly nothing, because they'd never found a laptop. Lee probably kept everything worth anything close to him in one safe place.

This drop-by was probably a waste of time, but worth a try. People were creatures of habit and tended to return to the familiar. She glanced up and down the empty hall, her nose prickling with its slightly musty carpet smell. She didn't see any security cams, and she'd brought her lock picks this time. First, she knocked on the dark brown door, feeling its peephole on her like an eye.

"Chan? Lee Chan?"

Nothing.

She knocked again. "Open up, Lee. This is the FBI."

Still nothing. She rattled the handle with one hand while reaching into her pocket for the lock picks with the other—and the handle turned. The door drifted open before her.

Sophie's scalp tingled. "Lee Chan?" she called into the darkened space.

She knew they'd locked the apartment after their earlier search. Without breaching the doorway, she pulled a pair of latex gloves out of her back pocket, snapped them on, and drew her backup weapon.

Using a finger, she reached over and flicked on the light.

The sterile little apartment was as bare and tidy as she remembered, but she thought she could smell something metallic, foreign. She could see into the spotless kitchenette from the doorway, and it was as shiny and empty as before.

There was only a bedroom and bathroom to check. Suddenly impatient with herself and this case of nerves, she strode into the room and over to the bedroom, turning the handle and throwing it wide forcefully. The door flew inward and bumped the wall.

Nothing. The pristine twin bed, made as tightly as any recruit's in boot camp, seemed to mock her. It was exactly as before. Lee Chan was long gone, probably with a fake passport.

The bathroom door was closed, too. She opened it, pushing it forward. The light was off, and she flicked the switch beside the door.

A horrific visual hit her, and a blur of movement. A blow hammered down on her extended weapon hand. Sophie cried out, the Glock dropping from her nerveless fingers, as a blade flashed toward her. She flung herself back, reflexes barely saving her, as a gloved hand, holding an open straight razor, slashed where she'd just been.

Sophie stumbled backward from the doorway, hitting the coffee table with the back of her legs as the assailant launched out of the bathroom after her. His free hand shot out and grabbed her by the throat, his momentum bearing her back, the coffee table levering into the back of her knees. She sprawled backward over it, borne down by the attacker's weight landing on her.

Stars spun in her vision, obscuring the man's face as she tried to break his hold with her good hand, writhing beneath him. He'd landed on top of her, sour breath inches from her face, his fingers squeezing her throat. The razor sliced down toward her, and she squeezed her eyes shut.

"Sophie." He breathed her name in the voice of nightmare. He didn't cut her.

She opened her eyes. She was looking into Assan Ang's face, congested with rage and adrenaline, his panting breaths burning her skin, his bloodshot eyes inches from hers.

His hand tightened and her breath shut off. His weight on her body and his practiced grasp on her throat were as effective as ever. A slow grin twisted his full lips.

"My Sophie." The razor caressed her cheek. "I didn't dare hope it would be you coming after me. This is just too good."

Sophie felt blackness closing in. A sense of hopelessness and inevitability rose up and swamped her. It was as if the whole five years between her escape and this moment had never happened.

"You're mine until I'm done with you," he breathed into her ear. Goose bumps erupted as she shuddered, gasping in vain for breath. One arm was trapped beneath him, one raised beside her head but still nerveless from the blow. Her heart lurched as his big hand depressed the nerves and veins in her neck, just as he'd done a hundred times in the past.

She was disappearing, conditioned by his assault and smothered by his weight.

He's going to kill me this time. She'd seen that in the exultant certainty in his eyes as he recognized her. Her heart felt like it was bursting. Her vision dimmed as he raised the razor.

The graceful Thai writing of the tattoo on the inside of her arm reflected on the mirror-like blade in an instant of comprehension.

Hope. Respect.

Her mind filled in the rest of the messages written on her body so she wouldn't ever forget them: *Power. Truth. Freedom. Courage. Love. Joy. Bliss.*

She had a lot to live for. She wasn't going down without a fight.

Sophie still had her feet on the floor beneath Assan's muscular bulk. She heaved, twisting to the side with all the strength of a thousand sit-ups, throwing him off and wrenching her neck out of his grip. He slashed at her with the razor as she rolled away. She felt the fire of its touch but didn't have the breath to scream.

He'd landed on his back on the coffee table. She heaved herself toward the bathroom. She had to get her weapon.

"Bitch!" He hurled himself after her.

Sophie grabbed the ceramic lamp on a side table with her good hand, heaving it at him. Assan dodged. The flying lamp splintered with a crash, and he leaped, grabbing her calf. She kicked, but he hung on, swinging the razor at her leg. It caught in the fabric of her pants as she dove into the bathroom. He pulled on her leg, a mighty heave, and she slid backward, her fingers scrabbling for purchase on the slippery floor.

She caught hold of the base of the toilet, grunting with effort. All of her hours in the gym paid off as she broke his grip on her leg with a powerful kick and heaved herself toward the weapon. She grabbed and retrieved the Glock, rolling over and sitting up, her back to the macabre scene in the tub.

"Drop the blade or I'll shoot." Her voice was a breathless rasp.

Assan was on his feet just outside the door of the bathroom.

"No, you won't." He swung the blade by its metal handle, holding her eyes with his dominating stare, advancing a step toward her seated position on the bathroom floor. "My Sophie. I've missed our games together."

"Stop. Now. This is your last warning." Her voice was thready. Her throat felt crushed.

"The new girl. She doesn't have your fight, your fire. You knew I'd come to you someday, didn't you? I told you I would. You're mine until I'm done with you." His voice, rich with silky threat, made her finger tighten on the trigger as he continued to swing the blade by its handle in a flashing, hypnotic arc.

She couldn't shoot him yet. She needed answers, needed to keep him talking.

"You got me. I totally didn't expect this. What are you doing here, Assan?"

"I came to tie up loose ends. On a number of levels." He inched another step toward her.

"So you were working with Chan?"

"He's been on my payroll since you met him." Assan seemed totally confident Sophie wouldn't hurt him. He tossed the blade from hand to hand. She found her eyes watching it instead of how he was advancing on her. "He gave me information. Information I used for various purposes. But he was going to talk."

"Lee spied on me?" Sophie whispered.

"I wanted to be sure you really went to those classes and were doing what you were supposed to, going where you were supposed to go." Assan shrugged. "You told yourself you could get away. Really, my dear, I thought I taught you better."

He'd definitely taken another step closer. Sophie's finger tightened on the trigger. She forced herself to relax, though her hands were shaking and her heart pounding so hard she felt sick.

She still didn't know enough. "Lee sold out the company? Were you behind the kidnapping of Anna Addams?"

"The beginning of a nice little shared operation with Chan." Assan's natural arrogance made him expansive. "Which, unfortunately, has to be put on hold. You thought you could touch someone else? I'm your first and only, Sophie. You belong to me." His eyes were hungry and invasive, roaming over her.

"No," Sophie panted. She could feel her cheek stinging as sweat ran into the scratch the razor had left on her cheek. "You'll never touch me again. I'll die first."

"Oh, that can be arranged." He actually laughed. He seemed to get larger as she felt herself shrinking, helplessness activated by all the times he'd tortured her. "I had to teach you a lesson, so I had the Boyz take out your boyfriend at the docks. They got the whole messy business on video for me. We can watch it together."

Bile surged up Sophie's throat in a choking wave. *Assan had been behind Alika's attack.*

He threw the razor as she squeezed the trigger. The detonation of the shot in the enclosed space deafened her. She felt a jolt of fiery pain.

The razor clattered against the bathtub as Assan crashed backward into the coffee table.

Through the ringing in her ears, she heard Assan moaning and cursing. She rose, one hand against her bleeding ear, and flipped her ex-husband onto his face, looking around for something to tie him with.

"You shot me!" He seemed genuinely shocked. She put her foot on his wounded shoulder and stepped down, a snarl twisting her lips. He yowled in pain. Her aim had been true—she'd gotten him right below the collarbone and shoulder joint, a painful but nonfatal wound.

She wanted him dead, but needed him alive—for now.

"Don't move." She left Assan gasping in agony and went into the spotless little kitchen, finding a ball of twine in one of the drawers. She hog-tied his feet to his arms behind his back, ignoring his cursing cries.

Finally, she stepped back, her whole body trembling and bathed in sweat. Her ear was still streaming blood, and she wondered how much of it was missing. She found a kitchen towel and held it against her head, setting down her weapon on the counter. She thumbed her phone out of her pocket and speed-dialed Waxman's private cell.

"Why are you calling me on your mandatory day off, Agent Ang?" her boss's voice was dry and crisp.

Sophie cleared her throat, but her voice was still reedy. "Because we've got a body." That first searing glimpse had shown her it was too late for the victim.

That shut Waxman up for a moment, but he quickly regrouped, rattling questions at her like automatic fire. Sophie gave him enough to get the rest of the team and the first responders on their way, and cut the connection. She pocketed her phone and looked down at Assan, putting off the moment she had to go and look at what was inside the bathroom.

"Thank God she's out of your reach, you sick scum," Sophie whispered.

Assan turned his head to look at her. "What?"

"Your new wife. She's free."

"What are you talking about?"

"I got word just a few hours ago. A friend did me a favor. She's down at the station in Hong Kong testifying against you as we speak."

"Whore! Bitch!" Assan thrashed, glaring. "You can't escape me. Wherever you go, I'll find you! I'll make you pay!"

"You can try." And Sophie stepped on his injured shoulder with her full weight as she walked toward the bathroom. His gasping screams were music as she looked at the bathtub from the doorway.

She shut her eyes, unable to process what she was seeing for a moment. The horror was just as bad when she opened them again.

Blood filled the bathtub, and there was a body floating in it. She could see short black hair breaking the surface of the red water, and the curve of a shoulder. Sophie breathed shallowly, trying to screen out the harsh reek of blood with its metallic aftertaste.

Deliberately not looking at the bathtub, she scanned around the rest of the small bathroom. White towels hung neatly folded. The sink gleamed, and so did the mirror. The toilet lid was closed, and a note on it was held down by a small black laptop. A bloody washcloth Assan must have been using to wipe up after the murder had fallen to the ground beside the toilet.

Sophie took a step toward the carnage and, her hands behind her back, leaned over to read the note, which was printed out on plain computer paper but signed in wavering ballpoint.

"I can't live with myself any longer. I sold out my friends and colleagues and the clients of Security Solutions who put their trust in me. This is the only honorable recourse left. In taking my own life I will right the wrong I've done. ~ Lee Chan."

"You'd almost got done staging this scene," Sophie said over her shoulder to Assan. "You pig." She made herself lean over the bath and verify that the body floating in the tub was indeed Lee Chan.

At least the young man's eyes were closed. Remembering Lee's eager grin, she felt a stab of grief for the enthusiastic young tech she'd studied with in Hong Kong a lifetime ago. She wondered where, along the way, he'd gone wrong—or if Assan had just got his hooks into him early, too deep to get out. She suspected the latter.

"I'm going to kill you. It's just a matter of time and place," Assan said as she reappeared.

Sophie leaned down and spat in his face. "You're only alive because I'm going to watch you lose everything, and suffer before you die."

* * *

The next several hours were a blur of the controlled chaos that follows death. HPD arrived, Ken, Gundersohn, and Waxman showed up, and lastly Dr. Fukushima, the Honolulu medical examiner.

One of the EMTs bandaged Sophie. The razor had scratched her cheek and taken a bit off the top of her ear. Her wrist was severely bruised. Her throat was the most painful injury, and there was nothing to be done for that but rest.

She gave a statement to the responding officers and detective about coming by the apartment, hoping to ask Chan a few more questions, and the attack that had followed. Waxman stood in the background, arms crossed on his chest. She dreaded talking to him.

"We already had a case open involving Lee Chan," she told the officers. "I'm taking his computer in. It has information we need for our case."

After a brief turf battle that the FBI definitively won, Sophie walked out of the apartment carrying the evidence-bagged laptop while Waxman was distracted by Dr. Fukushima, the medical examiner. She didn't look at the medical personnel working on Assan. No one had commented on her excessive use of restraint on an injured man.

In the apartment's doorway, she snagged Ken Yamada by his jacket sleeve. "Ken, I need to talk to you. About something other than this."

"What could be bigger than catching your ex as one of the men behind the craziness at Security Solutions?" But Ken followed her into the hall.

Sophie told him that she now had a general physical description of someone who had access to apartment 9C in the Pendragon Arches, had retrieved a package, possessed a black belt in some sort of martial arts, and was near enough not to have to change when he went to pick up something at the apartment.

"Who do you think it was?" Ken's even brows were pulled together in a frown.

"I don't know."

They both turned to look at Assan Ang being wheeled out on a gurney accompanied by two uniformed officers. He refused to acknowledge either of them, and Sophie shut her eyes until he passed.

Maybe she should have killed him.

"No. You shouldn't have killed him. It would have looked bad," Ken said. "He'll get what's coming to him."

She must have spoken aloud. "That's what I'm counting on."

"I was just going to call you from the kidnap building when Waxman sent us here to Chan's apartment. We scooped up some wrong on the fourteenth floor, all right. The room was being used to shoot a porn flick."

"What?" Sophie was nonplussed.

"Yeah. We all saw more than we wanted to when we broke down the door. Apparently that floor is available for all sorts of shenanigans. We're going to have to keep an eye on it through your contact at the building."

"Shenanigans?" A new word.

"Stuff like pornos. Not illegal, necessarily, but not savory either. We interviewed the man who booked the room and he said he found the number to call to reserve it on a forum. So if we can connect that with Ang and Lee, we'll have a lock on them for the kidnapping too."

"Assan admitted to me he killed Lee to shut him up, and that he was behind the kidnapping."

"We'll need to focus on building a case against Ang with what we can prove—which is that you practically caught him killing Chan, and then he attacked you. That should be enough to put him away for a good long time."

"We can be sure that what's on Lee's laptop is what Assan wants us to find. Probably frames him for everything. But there's still more going on." Sophie told Ken about the man who called himself the Ghost, leaving out the personal nature of their correspondence. "Maybe all we have to do to find the Ghost is watch apartment 9C."

"I think there's enough in what you've told me to get that apartment opened," Ken said. "We are, after all, still searching for Sheldon Hamilton, who's a missing person. Now you've found a second residence. Personally, I think Sheldon Hamilton's going to turn up floating in the bay in Hong Kong."

"I disagree. I think Hamilton disappeared on purpose. At the very least, there's some sort of operative using apartment 9C as a drop. Because of the timing, the pickup I saw could have been the surveillance transmitter that ended up being traced to my location and leading to the breach into my apartment." Sophie shifted from foot to foot in agitation, her wrist aching.

"I'm planning to bring all this to Waxman and see what he says."

Sophie frowned in frustration, glancing back toward the

grisly bathroom, where Waxman was still talking with the Medical Examiner.

"How about the two of us go to the Pendragon Arches apartment with the building manager, and get it unlocked? We need to see what's inside. I don't want it to be you and Gundersohn without me. I've tracked this beast this far. I want to find his lair."

"Beast? Lair?" She'd startled a snort of amusement out of Ken. "You talk about him like he's some sort of mythical creature."

"I've begun to think of him that way. There are so many layers to this. We're only seeing what he wants us to see. Getting this surveillance video is, I believe, the first real evidence that shows the Ghost." She could feel Ken wavering. "Please. I've never asked for a favor before."

"All right. But technically, you're still on leave, and going to be more so after Ang's shooting, so let me do all the talking. Meet me at the Pendragon Arches in two hours."

"Thanks," Sophie said fervently. "Oh, and I finally came up with an address for the shell corporation under Takeda Industries. Guess where it is?"

"Don't tell me. Apartment 9C."

"Right. Seems like that apartment is a handy location for all the 'shenanigans' of the top management of the Security Solutions."

Ken smiled at Sophie's use of his word. Waxman, done talking, spotted Sophie and strode forward to take the evidence-bagged laptop from her arms, frowning. Sophie cradled her wrist, wriggling it tentatively.

"You aren't back on the schedule until tomorrow, Agent Ang," he said coldly. "And then we have the investigation of this latest incident to deal with. I'll take these back to the office and log them in. What possessed you to come by here, anyway?"

"I just had this feeling about Chan. I didn't put it together with Assan—he wasn't on my radar at all."

"Assan is refusing to talk about any of it and has lawyered up. Dr. Fukushima, the ME, says Chan's body looks exsanguinated, which of course it is. The wounds on his wrists were deep vertical cuts—he bled out within minutes." Waxman was still frowning. Somehow Sophie knew his anger was because she'd come so close to being killed.

"I surprised Assan. He was staging Lee's suicide after he'd murdered him. If I'd come a few minutes later, he might have gotten away with it. A few minutes earlier, and I might have saved Lee's life." Sophie shook her head, regret tightening her already sore throat. She looked up to meet her boss's eyes. "Lee was telling the truth when he said he was afraid for his life."

"So Lee was the saboteur," Ken said thoughtfully.

"No!" Sophie exclaimed impatiently. "I don't think he had the—twisted sense of justice, the brilliance to be the saboteur. He was selling out Security Solutions' intel. But Assan confirmed to me that he killed Lee to shut him up, tie up a loose end. Lee was set up to take the fall for everything."

"On that note, go get some rest, Agent Ang," Waxman said. "We can sort the details out later. For now, we've got a body and a murderer in custody, and that's all we need to deal with right now."

Sophie turned away with one last pleading glance at Ken, who gave her a slight nod. He'd meet her at the Pendragon Arches later. Relieved, Sophie walked down the hall, cradling her wrist.

Chapter 30

The rotund building manager of the Pendragon Arches was clearly annoyed to have to leave the comfort of his office, but Ken's formal, no-nonsense demeanor left no room for argument. In front of the shiny door of 9C, the manager fumbled through a thick ring of keys.

Beside him, Sophie felt her pulse speed up. She'd gone home, taken a couple of Vicodin, napped like the dead and got up again when Ken appeared at her door. She'd draped a filmy scarf around her bruised throat, but there was no disguising the bandage on her ear, the Band-Aid on her cheek, the bruises left over from her fight.

But nothing was going to keep her from finding out who was in Apartment 9C. Her heart pounded. Not with fear. *Excitement.* She was so close to catching the Ghost.

"Well, before you get all hot and bothered finding the key, let's see if anyone's home." Ken reached out a finger and pushed the bell. It dinged inside, a genteel chime. The manager was still trying to find the right key when the door opened.

A shirtless man wearing red flannel pajama bottoms with kangaroos on them stood in the doorway, rubbing wet blond hair. A square-jawed, blue-eyed face looked at them questioningly.

Sophie tried not to notice the man's well-developed physique.

"George! What's the problem?" He had a light Australian accent.

"Ah, Mr. Remarkian. You're back," the manager exclaimed. "These FBI agents insisted on coming in to search this apartment. They say they're looking for Sheldon Hamilton."

"Oh, good!" The man's face cleared and he grinned. "So glad you two came by. I've had a communication from Sheldon and I've been on the phone to Security Solutions to tell them the crisis is over. Come on in." He made a welcoming gesture for them to enter, and the manager, emitting obsequious noises, removed himself.

"Special Agent Ken Yamada, Special Agent Sophie Ang." Ken introduced them as they stepped into the apartment, flipping open his creds wallet.

Sophie hesitated in the doorway, still trying to get over the surprise of finding Todd Remarkian in the apartment. The place was beautifully furnished in a modern minimalist style, with elegant silver carpeting and a luxe seating area in black leather.

Todd reached out to shake Sophie's limp hand, humor and concern in his bright blue eyes. "You look like you've been through the wringer." That Aussie accent was broader in person. His hand was dry and slightly callused.

"Hazards of the job," Sophie said. Her voice was still scratchy. "We've met—sort of. On the phone."

"Must have been a hell of a day!"

"It has been. We have news for you. But I'm surprised. I was here earlier and no one was home," Sophie said.

"Yeah. I got in from Hong Kong late last night and had to go out and pick up some food, run some errands. You must have come when I was out." Todd spoke over his shoulder as he walked toward the kitchen. "I was just fixing some tea. Care for some?"

"Sure." Ken surprised Sophie with his reply. The senior agent sat down on the leather couch. "Glad to hear there's some news of Hamilton."

"Oh yes. He called me on a visual linkup. Asked me to record our conversation for the board of Security Solutions and for you folks, once I told him he was being investigated as a missing person." Todd Remarkian's voice came back hollowly from the kitchen. Sophie heard some clattering noises. She sat tentatively on the loveseat adjacent to Ken and looked around the apartment.

The space had the professionally decorated impersonality of a corporate condominium, right down to a brass urn against the wall matching the ones by the front door. Ken quirked an eyebrow at her as Sophie searched for some personal sign of Todd's occupancy.

She spotted a discarded towel on the floor of the bathroom, a pile of clothing on the bed visible through the open door. On the coffee table in front of them rested a sleek silver laptop. Regrettably, it was closed. She longed to open it and see what programs he was running.

Todd Remarkian came back from the kitchen. He'd put on a T-shirt and he carried a designer teapot in hammered copper on a bamboo tray set with matching copper-colored mugs, sliced lemon and a ramekin of sugar cubes. He set the tea things down on the table and addressed Sophie. "Lemon? Sugar?"

"Black is fine."

Remarkian poured the tea and handed her a cup. Ken accepted lemon, and when they were all situated, he sat beside Ken on the larger sofa and opened the laptop.

"As Agent Ang said, we have news for you, too," Ken said. "Nothing good, I'm afraid."

"Oh?" Remarkian sipped his tea. His eyes were guileless, candid.

"Lee Chan was murdered today. By a man named Assan Ang." Sophie said, watching the blond man intently. "The killer's in custody."

Remarkian's eyes widened. His teacup clattered a little against the table as he set it down. "I'm so sorry to hear that," he said. "Chan killed. My God. Why?"

Ken didn't answer him. "We'd like to know all you can tell us about Chan. Okay if I record this?" He took out his phone and thumbed it to a voice-recording feature.

Remarkian made a gesture to Sophie, taking in her injuries. "Did he hurt you?"

"Not all of it," Sophie said. "Have you ever had dealings with Assan Ang? He's a businessman from Hong Kong."

"I'm aware of that name from our work in Hong Kong. Import-export, right? But I've never met the man." Remarkian knew something; Sophie could see it in the tight corners of his mouth.

"Someone is the saboteur, and someone is selling information within your company. We know that much. It seems Lee Chan was the leak," Ken said. "We got into his laptop today and found evidence he was siphoning off your clients' information and selling it to Assan Ang, and possibly others."

"I told you to look hard at him," Remarkian said directly to Sophie.

"How did you know about his financials?" Sophie asked.

"I suspected. I had bookkeeping put a bug on his account, if you must know. I froze him out of our client information days ago." Remarkian shook his head. "I thought he was the saboteur, too. Getting his jollies manipulating our less than legal clients into hurting themselves and making a profit off them at the same time."

"There's nothing in his computer indicating that," Ken said. "Though it might be safe to assume."

"Why don't you tell us your news about Sheldon Hamilton?" Sophie asked. "It could be germane to the case."

"I already called Frank Honing—of course, I had no idea about what you just told me. I left a voice message on his phone, and I called the rest of the board. We're having an emergency board of directors meeting later today to review and implement what Sheldon directed, but to start, I'll play this recording of our conversation this morning."

Sophie sipped her tea, and was startled to find that it was the strong flavor she bought at a specialty shop. "You drink Thai tea."

Todd, still fiddling with his laptop, glanced up and grinned, an attractive smile.

"Got a taste for it in all my time overseas. I have it shipped here to keep a supply on hand."

"It's different." Ken apparently didn't care for the smoky, dark flavor as he added sugar to his, stirring with a tinkling sound.

"Man. I'm still reeling about Ang and Chan. Shit. Do you know why Ang killed him?" Remarkian asked.

"Not for sure. We're interested in anything that you could tell us about that," Ken said smoothly.

"I have no damn idea, like I said. I had my hands full dealing with the Hong Kong expansion." Remarkian stood, pushed his hands through his hair in agitation. "Frank Honing is giving me a run for my money at the management level. He's a company man all the way, buttoned up tight, a real control freak. In fact, I anticipate the most problems from him with the changes this video calls for." He sat back down. "Let me just play this for you."

Sophie had to move over to join the two men on the sofa and get a look at the screen. She realized, as her shoulder brushed Remarkian's, that she was nervous to see the man she'd guessed was the Ghost.

"Hey Todd. Are you recording?" Sheldon Hamilton looked much as he had in the corporate photo Sophie had seen on the company website: dapper in a well-cut suit, short dark hair styled. He wore fashionable black-rimmed glasses and had grown a goatee.

Sophie narrowed her eyes, trying to glean all she could from the video.

He was sitting on a cream-colored couch. She could see that it was night through the window behind him. A constant flashing of neon signs in Chinese gave the location away: she recognized the familiar Hong Kong skyline at night, from a high-rise building.

"I'm recording," Todd's Aussie accent came through the audio.

"Well, it's past time I cleared things up. I'm making this recording so it can be circulated for authentication, as I imagine what I have to say is not going to be well-received."

Sophie felt a sense of familiarity looking at Sheldon Hamilton, though she was sure she'd never seen him before. Sophie kept her own facial mask in place as the video continued.

"I apologize for any inconvenience I've caused by my temporary disappearance. This recording serves as my legal affidavit transferring control of my shares of Security Solutions to Todd Remarkian. He is co-owner of our proprietary software, and will be taking over my role as president and CEO of Security Solutions." Hamilton held up a printed document. "Todd, can you zoom in on this? I'll fax it to you afterward."

The camera focused in on an official-looking document. Hamilton pointed to the signatures at the bottom. "Signed, witnessed, and notarized. This document transfers ownership of my shares in Security Solutions to Todd Remarkian. Todd, you've been a good friend through all of this. I trust you to carry things forward. And now, I bid you all good-bye. I will be living abroad for the foreseeable future."

"Any further words, boss?" Todd's voice again.

"Yes." Sheldon Hamilton's intense dark eyes seemed to fix on Sophie's. "I don't believe that justice should be blind."

His elegant hand reached out and hit a button on his laptop. The recording went black.

Sophie shivered, a tiny involuntary movement. She picked up her mug of tea, moving back to her place on the loveseat. She felt bereft, a feeling she hated.

Todd glanced at her curiously and then handed the document that had been beneath his laptop to Ken. "I think you'll see this is in order."

Ken took it, skimmed it, and looked back at the Australian. "Why? You must know more about what this guy is thinking. Why would he leave you everything and take off?"

"Sheldon is a builder, a visionary. He lives according to his own rules, always has. I've known him since we went to international school together." Remarkian shrugged. "I always knew he had very little interest in Security Solutions except as a way to fund his lifestyle and interests. He's a Renaissance man, likes to entertain himself by learning new things, perfecting his interests. He always told me he'd be moving on. I just didn't expect him to bail on me like he did in Hong Kong. It really rattled me." Remarkian picked up his mug, took a sip. "I've got to get ready for the most intense board meeting of my life, because I'm sure Honing's going to fight me. Replacing Chan is going to take some doing, too. I'm so sorry about him."

Sophie could see that he was. The tremble was back in his hand as the Australian sipped his tea. "Well, we need a copy of this document," Ken said. "And the recording."

"Done. I already forwarded them on secure email to your Special Agent in Charge."

"One more question." Sophie set her mug down and leaned

forward to make eye contact with Remarkian. "How long have you and Hamilton been planning this?"

The Australian appeared absolutely blank for a moment, then burst out laughing.

"You got me there. Don't quote me because I'll deny it, but this was always the plan. Like I said, Sheldon likes new challenges, likes the startup phase. But I want something solid. I want to build and guide this company, make it something great. I think we can do what we do, and do it better. And don't think he's giving me all this…" Remarkian gestured with his arms, encompassing the apartment. "for free. Oh no. He's retaining an income stream percentage payment off the company indefinitely. But you can't track it through the banks. It's all routing through offshore accounts."

"All right." Ken slapped his hands down on his gray gabardine slacks and stood. "I feel sure we're going to have more questions for you after we meet with our team, but this is a start. And good luck with your takeover of Security Solutions."

Remarkian stood, and Sophie did too. She'd left most of the talking to Ken, as directed, but her one question had been a good one, and he'd answered. Still, she felt deflated. She'd wanted something more. A showdown, some bigger closure.

She'd wanted to meet the Ghost.

Remarkian shook hands with Ken and the senior agent headed for the door. The blond Australian turned to her.

"Can you reach him?" Sophie whispered.

"Of course." Remarkian smiled. "What do you want me to tell him?"

"Good game," Sophie said. "I'm sorry it's over."

"Who said it's over?" And Remarkian winked.

Chapter 31

Sophie stood on the bluestone steps of the Addams family mansion several days later, holding the stuffed rabbit in her arms. She'd taken time with her appearance, putting on makeup to cover the worst of her injuries, but Anna's mother answered the door and recoiled.

"Oh my goodness, what happened?"

Sophie smiled. "Nothing much. Hazards of the profession." She held the rabbit out. "I called about returning this?"

"Oh yes. Please come in. Anna has been asking about you all the time." She opened the door wide. "Anna!" She called.

Sophie heard the pattering of running feet and smiled as Anna ran into the room. She would never have recognized the bouncy, pigtailed little girl who embraced her enthusiastically as the shell-shocked child she'd carried out of the closet.

"Sophie!" Anna exclaimed. "You brought Bun-Bun back!"

"He kept me company for a while, but he wanted to be back at your house," Sophie said, handing the rabbit over.

"He's all clean!" Anna embraced the rabbit. "Did he help you sleep at night? Because I have trouble sleeping sometimes."

"He did. He's very snuggly and good at helping people sleep."

"Let me show you my room." Anna towed Sophie down the hall. Sophie glanced back. Anna's mother was making tea in the kitchen.

"You go on," she said. "Let Anna tell you all about the book she's been making with Dr. Souza."

They went down the hall. Anna's room was at the end.

"I see you like rabbits." Sophie looked around at wallpaper covered with bunnies, curtains with bunnies, and bunny-themed bedding.

"Bun-Bun started it," Anna said. "I want to show you the story book I made with my counselor."

Sophie allowed herself to be pulled over to the child's desk. On it was a booklet made out of stapled sheets of paper. On the cover was written WHAT HAPPENED in wavering capitals, decorated by a drawing of a tall brown woman holding a girl wearing a nightgown in her arms. Orange wings came from the woman's shoulders, each feather drawn carefully, filling the page.

"The wings are supposed to be gold," Anna said. "But I just had orange. See, that's you rescuing me."

Sophie felt her eyes well up. "Nice," she said, blinking and looking away.

"No, look here." Anna tugged her hand, refusing to let Sophie's attention wander. "I want to show you how it was." Anna opened the booklet, and took Sophie through a visual narrative of her kidnapping.

The men who broke in through her window and took her.

The dark closet.

The scary noises.

Anna praying for her mom to find her.

The sound of guns.

The angel who flew down from the ceiling and fought the bad guys.

The angel carrying her out of the building back to her mom and dad.

"And that's you," Anna finished triumphantly. "I know you have to hide your wings most of the time, but I saw them."

"That's a beautiful booklet." Sophie didn't want to cry in front of Anna and scare her. "You draw really well."

"Dr. Souza says you aren't really an angel, but I know what I saw. Thank you for bringing Bun-Bun home." Anna went over to the bed and put the rabbit up against the pillow, much as Sophie had done at her own apartment. "Mom made a copy of the book, so this one is for you." She thrust the original booklet into Sophie's hands. "Mom said she was going to fix us a tea party snack. She saves the good snacks for when people come over."

"Okay." Sophie followed, towed along in the girl's wake, an ocean liner behind a tugboat. "But I can't stay long. I left my dog in the car."

"You have a dog? I love dogs!"

Sophie ended up in the back yard having a tea party with Anna, Anna's mother, Bun-Bun, and Ginger.

Later, replete with sugar cookies and tea, Sophie and Ginger bade Belle and Anna goodbye. Back in the Lexus, Ginger sat on the passenger seat as Sophie dabbed at the cut on her cheek, broken open from too much smiling.

"I could get used to being someone's angel," she told the dog, stowing the booklet carefully in her bag. Ginger thumped her tail in agreement. Before she turned on the Lexus, she checked her email.

The Ghost had written her back. Her taunt that she'd find him had worked.

"Good hunting."

She laughed, and put the car in gear. There were ghosts to catch.

Aloha dear readers!

If this is your first Toby Neal book, thanks so much for picking up *Wired In*, a whole new direction with a beloved side character from my bestselling Lei Crime Series. If you're already one of my reader *ohana,* thanks so much for taking a chance on Sophie Ang's story—I plan at least two more books in her series, and I'm so excited to write them!

Sophie first appeared in Book 4 of the Lei Crime series, *Broken Ferns*. She was so compelling that I gave her a point of view in the book—something I'd never done before or since—and then I had to keep editing back to keep the story focused on Lei Texeira, my main character. Sophie demanded her own book, and finally I gave it to her—and along the way, realized I wanted to do a whole new series with her as the main character...So if you enjoyed this one, sign up at http://www.tobyneal.net/ for new title notifications and keep your eyes open for *Wired Hard*, #2, and *Wired Rogue*, #3, in the Paradise Crime Series.

Thanks go to several people for helping with this complicated book: first, mahalo to my son Caleb Neal, who agreed to be my tech consultant. I'm not 'techie.' I don't have the instinctive connection with the Internet and its machines that Sophie does. After describing the plot and Sophie's job and the D.A.V.I.D. program, Caleb gave me all the information he could. I went ahead and wrote the book, making up stuff wildly—"can you really 'backtrace' another program? Could you track a location via the Internet? Was a program like DAVID even possible? Can you send data remotely from a hacked-into computer?" Frankly I had no idea—so it was huge good news when, after reading the book, Caleb explained how my made-up ideas were actual reality and gave me names for them—not only that, he enjoyed the book, giving me hope I'd be able to reach a new demographic of readers.

Secondly, thanks go to my wonderful agent Laurie McLean, who helped me with edits on the book and did her darndest to get me the right deal with it. Thanks, Laurie, you're the best!

Thanks also to talented novelist Holly Robinson, who gave me a lot of great feedback on deepening Sophie's character. Creating a woman like Sophie is challenging. Her abs alone could be intimidating to other women, not relatable enough, and Holly helped me see ways I could show the deeper sides of Sophie that we all share. I know I'd probably be intimidated, meeting Sophie in real life, thinking we'd never have anything in common...but Sophie has her wounds and struggles, like we all do, and she's trying to heal them. I'm excited to see that happen, and I hope she'll find love someday.

Thanks to (retired) Captain David Spicer, who was especially tickled at the name of Sophie's rogue data mining program! Mahalo for your help keeping my police work real.

If you liked the story, please leave a review. Especially important with a new series! It really helps readers find the books, and they are the best gift an author can receive. Until next time, I'll be writing!

Much aloha from Maui,
Toby Neal

Sign up for Book Lovers Club (perks, contests, chances to be an Advance Reader) or just for new titles at http://www.tobyneal.net/ and receive FREE, full-length, award-winning novel Torch Ginger!

Look for these Toby Neal Titles

Mystery

Paradise Crime Series: (Sophie Ang)

Wired In (book 1)
Wired Hard (book 2) coming 2016
Wired Rogue (book 3)
Nightbird: a Jet World Novella

Lei Crime Series:

Blood Orchids (book 1)
Torch Ginger (book 2)
Black Jasmine (book 3)
Broken Ferns (book 4)
Twisted Vine (book 5)
Shattered Palms (book 6)
Dark Lava (book 7)
Fire Beach (book 8)
Rip Tides (book 9)
Bone Hook (book 10)
Red Rain (book 11)
Bitter Feast (book 12)